For Mon
who absolutely loathes horror, bu.

PART I
THE RONIN

CHAPTER I

LEASHED

THE RONIN SWISHED HIS KATANA, flicking wet red to the wind. With silent pity, he sheathed the sword and whistled his mare over. Obedient hooves clopped from the woods, and the grey-washed steed emerged through the cherry blossom trees, halting with a snort.

'Good girl,' Hazukiro whispered, patting her neck. 'Come, Akumo.'

The ronin mounted the mare and tousled her mane. His eyes fell on the bodies below.

Three dead bandits lined the cobblestone road. Their blood trickled through a myriad of pink, fallen leaves. Hazukiro turned to confirm a suspicion. The last fortress of the island of Ijihan was still visible in the distance, its four towers shimmering in a haze of sunrise gold. The Teragaku Academy. He'd not long departed its gates and already his katana had found foes.

Hazukiro sighed. For these men to plan an ambush so close to dawn while the oniku roamed the skies at night? The islanders were growing more desperate by the day, it seemed. The ronin found himself wondering if the three that had met his blade were part of a larger group of brigands before the saving grace of sunrise.

Numbers dwindling in the night were simply a part of life now.

'*Lackwits*,' he muttered, tapping the hilt of his sword.

The blade held a thousand bloodied secrets along its edge, and Hazukiro carried the weight of them each time he ventured out. He looked back at the pooling corpses. A few more fools wouldn't make it any heavier, he decided. He clasped the reins and nudged Akumo along.

Autumn neared its end, and Hazukiro wore the warm serenity of the sun like a cloak. Akumo flickered her ears at the swirl of vibrant leaves fluttering about them, carried by gentle crosswinds. The ronin forced himself to savour those moments. With a constant storm in his mind, the actual calm was difficult to appreciate.

Every islander knew that sunlight hindered the oniku. A graceful boon. Its presence was always warmly welcomed. Akumo cantered along while Hazukiro indulged in the glow of the sun that kissed his neck.

A few miles further, the stones on the road began to peter out. The path eventually became a wider stretch of dirt. A worn guidepost stood on the road's fork under arched blossom branches. The etchings on the sign may have been legible some years prior; now the weathered wood marked yet another reminder of Ijihan's decline. The roads had been ravaged in the seven years since Blightfall, but the ronin knew them by heart. His past saw him travel them for decades. He grunted and dismissed those intrusive memories.

Akumo slowed down and pawed at the path. Sharp and uneven stonework meant uneasy, jilted hooven steps for the mare. She snorted in protest. Hazukiro eyed the road, seeing that it only worsened as it approached the village.

'They really do need to fit you for some new umagappa.' He clicked his tongue. 'This way.'

Hazukiro steered the horse off the path and towards a wide green glade that stretched into rolling hills.

'To your heart's content, then.'

With a snort and a jolt, Akumo galloped on. The grass merged with sun-pressed pampas fields, and a flock of ravens took flight when the mare burst past in a flurry of grey. Before long, the hills grew narrow, the treeline of the forest closing in. Akumo slowed to a gentle trot when she returned to the main road.

Hazukiro tilted his head. He heard strange voices on the wind, sounds that made his horse uneasy. He pressed his heels to Akumo and rode on until the village was in view.

'Fushumaka.'

The main road passed through the farming hamlet, dividing its thatch-and-wood homes. Two fields skirted each side of town, one lined with rice stalks in shallow waters, the other a desolate mound of charred pyres and black stumps near a lake. Three women were huddled in prayer around a single pyre, a plume of black smoke billowing from it.

'The night has wrought ruin,' Hazukiro hung his head. 'And so shortly after the last attack.'

Several other villagers had formed a working line from the lake to their warehouse, passing along large pails of water and soil. They sang solemnly as they worked, an old hymn that humbly asked Kesyoka, the goddess of Light, for her divine protection against the Dark. Ankle deep in the cold wet with slouched backs, even the elderly toiled away.

Hazukiro had seen this before on his excursions. Rain and mud, in thickness and volume. These seemed to be the only things that masked the scent of blood from oniku. Plastering buckets of mud over yourself and your home wasn't as foolproof as sharpened silver, but it still reduced the risk of attack come nightfall. And as the ronin drew closer to the village, the voices he'd heard on the wind became painfully clearer. They were the wails of the women at the pyre, crying over loved ones lost.

Murmurs and whispers broke out amongst the residents when the ronin arrived at the village edge. Elders beckoned and ushered children indoors. One small boy was sent off sprinting towards a larger minka house, presumably where the village elder lived.

Hazukiro halted his horse at the small gate and met his hands on his lap. He bowed his head, awaiting the usual cold welcome.

Fushumaka, so close to the Teragaku Academy, had not faced an attack in over a year. And now the villagers were enduring the aftermath of a second attack in one month.

Something sinister was at work. And it apparently wasn't worth the time or resources of the Blood Spectors. Instead, they had sent a ronin desperate for redemption to document the attack.

Someone the daimyo had dubbed '*Leashed*'.

A branded prisoner.

CHAPTER II

WITHERING

THE VILLAGE ELDER STORMED towards the gate, brandishing a blunt blade. Four younger men followed closely behind, each one bearing their own weapon. Hazukiro remained silent and examined the approaching villagers. They projected the look of angry men, but the ronin knew these to be shallow masks, barely covering the truth beneath. These were men with tired and fearful faces. He couldn't blame them. The night had been harsh, and daybreak had only just graced them with its presence.

And now, in the midst of fresh mourning, an armed stranger splattered in blood had arrived to disrupt their brief peace further.

'We've nothing left for you to steal!' The elder stomped forward and flicked his hand as if he were dismissing a gnat. 'Off with you!'

The ronin took care to study them further. They clearly weren't warriors, but Hazukiro knew that a man desperate to preserve what he had could be just as deadly if underestimated.

As he always did, Hazukiro studied their hands first.

They each clutched a crude farming tool. One man gripped a scythe scathed by decades of harvest. Another, a sickle, chipped at its point. The other two both held spades, muddied and rusted. The elder was the only one who held a sword, and even that had seen better days. Or worse, the ronin imagined, given the age of the man. He must have seen his fair share of skirmishes, local and abroad. The theory matched the old man's gaze. Tired, but undeterred. He halted at the gate and looked up to the stranger astride his horse.

'Leave us,' the elder's voice hardened. 'Can you not allow us a moment to mourn before you pilfer through our fields?'

Hazukiro glanced at the armed farmers. They glowered in agreement, signalling him off with their blunt tools and sour faces. The ronin scoffed and reached into a saddlebag. The men stammered. The elder raised his sword high.

'Careful, stranger...'

Akumo huffed in fright. Hazukiro patted her neck and continued his rifling, dismissive of the blade in his face.

'Here.' The ronin produced a large pouch and tossed it to the elder. It jingled when he caught it.

'I am called Hazukiro.'

The elder shook the pouch at his ears.

'I ride on behalf of the Teragaku Academy.'

The pouch was knotted closed with twine and a bronze token. The elder rubbed his thumb over the familiar sigil; a four-towered fortress ensconced in roses. At the castle's base, a pair of lions rested while three ravens soared above.

The elder looked up at the stranger, eyes askance.

'They send a Blood Spector *now*?' he spat. 'Could've used your blade last night when the demons fell upon us. How will *this* aid us from that?' He tossed the pouch of silver aside with a clink.

'Melt it down for all I care,' Hazukiro said. 'Have you a smithy? Forge it into something stronger than shovels.'

Raised brows all around saw the elder open his mouth in protest.

'And I'm no Blood Spector, tonomori.' He steeled his voice. 'I am only a scribe.'

He removed his black straw hat and set it on the saddle's pommel. Small, violet baubles lined its rim. They dangled and chimed when a gust of wind lifted Hazukiro's unkempt hair. His dark locks waved before settling and framing the brand on his forehead.

Squinting, the elder stepped forward. The pale grey of his old eyes met the ronin's, dark as deep waters.

'A disgrace is what you are, then.' The elder studied him in return. 'With a blade at his side? So the Academy armed a criminal and let him loose, is that it?'

Murmurs broke out between the men. One explained to the younger of the four that this particular brand, a symbol representing two clashing katanas, meant that this man had committed an act of tremendous dishonour against the Maija Empire.

Hazukiro sighed and scratched his beard, a blend of black and grey, as he allowed the startled farmers to draw their conclusions. He knew what he had done. It was not worth losing daylight over, he believed. While his men bickered, the elder examined the criminal with fresh eyes.

He wore hakama over a tattered kimono; black, crimson, and tattered all over. On his back, he stored a wakizashi, and at his side, his katana. A row of four kunai lined the bandolier across his chest, and more were slung in pouches along the left side saddle. The assortment of curiosities on the right side saddle contrasted the left. Fashionable satchels made of special grade leathers and silver buckles housed journals, scrolls and ink. Each satchel bore the symbol of the Teragaku Academy. Hazukiro caught the elder's wandering eyes.

'The roads are perilous,' he explained. 'May I dismount and speak my piece, tonomori?'

A silence rode on the wind between them before the elder eventually offered a resigned sigh.

'We've trouble enough with demons at our neck.' He turned and signalled the men to lower their tools.

The ronin nodded and dismounted, sending Akumo off to graze. She found a fresh spot of green and tucked in.

'Keep those blades sheathed and follow me.'

Hazukiro offered a shallow bow that was not returned. The elder picked up the pouch of silver again, bitter with the knowledge that he had to swallow his pride for the sake of his people. He tossed it to the young man with the sickle.

Hazukiro cleared his throat. 'The Teragaku hopes these funds will contribute toward any damages sustained or any livestock lost. You may use the token at the Fortress gates to be allowed in for trade for the morning or afternoon. The token does not permit Sanctum for the night.'

The old man scoffed. 'That sounded rehearsed.'

'I never said it wasn't,' the ronin sighed, turning his attention to the young man counting the coin, scowling.

'Take the wagon and get as much straw and lumber as that pouch will buy,' the elder commanded, watching the man fuming. 'Go now, Zenso. While we've daylight to burn.'

'Why not send a Blood Spector to dispatch the terrors entirely?' Zenso burst. 'If the Teragaku truly wants to help us lowlifes while they cower inside their gilded cage, then the least they could do is send us some real help.'

'I've no ken of the Spectors' business, boy.' Hazukiro turned back to the elder, someone with some shroud of sense and patience. 'As you say, daylight withers. Allow me my duty and I'll be on my way.'

'Go, Zenso,' the elder shouldered past the men. 'I will not ask again. No one is coming to save us.'

The elder led the ronin along the banks that skirted the village, towards the charred fields of pyres.

'I need to speak with any witnesses, anyone who can give me a detailed account of the attack. If there are bodies from last night I must examine them too.'

The old man chortled in disbelief. 'No poise or grace from the *dis*graced, eh?' He shook his head.

Hazukiro's cold stare was his answer. The old man looked to the hilt of the stranger's katana, the branded sigil on his forehead.

'You'll want to talk to the girl,' he conceded. 'Runi. She saw *them* last night.'

Hazukiro nodded and followed the old man through burnt-black grounds brimming with mounds of brittle wood and ash. Three women stood at a pyre, continuing their prayersong from earlier.

'I would leave them to their mourning, but. . .' Hazukiro said softly on their approach.

'Daylight,' the elder sighed knowingly. 'Let me speak to them first.'

Hazukiro felt a sharp tug on his kimono then. His hand quickly found his sword hilt.

'Please, good warrior.'

Hazukiro looked down to see a young woman on her knees. Her cheeks were tear-smudged and her hands were black with soot. Her voice and fingers trembled, clasping his clothes as if he were moments away from abandoning her.

'Take your sword to these beasts' hearts, won't you?' she pleaded. 'I cannot lose another child. . .'

Her words shifted to tears and she fell to the ground, sobbing into the soil.

Hazukiro hovered an uncertain hand.

'I. . .have been sent to help.'

It was not a lie, but he could promise nothing more. He was no demon hunter, and only the Academy knew what their Blood Spectors were doing in these harrowing times.

'Ronin!' the elder called. 'This is Runi. The witness.'

Two other women bent down beside the sobbing mother, rubbing her back and lifting her to her feet. One cast a glare at the ronin as if he'd struck her to the ground. He considered saying something, but Runi approached him.

She looked to be about twenty years old. She wore a kimono that was once white, now stained brown and grey.

'Elder Hutaka tells me you're from the Academy.'

She wiped away a tear and bowed deeply. Hazukiro reciprocated.

'You're here as—' The woman's tongue staggered when she noticed the ronin's forehead branding. Her words trailed off.

'As a scribe, yes,' Hazukiro pressed on. 'I'm to document the attack. Please pardon my intrusion on the rites, but the Academy requires knowledge of the comings and goings of the oniku.'

Runi nodded in understanding.

'I'm not entirely certain if Kesyoka listens to her devout these days. At least the Academy is doing something to fight the Blight. Swords are useful, but knowledge is invaluable.'

She looked to the heavens in contempt, then cast a tiresome gaze to the smouldering pyre.

'I've burned more bodies than I care to count. My husband included. All within too short a span.' She wiped away a tear and defiantly nodded. 'I tire of the withering. The island. Its people. Resources. I'd be glad to offer my help.' She rubbed her shoulder and winced.

'Thank you.' Hazukiro whistled and Akumo came trotting through the black bleak.

'The elder says you saw them last night?'

'Yes.'

'How many victims were there?' He opened a satchel and produced a leatherbound journal, stuffed with loose papers.

'Three,' she sighed. 'Two were killed.'

Hazukiro froze at that. 'The third still *lives*?'

'Unlikely.' Runi breathed deeply, clutching her chest. 'She was *taken*.'

Hazukiro watched as the widow spat on the ashen soil.

'I cannot bear to stand here a second longer. Follow me.'

CHAPTER III

TARNISHED PYRES

RUNI WELCOMED THE RONIN into her home, away from the smell of smoke and bone.

'Please,' Runi offered him a seat on her goza mat. 'Tea?'

'I cannot stay long.' Hazukiro laid his journal down and flipped to a blank page.

He popped off the ink well's lacquer lid and dipped a fine brush into it. Runi sat in front of the ronin, placing her hands on her legs and tapping her fingers.

'If you would,' Hazukiro urged.

'I'm sorry,' Runi stuttered. 'The black of that ink. It's like their *eyes*.'

Hazukiro wished he had the time or patience to be timely and patient, but he did not. People had been living in an endless nightmare since Blightfall. Every sighting at night was nothing short of terrifying. For everyone. From children to regular farmers to seasoned soldiers. Even he could not deny the chill the demons accosted him with a single stare.

'The attack,' he pressed.

'O-of course,' Runi stammered, stiffening her posture.

She took a deep breath and the ronin dipped his brush again.

'I get these headaches. Since I was a girl, I've found myself fainting at unpredictable times. It used to happen once every few years, but lately, I've been pass—'

'The *attack*.' Hazukiro tapped the blank page with a stern finger.

'I fainted outside the village,' she shifted her knees, agitated. 'And I only woke up again at sundown.'

The ronin made a note but no apology.

'Continue.'

'When I came to I saw the sky and ran. I was dizzy. Disoriented, I tripped over something. A rock, or a root?'

The ronin glared.

'I fell face down into the lake. I slipped trying to get to my feet. That's when I heard the hissing.'

Hazukiro nodded, his eyes fixed on the words he jotted.

'Shallow end? You were covered in mud and they ignored you.'

Runi nodded, took a sip of her tea, rolled her neck anxiously, and continued.

'One of our cattle had wandered off yesterday morning. Some of the boys went out to find her, but Elder Hutaka called it off in the afternoon. Anything beyond the village can still be dangerous during the day. And so the boys all returned. One of them, Kirito, ventured back into the woods, despite the elder's wishes. Poor boy. Only fifteen. He considered the cow to be valuable; to be worth the risk. I—'

Runi brought filthy, ash-laden hands to her face and sobbed softly.

'I'm sorry,' she managed to whisper.

After collecting herself, Runi regaled the tale and Hazukiro documented the details. When she had finished, she shakily drank her tea while the ronin lightly blew on the ink. He reread the account while it dried.

The boy had returned with the stubborn livestock, moments after sundown. Fearful, the boy's sister ran out to meet him, brandishing a pitchfork. The oniku swarmed them. The boy and the cow were torn to shreds in seconds. The swarm *took* the girl, Kamo. Swooped her from the ground and headed north into the night. From there, Runi claimed that she lay in the mud until she could summon the courage to scramble back into her home.

'Your story has been helpful,' Hazukiro said, packing up his things. 'But you made no mention of your shoulder.'

Runi finished her sip and frowned. 'My shoulder?'

'You've rubbed it three times,' the ronin said matter-of-factly. 'Once at the pyre, and two during your tale. It's difficult to stay the true ambitions of our hands when our tongues run wild with worry. You tried to hide it. Caught yourself doing it the second time and attempted to pass it off as a crick in your neck.'

'I–'

'Is it a scratch?' He stood, startling her enough to drop her teacup. 'Or a *bite*?'

A small child, close to five years of age, revealed herself from a hatch in the floor.

'Mama?'

'Soto!' Runi rushed over to the girl and cradled her in her arms. 'I told you to stay put until I came to get you!'

'It *smells* down there, mama.'

Runi turned to Hazukiro.

'Show me,' demanded Hazukiro, placing a hand on his hilt. 'And move away from the child.'

'Please,' she began. 'Please don't take her from me,' the woman whimpered. She gestured softly with a trembling hand. 'She's all I have since I lost my son last winter.'

Hazukiro stifled a deep sigh.

'I feel fine,' Runi insisted, a croak in her voice.

She carefully slipped her shoulder out of her kimono. Hazukiro leaned forward and noticed the patchwork of bandages, then withdrew with pursed his lips.

'What's wrong?' the child asked. Runi swallowed and swayed her head back and forth. 'Dear child, I—'

'You and your mother were very brave last night,' Hazukiro cut her off and softened his stance.

'I've no authority to condemn anyone.' He dipped the brush back in the ink.

Runi thanked him with her eyes.

'Take this,' he said, retrieving and handing her a small gourd. He whispered so the child would not hear.

'Your bandages have soured purple. A talon nicked you while flying over?'

She nodded.

'You've let it fester overnight. Soak this into your wounds and apply fresh bandages. Remove it after a week. It should work.'

She fell to her knees graciously, grasping the ronin's hand. He recoiled. She bowed in apology and returned to her feet.

'No one need kneel before me.' He sounded firm, offended even.

'Thank you,' she cried softly. 'You have no idea how much this means to me. To us.'

'Keep this to yourself,' Hazukiro said. 'I have no more.'

Of course,' she said. 'But what if. . .' she hung her head.

'What if it has already spread?'

Hazukiro turned to the child, then back to Runi, resigned.

'Then you must do what is right,' he said, tapping the hilt of his katana.

She nodded in solemn silence and bowed once more.

***

Hazukiro made his way to the shrivelled remains of the cow carcass and knelt beside it. Puncture wounds riddled it like a sinking ship, its once chestnut hair a sickly pale grey. Its gullet and hind legs had been torn off completely.

'You there,' a man called.

Hazukiro turned to see a villager stumbling towards him, shaking arms laden with logs. He dropped them with a whistle and wiped his brow.

'Best you clear off, I'm about to burn the tainted meat.'

Hazukiro took to his feet and glanced over the sapped beast again, then nodded to the man and called Akumo over. She came running beyond the hills and stopped at his side with a gentle whinny. The ronin donned his straw hat and put away his pouches while the man began stacking the wood.

'I saw you toss the elder some silver,' he said, secretive and soft as if speaking to the lumber. 'We appreciate the aid, stranger. Take care on the roads.'

Hazukiro scratched his beard and nodded before climbing into his saddle.

'Tell me,' he said, turning Akumo about. 'Why burn the cow here, and not at the pyres?'

The man sighed and stacked two logs, his eyes locked on the animal. 'This is where it fell. Where it spilt offal and bled into the soil. Even the pyres are no doubt tarnished. It *all* needs cleansing.' He spat. '*Kynzo* has tainted this ground.'

He emptied a pouch of powder over the carcass and clapped the dust from his hands.

'Kynzo?' Hazukiro raised a brow. 'That hellish tale that was created to scare children?'

'No,' the man's voice grew dark. 'The demon lord is as real as you or I.'

He began positioning the logs around the cow, then over it, row by row.

'Believe what you will,' the ronin remarked.

The man chuckled as he worked. 'You doubt *that* but report on the active dealings of the dead? People who were once alive, now wearing the skins of demons, prowling the night? Make no mistake, stranger. Ijihan is being *punished*.'

He sparked the bundle and watched the flames rise.

'And we deserve it.'

CHAPTER IV
A TIME FOR WOLVES

THE ISLANDERS OF IJIHAN knew the sun to be many things.

For most, the miraculous orb bore the radiance of Kesyoka, the goddess of Light. Some saw it simply as the agent of passing cycles, marking time and toil, the dawn of wars, or the prospect of peaceful days. To others, a bountiful paintbrush that smeared the sky when it rose and set; a sight always worth soaking in with family.

But for the seven years since Blightfall, every islander agreed on one thing.

The sun was their saving grace.

Hazukiro looked up, squinted, and estimated the time before sundown. His estimations were near-perfect. They had to be.

Akumo snorted and shook her mane while the ronin mulled over the morning's events.

'Ajina North. Roktao. Gojikao. And now Fushumaka. Mindless as they are, the pattern is too plain to ignore. The oniku move north before first light. And this time they'd taken someone with them.'

Hazukiro stroked his peppered beard, then sighed.

'That's what the Spectors are for. Let them wet their blades and face the night.'

Hazukiro returned to the forest path. He thought back to Runi and the vial he had given her. Though the sun shone strongly, it was unwise to traverse the island without ground wasari, a hardy plant that slowed the spread of demonrot, if blanketed over the bite or scratch properly.

The ronin passed by trees and scoured them, hopeful. Wasari often grew in clusters among the thick entanglement of roots of larger camphor trees.

He slung an empty pack over his shoulder and dismounted his mare, entering the woods. Walking underneath enveloping trees, his ears pricked to a soothing sound.

It was the honeyed melodies of the violet songbirds. They hopped and fluttered between branches, exchanging chirps and tunes. Hazukiro removed his hat and stopped to both admire and envy them. They danced about, content and free, while the sun pierced the treeline and brushed the ronin's branded forehead. He exhaled deeply and dropped to his haunches, searching the roots. He took careful time to enjoy the earthy undertones of the rich soil as well, another luxury he'd missed from inside his cell.

After a few moments of unsuccessful sifting and patting around, he finally gripped a promising wet root and tugged.

Wasari.

He shook off the soil from the small uprooted bundle and placed it in one of his packs. A sharp neigh cut through the trills of birdsong.

'Akumo.'

Hazukiro sprinted back towards the road, his hand on his sword. He leapt onto the path and shot his head both ways. No one, save for Akumo shaking her head. Cautiously, he approached the horse, glancing over his shoulder as he moved. Hazukiro stroked her snout and whispered familiar and gentle words until her whinnies softened, but she was still uneasy.

'What did you see, girl?' He wrapped his fingers around his hilt with an iron grip.

'Show yourself!' he called out.

An arrow answered, striking the ground at his feet. Looking up, he spotted a man in a tree balanced on a wide branch, bow in hand.

'Hands off that sword,' a voice from the forest demanded.

Several men emerged from the thickets on both sides of the road. They moved with a familiar defensive stance and brandished sharpened swords that shared an insignia and gleamed terrifically. The men were all lightly armoured as well, fitted with leather cuirasses, boots and greaves. Not bandits, probably mercenaries.

The archer in the tree readied another arrow. The others callously conversed as they inched closer.

'Packs on his horse,' one of the men remarked, pleasantly surprised. 'Packs on his back. A lot of cargo for one man.'

'Seems greedy, even,' another man said, stepping forward with his sword arm outstretched. 'Best to distribute the goods evenly among the people, hm?'

Hazukiro softly exhaled. 'Let me pass. Allow me that, and I'll allow you to go and find shelter for the night.'

He returned his hand to his hilt. The archer drew his bow and aimed, waiting for the word.

'Ha,' scoffed another. 'I don't know which corpse you looted those weapons from, but you don't look like much to me.'

The leader strode forward and his men stepped with him, shrinking their circle around the ronin. He was a thin man, with paler skin than most, sickly even. He took a careless swig from his gourd and looked down at Hazukiro's hand, still clasping the hilt firmly.

'Try it,' the man spat, his breath sour with saké. 'You'll feel that arrow before you've freed your blade.'

Hazukiro hid his disdain at the scent and moved his eyes between the men. They were roughly the same size, positioning their weapons at the same height. And, save for their archer, they wielded only swords. Two had daggers strapped to their belts, and another had a small axe strapped to his boot. These secondary weapons were strapped in securely though, Hazukiro noted.

Difficult to free in a bloodbath without fumbling.

It wouldn't matter if he was quick enough.

'Look. You've figured us all wrong, traveller,' the leader said, his tone softening. 'We do honest work. Keep the villages around here feeling secure. Do you follow? They toss us some coin, and we brandish our blades and bow deeply. Folk sleep better knowing their borders are lined with scarecrows. Had no bandit attacks in months, see? But they're no fools. They know we can't stop a swarm of the dead. And what do you do? You come strolling in with silver and promises. Mentioning the Academy. Getting their hopes up.'

He took another sip.

'Empty words, I'm sure.' He wiped his chin. 'Probably duller than that blade. But still, you've gotten them thinking now, haven't you?'

The other men nodded, scowling. Their leader continued his rant.

'Maybe we don't need to fork out for those mercenaries,' the man mocked. 'Maybe the Blood Spectors will come, once they figure out how to stop the demons for good! Fellow's doing research, helping us! Bandits will be nothing, then. The Teragaku will help us!'

He took another swig from his drink and his voice fell dark. He locked his deep, gaunt eyes with the ronin's.

'All you've done is given them false hope and taken money from *our* pockets.'

'You monger fear,' Hazukiro retorted sharply. 'There are no bandits for them to fear because you've taken on that role yourselves. Under the guise of extorted protection. You're no better. Arguably worse. A bandit is a wandering wolf, banished from his pack, feeding once and moving to its next meal. Desperate and foolish. But the pack? The pack prowls its territory. And they bleed it dry.'

The men broke into laughter. Some applauded sarcastically, and Hazukiro looked for an opening. They still stood firm, laughing but not softening their stances. The ronin pursed his lips.

'And which are you, traveller?' the leader trailed off from his chuckling. 'The elderly, sickly, retired hunter of the pack? With claws withering away? Faded fangs? Too comfortable for too long under the roof of his superiors, eh?' He pointed to the ronin's forehead and scoffed. 'Someone's *dog.*'

He gestured to his men. 'Least we're free. And one thing's clear. The Blight has kept the sheep trembling.' He folded his arms and wore a sinister grin. 'It is a time for wolves.'

There was a grain of truth to those words. And though what he'd said had bite behind it, Hazukiro kept his composure. A distraction of the mind could be as lethal as a misstep in a skirmish of swords.

'The fact remains, traveller,' the leader continued. 'Your little intervention has sucked us drier than the oniku. Our pockets are empty. How about helping *us* out?' The men chuckled again. 'It's nothing personal. We're all scraping by on this island. You came back quicker than we expected. All we found on your horse was paper. Listen to me carefully.'

He pointed to Akumo. 'Burn those notes. We'll not have hope restored just yet. Then, dig around in those packs for something shiny, and hand it all over,' he took another careless swig of his drink. 'And in return, we'll cut your throat quickly instead of leaving you to the night.'

'Very well,' the ronin conceded, and the mercenaries grinned victoriously. Hazukiro had hoped that the drunken nature of their leader would lead to his guard dropping, but he'd kept it up for the entirety of his musings. The ronin would have to make his own opening.

'Catch.'

Hazukiro moved swiftly. He reached for his satchel of fresh papers with his left hand. He sent them into the air, blanketing the bandits in a haze of white. In the same breath, his right hand drew his katana. The leader was the first to taste steel. The blade sliced his belly open, end to end. Before he fell, Hazukiro steadied his footwork and held his blade up. The expected arrow hurtled but skimmed off the katana. The papers fluttered still, and the archer would need a moment to nock another arrow. The ronin exhaled, then moved. He whirled through the men like a fanciful ribbon. His blade sliced, digging deep, pouring red as he danced. The last of the papers settled on the leaves below, most of them painted red. Hazukiro's ear twitched at the familiar pull of a bowstring. When the arrow soared, he spun on his heel and flexed, thrusting his elbow up. The steel sliced true, splintering the arrow in two.

The agitated archer growled. '*Why won't you di—*'

He froze, cold, to find a small kunai blade stuck in his throat. He fumbled for it before his world faded black. Hazukiro wiped his bloodied blade on his sleeve as the last of the men toppled from the tree.

The ronin looked down at his attire, smeared in red splotches. A painted target for the creatures of the night, so shortly after the previous smattering of blood had dried.

After cursing under his breath and calming Akumo down, he mounted his mare and headed for the nearest river.

* * *

Fearing the attack had cost him precious time, Hazukiro pressed his heels into Akumo's sides and surged on. The sun slothed toward its inevitable hiding place as they kicked up dust. Not more than an hour of travelling west, the pair halted at the sight of something blocking the road ahead. A massive fallen tree.

'Another ambush?'

The base of it was charred and black with a crack running up the trunk. The storm from the night before had claimed the tree with a fantastic strike of lightning. Too thick and riddled with scraggly branches to encourage Akumo to leap over, Hazukiro wasted more time manoeuvring the horse through and around the bramble beside the road, setting him back even longer. Finally, back on a steady path, Hazukiro calculated another half-hour to the river and back, cleaning included.

It was risky, but not as risky as riding through the night covered in blood should anything else hinder his journey. Such was the life of an expendable scribe. Oftentimes he had to make camp overnight, due to some or other hindrance along the treacherous paths between villages. Other times, mainly due to distance, he was forced to take shelter in any manner or method that worked. Drenched in mud, sealed off in a cave, or in some windowless, abandoned home's cellar was often enough of a barrier to blind most oniku. But being wounded, or covered in someone else's blood, was like waving your arms from a smoking cookpot.

'The river,' Hazukiro sighed in relief. He dismounted Akumo and searched her for bloodstains while she grazed.

'You're all clear, but could do with a bath nonetheless.'

Akumo whinnied in protest.

The river's banks had clear lines of sight. Only reeds and flowers grew at its edges, with glades of open grass reaching out before joining the forest and its roads again.

Still cautious, Hazukiro placed his blades among the reeds closest to the bank and disrobed. The water's cooling touch was a soothing welcome. The humidity had been high of late, especially for the final days of Autumn. Villagers were often heard to be pointing blame at the upcoming winter *blood moon*, stating that it brought foul omens. Humidity. Drought. *Fire.*

And though the presence of the sun usually felt comforting, it always took its toll after riding on the road for hours on end.

Hazukiro took a final glance about, then submerged himself in the waters. He burst through the surface and pulled leaves from his hair that the storm had swept into the river. He pulled his clothes into the waters, dipping them then wringing the red out. After repeating this several times, he emerged from the river and traipsed the clothing over the back of Akumo. This was not the first or even the tenth time something had tarnished his attire, and so the ronin dug into a pouch and produced his one spare kimono, plain and navy, with the same sigil of his forehead embroidered across the back of it. Once he had tied his hair back into a bun and secured and fitted his weapons, he patted Akumo's snout and mounted the horse.

'Drink?' he tugged the reins in suggestion towards a clear puddle of water, not tainted by blood.

Akumo sniffed the air and pulled away. Hazukiro shrugged and gently nudged her side, and they sped off back onto the path.

Though the road back to the Teragaku was fairly straightforward, it would still take another hour, give or take. But the orange glow of the early evening sky, and the Blighted sun that engorged it, had already begun to taunt him.

CHAPTER V

DUSK

'TARNISHED PYRES, THE SUN is moving fast,' Hazukiro muttered as he drove his heels into Akumo. She whinnied and pushed through, groaning. The ronin stroked her mane apologetically as he teetered on his saddle, squinting at the sun. With one hand clasping and steadying himself with the saddle's pommel, Hazukiro reached for one of the baubles dangling from his straw hat.

'*Kuyo ni ma,*' he whispered to the wind.

The bauble flared a piercing, violet hue. He reached for the other three around the hat's rim, repeating the phrase for each ornament, lighting them up like a sphere of burning bellflowers. Folding open Akumo's blinders, he ignited the small huelamps at the base of those too, then several more around her throatlatch and curb bit. Lastly, he sparked the four near the base of the stirrup leather. With the growing shadows across the forest glades, their gallop dissolved into hazes of bright purple passing swishes.

The trees grew fewer the closer they got to the Teragaku. With enough hollowed-out trunks and overhead cover, Blighted black birds had taken to burrowing inside oak trees during the day.

Ikari crows. The first vermin made vicious by blood.

Two years ago, one afternoon, two wanton Academy students neglected their lessons and fancied a secret stroll instead. Snickering off into the thickness of the woods, they tousled under a hollowed-out oak. This had drawn the attention of a small, nestled flock. Ikari. Blighted crows. The day was just cloudy enough. The branches and its leaves were just thick, and just in bloom, enough. The ikari cawed and clawed, swarming the students. They fed quickly, ripping skin from bone, leaving only ravaged remains. It took only seconds, and by the time a ray of light had broken through the clouds, banishing the flock back into the shadows in a mad flutter of ichor-stained feathers, it was already over.

After that, the Academy cut down every tree within a three-mile radius of its walls. Because of this, the hill that the Teragaku sat upon was especially visible, even more so now with the faint violet aura that shielded it.

The lamps adorning Hazukiro and Akumo's attire were a thumbprint in the monstrous hand that was the School's defensive lights. In a time when Ijihan fought alongside the mainland, and the wars of men mattered more, the estate was once a fortress. Four ivy-plastered towers rose from its grey walls like stone fingers. The outlines glowed a satisfying purple hue. Hazukiro breathed relief.

'Almost there, girl,' Hazukiro reassured himself more than the mare.

It was only a moment after these words that he heard Akumo make a fretful sound. One he had only heard once before. He was taken back to his training when he was young.

When he did not properly maintain the iron horseshoes of his war horse.

He cursed himself for not checking her tack and attire after his encounter with the mercenaries, though he swore he remembered doing so with due diligence before the trek. Akumo whinnied in annoyance, her knees nearing a buckle. Hazukiro eyed the fortress and the fading sun ahead. He hesitated, resistant to press his mare so hard. Then Akumo cried out.

Her knee bent and she faltered, fumbling to a stop. Her back legs skid on the road, kicking up dirt. Hazukiro was flung free. Akumo fell to her side and smashed three of the huelamps. The ronin cushioned his fall with his shoulder, dislocating it. He scrambled to his feet, realising he'd also torn his kimono. A few scrapes, he noted, but nothing trickled down. He groaned, slamming his back onto the road to pop his shoulder back into place. Stifling cries, he rushed to Akumo. His leg trembled and buckled. From the harshness of his fall or the agony of age, he couldn't quite tell. But he pushed through it all the same to reach his distressed mare. He dropped to his knees beside her, wincing, and began tenderly testing her joints.

'You're luckier than an iris garden, girl,' he sighed. 'Nothing broken.'

He tried to hurry her to her hooves, apologising again. The sun's gold faded further. 'We have to go. *Now.*'

Akumo protested and gently rolled her back against the road, snorting. Hazukiro glanced over his shoulder. The shadows of the forest behind him grew longer like an army of yearning arms. It didn't need to be sunset for danger to take flight. Keysoka's light just had to pass beyond the Eastern Hills. At least for anything prowling from the west. He muttered to himself and examined the hoof. The shoe had been tampered with. It was half-torn off of Akumo's hoof, and the shifted iron had roughly grazed the soft tissue of her sole.

'Blood...' The not-so-distant trees stared darkly. 'And I've done nothing but push you.' He cursed under his breath.

'Up, Akumo!' Hazukiro cried, shaking vile thoughts. '*Up*!'

The horse lay still, save for the sharp movements of her brisk breathing. Hazukiro tried smacking her hind leg, but it only reeled and kicked in place. The sun slunk lower, casting narrow rays like a squinting stare. The ronin cursed louder. *Dusk*.

His muddled mind grasped at possible options. A mob of intrusive thoughts clambered for attention. He slowed his breathing and recalled a practice he'd learned from his time in the Shogun's service. The art had a specific name he'd long forgotten, a brief passage among hundreds in the handbook he had to memorise in four languages. But the practice itself had become a permanent piece of him.

The Hush.

Hazukiro exhaled deeply. His eyes shifted back and forth behind stiff lids. A moment passed and he opened them. The ronin's demeanour dissolved from panic to calm with the finesse of a fading cloud. His mind stopped seething. His thoughts that had been swirling with the wildness of a flickering flame had now been silenced. Only a tender wisp of smoke remained. He searched his mind for any leftover, sprawling noise. Any scatterings tearing him from his focus. The chaos was quiet. Extinguished. *Hushed*.

He stomped out any lingering licks of flame. Smoke. Ashes. *Quiet*.

He was familiar with the art. It only took a matter of seconds to both unveil and use it.

'Gods, girl.' Hazukiro turned to Akumo, his voice calm. 'I am sorry about this. I know it stings.'

The ronin swiftly stepped over the horse and knelt beside her. He patted her side gently as he pried underneath for the nearest satchel lodged under her. He dug around the pack, ignoring the shadows that were lapping up the road. Everything else was only noise.

Noise he'd silenced.

'Here it is,' he pulled out a small cylinder nestled in a strap. Removing its cover revealed a sinister-looking needle and a small, swirling dose of an olive-green elixir.

Hazukiro awkwardly manoeuvred one leg over the saddle, positioning his backside as much as he could into his regular riding position. With one hand he clasped the pommel, and with the other, he injected his horse.

Akumo whinnied and sprung up, fumbling and panting. Hazukiro, jerked by the sudden motion, held onto his half-lit hat and shifted his weight to balance himself as Akumo steadied herself. She dashed down the road, bursting through any pain or discomfort.

Hazukiro watched the last shreds of sunlight flicker over the horizon.

'Faster, Akumo!'

The sight of the Teragaku towers grew closer, those stone fingers beckoning with the promise of shelter. Akumo snorted with each hoof clop on the hard, stone road. Hazukiro looked over his shoulder, and a surge of chills throttled his stomach.

The sun had set, and a cacophony of screeches followed it.

Hazukiro looked ahead to the fortress, somehow further away now. Its purple hues seemed dimmer. The Hush began to falter. Small flames surged higher, and he scoured his mind in the panic to stomp them out again.

'Damn it.' He tore his katana free and glanced back.

The ikari emerged from the forest's edge, a flutter of tar-black wings. The flock spiralled upwards as if a tornado had swept up a choir of crying souls.

One by one, several larger ikari tore away from the swarm and swooped towards the lone rider. The evening air was cool, almost chilling astride a horse in full gallop. But even as its gust brushed over Hazukiro, the undeniable stench of the approaching creatures hung in the air. Tainting it. On foot, the smell would mean you were already seconds away from becoming a burst of spleen and bone. But Akumo surged on, spurred by the needle's mixture. Hazukiro hoped the flaring baubles jostling wildly in the wind would be enough. Feeling for them around his hat's brim, he noticed that more of them had shattered in the fall than he'd expected.

A sharp screech tore his attention. The bird swooped down, talons primed, eyes hungry with red.

'Faster, Akumo!' the ronin commanded.

The creature's beak parted and split open like a beasted flower blooming. Inside hosted a coil of black fangs, extending like a hundred tiny needles as its maw widened.

'Back!' Hazukiro sliced the air.

Akumo leapt a cragged stone in the road. Hazukiro was forced to steady himself mid-strike. The ikari screeched, frustrated, and swooped again, snapping at the air. Its wings flapped faster, then settled itself into a consistent glide behind the ronin, gaining on him. Hazukiro reached for his hat and tore one of the baubles from it, swiftly wrapping its ribbons around his armed wrist.

'*Back*, demon!' he swiped again, this time a purple hue arcing with the curve of his katana.

The oniku hissed like a doused fire. It drew back for a moment, still in flight, then sharply broke off and rallied with its swarm. Several others broke off in its stead and began to pursue the ronin, huddled some distance behind him. They edged closer in what seemed like a coordinated attack pattern. Hazukiro used the moment to look forward. The fortress gate was winding upwards.

He could hear a clamour of voices barking orders. Behind the walls, a series of violet lights triggered one after another. Another two smaller towers hugging the arched gate lit up with a luminous hue so bright it was almost like staring into the sun. A lone figure stepped out from the gate. Hazukiro squinted, unable to make out who it was.

The figure shouted words that were lost to the wind. Akumo surged on. The voice called again, louder.

'Duck!'

Hazukiro lowered his head just in time to see a wooden stakespear hurtle past his head like lightning. It lanced a large ikari. It cried, frumpled its wings and crashed against the stone road.

'Ha!' the spear-hurtler howled. 'Not even ikari are as thirsty as my spears!'

Hazukiro shielded his eyes as Akumo dashed past the gate's lights. The Blighted birds faltered, hesitant, the lights growing too near, too impending. When the hue started to sizzle their feathers, they screeched and retreated into the night.

The spearman paid the ronin no mind when his horse shot past him. He readied another stakespear, grinning like a madman. The lights behind him glistened along his exposed skin, accentuating his tall and tattooed frame. Only the bottom half of his torso was armoured. Greaves, tassets, obi and boots, all bloodred.

'Itaro...' Hazukiro realised.

The Captain of the Blood Spectors.

The gate began to lower. Muffled voices frustratingly called the warrior back inside. He ignored them all, hurling another spear and scanning the dusk sky, but the swarm swirled and fluttered towards the woods.

Disappointed, Itaro grunted and slipped under the gate as it shut. He turned to Hazukiro gingerly dismounting his horse.

'Leashed!' Itaro boomed. 'Bring something bigger back next time.'

CHAPTER VI
A DANCING TIGER

JUST BEYOND THE GATES, the ronin stabled Akumo. She brayed and fidgeted incessantly.

Hazukiro rubbed her snout profusely, offering up bundles of hay and soothing tones to no avail. She reared her head at every advance. Her restless writhing began to unsettle the other horses, and before long they joined the commotion, stomping their hooves.

'Leashed! What in Kesyoka's holy name is wrong with your mare?'

Hazukiro turned to face Horsemaster Bokao. He was a weathered man, nearing sixty winters, though he still stood as tall and sturdy as his war horses. He snapped his fingers and several stablehands came running over. He barked orders to each of the boys, and they bowed and tended to the fussing horses. The ronin sucked his teeth and exhaled.

'Master Bokao,' Hazukiro half-heartedly bowed. 'Spooked, I can only assume. We'd narrowly escaped a swarm of ikari outs—'

'Nonsense,' retorted Bokao. 'My horses don't shamble like that after a sighting.'

He studied Akumo. The mare was wrestling the efforts of a skittish stablehand.

'She's stabled!' He stroked a braided white beard. 'She's warm and fed. Should be calm as a gecko in the sun.'

Hazukiro simply bowed again, anxious to end the interaction.

'I will settle her, Master Bokao, you may return to your quarters and—.'

'Oh, *may* I?' He brought his face inches away from Hazukiro's.

The ronin tried not to wince. The man smelled like a neglected stable stall.

'You're lucky the daimyo wants to see you, else I'd have a few more choice words for you, rat.' He spat and approached Akumo, waving the stablehand away.

'Kiraku!' Bokao called.

A young boy dropped a hay bale and sprinted over.

'Ser?'

'Take the prisoner's notes to the Academy.'

The boy nodded and turned to Hazukiro, holding out an expectant hand. The ronin reached into his satchel and handed the scribed accounts of the day. After a quick bow to his master, the boy ran off through the streets.

The horsemaster stroked Akumo's snout.

'The daimyo is waiting, leashed. *Go.*'

Hazukiro gave another uncomfortable bow and turned about, brushing his bruised shoulder against someone.

'Captain Itaro,' he said, surprised. 'Thank you. For your aim.' He gave a grateful nod.

The towering man smirked and placed a hand on Hazukiro's shoulder.

'Cut it a little damn close, didn't you?' He flashed a flippant smile.

Hazukiro couldn't recall the last time he'd seen a Blood Spector that wasn't clad in his crimson armour, head to toe. The captain must have been off-duty when the bells chimed. His chest and arms were bare, a canvas of needle ink creations, each tattoo telling a tale of his exploits against the Blight.

'I apologise, captain. For forcing you down from the Spire to tend to—'

'Not that,' he lowered his voice and motioned to the horses. Hazukiro feigned confusion.

'I'm afraid I don't follow.'

'Stop.' Itaro pointed at the grey mare. 'The *yuzai*.'

Hazukiro held his tongue, his shoulder still clasped in the grip of the captain's monstrous hand. Itaro leaned in, digging his fingers deeper.

'Those syringes are meant for the Spectors' steeds. Not for the likes of a treacherous snake such as yourself.'

The ronin held his tongue. Itaro did nothing to hide his disdain.

'If it weren't for the daimyo, you'd have been executed years ago.'

The captain released the ronin and shouldered past him.

'Don't keep him waiting.'

* * *

Breathing in the brisk evening air, Hazukiro made his way through the market square. The stalls sat in a quiet cluster. Windows and shutters had been bolted down for the evening.

He often imagined himself there, walking freely and aimlessly during the day. He'd browse the fruit stands, and converse with those he would call his neighbours. He'd peruse the wooden coffers holding his favourite seasonings, choosing which to bring back to his simple home, then cooking and offering up generous servings of baked salmon and sticky rice to his family and friends.

A swift breeze intervened and tore him back to the present. To the fact that he would never experience the bustle of friendly folk. The smell and sizzle of savoury foods being prepared. And beneath that despair, an even sadder truth simmered.

Hazukiro did not believe for one second that he deserved it.

Any of it.

At the edge of the square, the stone streets branched off into dirt roads, all muddied for the evening. On the left, smoke billowed from the mills, furnaces, and mines. In shifts, every day and every night, workers did their part for the upkeep of humanity. Those operations focused primarily on the mining of silver ore, the infallible element proven to sizzle the skin of any oniku. Weapons were made. Defences strengthened. And beyond this timeless art of Ijihan islanders, another kind of craft had resurfaced since Blightfall.

Artificing.

A once-illegal practice. But with no enforced regulations from the mainland, the daimyo granted his smiths permission to delve into the forbidden arts of *majik,* called *magikare* in the Maiji tongue. Across the realms, people had different names for it.

Borui.

Tizu.

Elmence.

And with free rein comes progress. Smiths became artificers, or *arkinists,* learning the science of harnessing the light of the sun itself, an art Hazukiro could never inquire about, though he was certain it would go over his head regardless.

Opposite the labourers of silver and steel and the minds of magikare, the soldiers' barracks stood tall.

Swords clanged and armour clashed from inside their walls. The Teragaku mandated night training a necessary task for all would-be Blood Spectors. Passing the noise, Hazukiro moved through the residential area. Something caught his eye from one of the homes.

A small doll sat at the window sill, positioned to look as if it were basking in the moonlight. It resembled a tiger, with scruffy orange fur and painted black stripes. A tiny hand reached up to grab it but missed. A small boy, no older than three, carefully propped himself up onto something and successfully snatched the toy. He placed it on the sill again, this time gently holding its white cotton paws, bouncing it along, encouraging the cat to dance. Hazukiro couldn't help but smile, his wrinkles scrumpled into that of a kind old man. The sight took him back to his childhood. He recalled the tale of *The Dancing Tiger*, a play the kabuki would put on for the children with puppets and fireworks.

The young boy's eyes glanced beyond his toy and he noticed the ronin in the muddied street. He paused for a moment, and then his briefly baffled face broke into an honest, gleeful smile.

He had an audience.

The boy waved and made the tiger dance wildly, flipping it this way and that. Hazukiro choked a laugh and stifled a tear, silently mimicking clapping hands.

'Wonderful,' he said quietly, knowing he couldn't call out.

He raised his hand and mimicked a royal wave like the one the shogun in the play would give with stringed hands. The sentiment was pulled away by the boy's mother. She shooed him back inside with a tongue click. The woman looked down to the street, saw the ronin, and spat. The shutters slammed. Hazukiro's wave staggered. His hand dropped with his smile, and he shuffled towards the temple.

CHAPTER VII

THE DAIMYO

THE RIDING AND HINDRANCES of the day were starting to take their toll. He was already dreading the temple's thousand stairs. In all likelihood, they couldn't have been more than a couple of hundred steps at most, but even that amount felt too daunting tonight, as wide and steep as they were.

As his knees bent Hazukiro felt the cruel twinge of age in his joints. The strained tugging of his calves. He pushed himself up and through the rising chill of the evening.

The daimyo's personal guard stood at the summit of the stairs. The *Umawari*. They stood before the daimyo's temple, tall and strong in their thick, orange armour, the colour of a crisp sunset. Even now after sundown, the curves and plates of their attire gleamed in the light of the moon.

The daimyo's hall was a small, square temple with four marble pillars encompassing it. Red tsubaki flowers sprouted in downward spirals from their golden tops. Hazukiro had always wondered if some sage or scholar at the Academy had been responsible for conjuring some form of sustainable magikare that had allowed these plants to grow and thrive without soil. Another question he'd have to leave forever unanswered.

Two large, bright red doors stood behind the Umawari. Hazukiro approached, bracing himself for the verbal assault.

'Halt!' one of the Umawari boomed.

'Step aside, you know who I am.' Hazukiro strode forward.

He felt the sharp end of a halberd's blade against his collarbone. Gentle as it was, it still drew a trickle of blood.

'State your name and title,' the Umawari said, firm as an oak.

A speck of anger stirred in Hazukiro. *Dutiful bootlickers*, his eyes whispered.

'Hazukiro.'

The other guard spoke up. 'Of?'

His helm and mask covered his face, but the ronin could feel the mocking grin beneath.

'Of nothing.' Hazukiro flatly replied.

The first guard repositioned his halberd, ensuring its edge nicked the ronin's cheek. Hazukiro winced in silence and passed through, giving the guards no further satisfaction.

The temple doors bore large bronze knockers resembling twin lions. He clasped one and pounded on the door. Another Umawari from inside the temple opened the way and the ronin stepped through the alcove.

'Daimyo Gutaka.' Hazukiro bowed.

'Step forward,' the local lord commanded.

A long, woollen rug split the temple down the middle. The left side of the room boasted a collection of items from before the Blight when the daimyo had served as a Mai-Ajin samurai. His old, black armour hung inside a dusty glass display case. Many katanas hung above and around it in gold kazaritachi mountings. The walls also housed several famous paintings, strung up and encased to protect their fine paper frames, delicate kozo and gampi originals. The first art was something familiar to Hazukiro, a commissioned acrylic piece of the former Shogun and his three favoured wives amidst the Wisteria Woods. The second was an odd piece to display, for it held a harsh reminder, but it was famous among the Isles nevertheless. It was a black ink piece depicting a battle with the Njörkin, a war that saw the defeat of half the Mai-Ajin samurai two decades ago. The artwork used pig's blood for the red, the only colour in the piece. The final piece hung closest to the daimyo's throne. A simple watercolour piece, far smaller than the other commissioned works. It showcased a simple sunset, with the flag of Ijihan flapping in the wind on a hill, a violet banner with a thorned rose bush at its centre and vines of red as the frills of the flag.

The right side of the hall was a stark contrast, adjourned with the daimyo's fine silk clothing, and a small array of weapons forged by silversmiths. Another impressive set of armour hung preserved inside a case of oak and glass. It was clearly polished and cared for often, gleaming black and navy blue, the colours of the night. Originally it belonged to the one known as the *Valor Noctis*, the first Blood Spector. Hazukiro wondered if Gutaka had ever wielded such armour or weapons himself.

Gutaka sat, plump as ever, at the end of the hall amidst a sea of satin pillows, smoking paraphernalia, and several golden cages housing singing canaries. A silver platter of wines rested on a stool nearby. As if he didn't look comfortable enough, he also wore yellow, silk robes that flowed and traipsed across the polished marble floor.

'Approach the throne, prisoner,' Gutaka beckoned with a careless wrist flick.

Two more Umawari stood beside their lord, halberds in hand, watching the ronin like hawks as he approached.

'Gods, look at the state of you,' Gutaka gawked. 'Come now, I've waited long enough to hear today's reports. What have you to say for yourself?'

Hazukiro humbled himself and took to his knees before the daimyo.

'Sincerest apologies, my Lord.'

'Your report.'

'Another attack at Fushumaka,' he complied. 'Two casualties. One, a boy. The other, livestock. And, strange as it may sound. . .a girl was taken.' The bodies were being burned when I arrived.'

'By the *oniku*?' The daimyo sat up, toppling pillows over. 'Very strange indeed. Perhaps they've learned to savour things for later?' He snatched a silver cup of wine and chugged, spilling red over chins.

Hazukiro bit his tongue and kept his head low.

Gutaka wiped his face.

'Nothing of any new breeds?' the Lord asked, curiosity piquing.

'Nothing,' Hazukiro kept his head low. 'I distributed the Lord's generosity after collecting the account.'

'Bah!' The daimyo sneered. 'A simple journey, then?'

Hazukiro thought back to Runi and her bite. He nodded.

'Then tell me this. How is it that you are so very, *very* late?' The daimyo stood, his voice growing angry.

He walked over to the kneeled prisoner. 'So late that you would bring down a *swarm to our gates?*'

He smacked Hazukiro's head with the back of his hand.

'The journey back, my Lord,' Hazukiro spoke with composure. 'I was slowed by bandits. My horse stumbled after they tampered with—'

'Ah, so your beast is to blame, then?' the daimyo flouted. 'A lame animal is unfit for its duties. What's the point of it then if it cannot carry out a simple day's—'

'*No!*' Hazukiro half took to his feet.

Halberd blades flashed. The daimyo raised his brows, stunned at the protest. Hazukiro looked around. The Umawari were half-lunged, weapons pointed at his throat. He sighed and stooped back down to his knees.

'Akumo is not to blame. I—'

'So you'll take the mare's lashings then?'

Hazukiro looked up and met the daimyo's gaze.

'I will.'

Gutaka nodded and the guards stood down.

'There was a time when you served with pride, donning that armour.' He sat back down and sunk into his cushions, exhaling loudly.

'Until you smeared your ledger red. Now here you are, taking the punishment of an animal.' He took a sip of wine and soaked in the painting of the shogun and his wives, smiling amidst the terrific trees of the Wisteria Woods.

'As well you should.' He flicked his wrist and returned to his smoking pipe.

'I am growing increasingly tired of seeing your face, leashed.' The daimyo turned to one of the guards.

'Five lashes in the barracks courtyard. Let the trainees see what happens to those who fail in their duties and bring death to our doors. Escort him, Jinaro.'

The Umawari nodded, snatched Hazukiro by his arm and violently tugged him up, then shoved him across the temple and out of the doors.

CHAPTER VIII

LICKED WOUNDS

'HERE HE IS...'

Jinaro forced the ronin down, slamming his knees into the concrete courtyard of the Teragaku Dojo. The Umawari flung the straw hat into the dirt and snatched Hazukiro's hair as the trainees gathered around him.

'Look at them,' Jinaro snarled, yanking his gaze upward. Hazukiro took in their faces.

Young. Eager. Naïve. Likely full of foolish ideas of status and grandeur. They encircled him now, a ring of reminders of a regretful and wasted lifetime. One he was forever itching to be rid of it.

Instead, the ronin stared into the eyes of these soldiers, hungry for blood, like looking into a memory made manifest. Jinaro looked them over as well, his glance brimming with pride.

'I'm pleased to see several fresh faces.' He wrapped more hair around his fingers, tightening his grip on the prisoner as if he were a disobedient dog. In unison, the trainees bowed to the Umawari. It was, after all, the most esteemed rank after Blood Spector. Either way, you were serving Ijihan in the most respected way.

'Thanks to brave men like you who are willing to risk their lives for our people, we won't have to rely on the aid of prisoners before long.'

He let go of the ronin and spat in his hair.

'We should never have had to invoke such a ploy in the first place. And *that* is why what you do here is so vital. You there!' He pointed to a frightened young face. 'Show me this prisoner's back.'

The boy bowed, dropped his bokken, and hurried forward, kneeling beside Hazukiro. He produced a wakizashi, tore into the kimono, then cut and stripped the ronin bare. Abrasive and cold wind crashed against it. Goosepimples outlined a patchwork of faded scars.

Jinaro praised the trainee's swiftness with a nod. 'Your name, boy?'

'Acolyte Kiyo, Umawari Jinaro,' he bowed, his heart drumming.

'Kiyo. How old are you, boy? And how long have you been training with us?'

'I'm eighteen. I've been here for three weeks, Umawari Jinaro.'

'Eighteen. Three weeks,' Jinaro repeated. 'Hold out your hands.'

The boy complied without question. Jinaro brushed his thumb along the inside of Kiyo's hand, then turned and held it up for the other acolytes to see.

'Calloused palms already! You push yourself, don't you, boy?'

'Yes, Umawari Jinaro.'

'Why?' Jinaro turned to the others.

Hazukiro kept his head down, waiting for the little power-hungry show to end. Jinaro enjoyed milking every second of it.

'I wish to join the ranks of the Blood Spectors, Umawari Jinaro.'

Jinaro placed a proud hand on the boy's shoulder.

'*Silver and sword will end the endless.*'

The other acolytes, beaming with pride, repeated the mantra of the Spectors.

'I am glad to see young Kiyo is taking his duties seriously, with the severity necessary. If we falter, our island will fall. A weak link will snap and lower any drawbridge, and *let the flood in.*' He kicked Hazukiro right in the ribs, toppling him to his side.

'This is the *traitor* who led the oniku right to our doorstep this evening. He has gracefully allowed us to make an example out of him. I want each and every one of you to remember this. Weak links will not be tolerated.'

He grabbed Hazukiro's arm. 'Back on your knees, *leashed.*'

The ronin calmed his mind and entered the Hush.

Hazukiro had known pain. He'd felt the invasive end of a sword. The jolt of an arrow. But beyond the blood shed in battle, a pain he'd chosen to endure, nothing stung more than the agony he'd felt the day he lost his—

'Remember. . .' The bullwhip cracked the air asunder, its split tongue searing skin.

'Your. . .' Jinaro swiped with grit, lashing a line of red.

'*Place!*'

The third slash covered the largest area. Its sting warped and welted his skin from shoulder to side. The whip's end tore open a path of blood like a blade through paper, then fell back to Jinaro's side, dripping.

Hazukiro had *known* pain.

He was still human. His back stung like boiling rivers bubbling over. He winced as he solidified his mettle, ensuring he remained grounded within the Hush.

'Burn this image into your mind!' Jinaro cried, raising his arm again. 'Harness it. Recall it as you would a technique when wielding your sword. Remember what happens when you *falter*!'

The fourth lash struck. The whip cracked again, and a bit of the cracker nicked his neck. Hazukiro wobbled and fell hard on his elbow. Before he could adjust, the fifth and final lash completed the canvas of red.

He thought of *her* again. And twice was enough. He exited the Hush and let in the pain; that agony that demanded to be felt all over his burning back.

'*I deserve this. . .*'

He flicked a strand of hair from his eyes, sticky with sweat and blood specks.

'Is that all?'

'What was that, *leashed*?' Jinaro spat.

Hazukiro turned with a tremble. His body suffered, freezing from the air, burning from the blood. Despite all that he still wore a strange, dark smile.

'All that time standing in front of a temple has left you soft.'

Jinaro showed no sign of simmering. He approached the ronin from the front and dropped to his haunches.

'Daimyo Gutaka ordered five lashes. You have been dealt *five lashes*. Unlike you, I have no interest in defiance.'

He stood up. 'That being said, if you truly are so adamant to die I will see what I can do.'

He pulled the ronin to his feet and turned the prisoner's bleeding back to the acolytes. They stared in silence.

'Remember this. Defiance will only bring you pain and regret.'

Hazukiro hid a smirk.

'The bastard was right about that.'

* * *

The walk back to his cell was made more painful by the occasional sadistic spear prod from Jinaro as he escorted him. Hazukiro heard the brewing of thunder above and prayed for rain to wash over his back. None came.

The prison was nestled on the outskirts of the residential district, just before the Spectors' dwellings. As the second largest of the Teragaku's four towers, the Blood Spire served as the personal quarters of the elite Blood Spectors.

'A leashed for you,' Jinaro shoved Hazukiro off to the warden and departed without another word.

Once the prison gates closed behind the Umawari, the warden rushed over to the battered prisoner.

'Gods, what's happened to you?' He clasped Hazukiro's shoulders and turned him around, hissing his teeth at the criss-cross cuts. 'Those damned fools. Quickly now. There are bandages in my office. Can't leave those open like that.'

'Thank you, warden,' Hazukiro winced.

'Don't thank me,' he said. 'What happens beyond these cells isn't my business. But you come in here like this? Well. It is my business to keep you alive.'

He shook his head at the scars, fresh and old alike.

'Even you, *Deathwish*.'

* * *

A cold week passed, and Hazukiro spent each of those days inside his cell.

Recovering. *Simmering*. Fitful sleep. Nightmares scratched and scraped inside his mind.

He turned in his bed, restlessly raging against the tempest that assaulted his subconscious.

The attack came in unforgiving waves.

Cities he'd never seen were burning. Screams and cries left unanswered. Towers of green and gold crumbled like sand. And in the centre of billowing storms of fire, a hovering figure, dark as the night.

And though faceless, it smiled.

Heavy eyes surrendered. Hazukiro woke in a sweat, disoriented. The battle inside his head now lost.

He rubbed blurry, burning eyes, and his reality flooded back with the madness of a sea storm.

The stench of the prison. The chill of the stone floor beneath his threadbare clothes. Fresh cuts that flared in a symphonic flurry when he heaved his beating chest.

In a moment, he'd left one hell for another. He let his reeling mind reset.

The fog of war lifted in time, the thrum of his wounds eventually pulsing slower. The small slot of his cell door scraped open. A heavy hand flung in a wooden bowl that whirled and spilt its contents before the latch clanged shut again. Pulling himself up, Hazukiro carried listless legs to the porridge. With a deep sigh, he sat in the middle of the room, as far away from each wall as the cramped space would allow, and began scoffing down the gruel by hand.

A small, barred window allowed a sliver of moonlight to pass through Hazukiro's cell. Hungry as he was, he ensured that he'd left a small portion of food in the bowl. He gently placed it in the corner of his cell. The pain persisted, and the ronin knew there was nothing left to do but go back to sleep. He gingerly crawled on top of the tattered tatami and shut his eyes.

He dreaded the hells he'd face in his dreams. Anxious thoughts took root in his gut and swarmed with a hot chill. A sudden gentle and curious mewl came from the window. Hazukiro shot his head up, then winced and cursed himself for the rapid movement.

A stray cat stood at the window, its slender body between the bars. He blinked at the ronin with his one eye, then leapt down with a pronounced chirp.

'Linku,' Hazukiro smiled, breathless. 'My only friend.'

The feline was black, save for its stomach, filthy white. He approached the straw mat and curiously sniffed the ronin's fingers. With a soft meow, he began licking them. Hazukiro chuckled at the ticklish touch.

'I left some in the corner for you,' he gestured. The cat dropped to mimic Hazukiro's position, lying on his side and baring his belly, purring.

'Very well. Business first.' Hazukiro stroked and scratched Linku's scruffy head.

When the cat decided he'd had enough, he took to his paws and scurried to the edge of the cell, bobbing his head around the bowl before eating its contents. Lapping up the last piece, Linku stretched his legs and scampered back to the ronin.

'You have no idea how good it is to see you, little one.' Linku curled up into a black ball behind Hazukiro's knees. Moonlight shifted along the cell floor as time passed, and they fell asleep.

In that moment, the pair felt content, and a bit warmer than before.

CHAPTER IX

FANG OR BLADE

'STAND ASIDE! THE SPECTORS are *bloodbound*.'

The Umawari belting the command dropped to one knee and fixed his eyes on the floor. Though agents of law within the walls, the temple guard paled in comparison to the renown of the Blood Spectors. Wrist-slappers and wine-bearers, most fortressfolk would mutter about them.

But the Spectors?

People looked at them with admirable eyes. Every soldier was respected. Even *worshipped*. They came through when an entire pantheon of gods had not. When the shogun cut Ijihan's ties with the mainland, they were the ones to take up silver swords and stand for the island in its darkest nights.

A party of five horsemen strode through the bustling day market. They were clad in crimson, head to toe, their armour marked with the ancient script of the Holy Book. Residents parted in reverence for the riders. A young woman dressed in white approached the lead horseman and offered up a violetstem bloom.

Captain Itaro removed his helmet to sniff the flower. He nodded in thanks and trotted on, leaving the blushing woman beside herself. The company pressed through calls of praise and encouragement, sauntering down the streets before coming to a stop at the main gate beside the stables. Itaro noticed the horsemaster, who was muttering to himself as he saddled up a sixth horse.

'Bakao!' called the captain.

The old man gave pause and fastened a bridle buckle.

'Will you be joining us on this hunt?'

The old master shook his head, as if in utter disbelief.

'Not I, captain.'

* * *

Invasive iron clangs stirred the ronin. Groggy, Hazukiro sat up to see the warden, tapping the hilt of his sword against the cell's bars.

'Come on then!' he bellowed over the banging. 'The daimyo wishes to see you.'

The warden ceased his rattling and sprung open the door. Two large guards poured into the cell from behind him. They wore ash-grey armour and bore steel naginatas, their broad blades pointed at the prisoner.

The ronin rubbed his eyes and groaned. He clenched his fists when he gingerly took to his feet. The burn of the lashes had mostly subsided, but he still felt the throb of bruises when he tried to stretch his jaded joints. Linku had scurried off in the night, leaving only black hairs.

As a small silver lining, he noticed that his food bowl had been completely picked clean. It eased his ache a little knowing the stray had left with a full belly.

Growing impatient, one of the guards prodded the prisoner with his weapon's hilt.

'Yes, yes!' Hazukiro spat. 'I'm getting up.'

The warden tossed the prisoner a fresh kimono. Confused, Hazukiro put on the fresh clothes. They were warm, thick, and made of far sturdier cotton than he was accustomed to. He cast a gaze like thrown daggers at the warden, eyes shrouded in scepticism.

'Would you mind telling me why I've been *granted* another audience with the daimyo? So shortly after his royal fanciness graced me with one so recently?'

The bottom of the naginata, hard and merciless, knocked against his skull.

'You were told not to harm him. Out. Both of you.'

The guards left in a huff with itching fingers.

'Everyone wants a piece of you, it seems.' The warden produced a cup of tea and a bowl of food, both still steaming.

Hazukiro nearly dropped his guard at the sight. Eggs, sprinkled with spices, ran yellow over a steaming bowl of hot rice and vegetables.

'A final meal?' he said, eyeing the bowl.

The warden chuckled. 'That is entirely up to you. Please.'

He extended the bowl, placed two chopsticks inside, and shook it gently.

Nodding his thanks, Hazukiro accepted the food and indulged in the hot and flavourful symphony that sang along his taste buds.

'I feel like a decorated duck, prepped for a feast to be held by my betters.'

The warden watched as the ronin scoffed down the meal.

'We haven't the time for another of your convoluted analogies, ronin. Besides, it is not my place to say. I was told to rouse you, feed you well, provide you with new clothes, and escort you to your audience personally. Your fate beyond that is out of my hands.'

He brushed his palms together in a show of dismissal and leaned against the cell wall.

'And you don't want to summon your guards back for that?' He smiled and slurped down his food.

'You don't seem the kind to bite the hand that feeds.'

Hazukiro savoured the last of his meal and washed it all down with the honeyed tea. Flavours quelled the worry of the daimyo's sudden request. Despite everything, Hazukiro felt content, even inside those four filthy walls.

Replenished. His stomach sighed. He tried to hold onto that feeling the way he had savoured every bite.

'Thank you all the same.'

He placed the bowl down beneath the window, a small portion of egg white and rice heaped in its centre.

'Lead the way.'

Passing through the fortressfolk, all going about their day, was a bittersweet experience for the ronin. He'd longed to be a part of it, while constantly deeming himself unworthy of such a frivolous life. Though, with the warden at his back, and the eyes of many a mumbling resident, it was not too far off from what he'd often envisioned.

To Hazukiro's surprise, he did not have to make the long walk up the stone stairs. Daimyo Gutaka stood at the bottom step with two of his Umawari at his sides. He held the ends of his fashionable frills in a delicate bundle like a woman nervous about muddying her kimono. He seemed out of sorts, like a frail fox among wolves. Hazukiro wondered just how often he had strayed from his temple to the town below, or beyond the walls for that matter. His entire worldview was brought to him by scribes. Facts expressed through simple ink and paper.

'Ronin,' Gutaka spoke impatiently.

'Forgive the delay, my Lord,' the warden spoke. 'The prisoner's wounds needed fresh bandages.'

The daimyo nodded and dismissed the warden. Hazukiro watched his keeper leave, then turned to Gutaka. The ronin stood stern, expecting a tongue-lashing for something or other. He could only guess.

Instead, Gutaka descended the steps, approaching the ronin with soft eyes and open palms, sighing deeply. The Umawari remained on the steps, vigilant.

'Horsemaster Bokao has informed me that your mare was indeed tampered with,' he said, *almost* apologetically.

'She has been refitted with the finest iron bracing for today's excursion.'

'Excursion?' Hazukiro's voice dropped. 'My Lord, forgive me, but I humbly request time for my wounds to fully—'

'I'm afraid time is not a luxury any of us can afford.'

Gutaka leaned in and opened his mouth to speak, then winced and took a step back. He gestured to the steps and took a seat, jostling his frills and straightening his posture. His face formed an uncomfortable smile and he motioned for Hazukiro to sit beside him. The resigned ronin sighed and sat down.

'You seek to regain your honour, ronin,' the daimyo stated, as if deploying empathy.

Hazukiro nodded, knowing the weight it carried on his *own* shoulders. But to this man? A pompous fool with a heart of avarice? Hazukiro couldn't help but feel he was stepping into a trap led by the wiles of a greedy fool.

'What more would you have of me?'

'You've expedited your sentence greatly with your risky role as scribe. For the benefit of your land. On behalf of *your people*!'

Hazukiro glanced at the daimyo's corpulent belly and held back a snide comment about '*benefiting*' that brewed on his tongue.

'Despite all this, *Hazukiro*,' the daimyo continued, 'I must now ask one more thing from you.'

Hazukiro mulled over the words in silence. Gutaka pursed his lips and tilted his head, anticipating a response. The Umawari tensed, halberds clenched in orange hands.

'My Lord, I *am* indebted,' Hazukiro finally said between tight teeth. 'Until honour is mine again, you need only tell me where to go.'

'Ah, well, this will be quite different.' The daimyo straightened his posture and the creases in his clothing, then leaned in to whisper.

'You've a military background. Skill with a blade. The level-headedness of a samurai, and you've aged like the oldest wine in my private cellar. Impressively hale.'

Hazukiro allowed the daimyo to continue, sick with the thought of any one man owning a private cellar space while villages faced fangs in the night.

'Which brings me to my point.' He cleared his throat.

'Assist my Spectors on a hunt of a bizarre nature, and you *will* be pardoned from your prison. Though, you will still serve the Teragaku. Just not from within a cell. Is that clear?'

Hazukiro's well-versed facade smiled and he bowed deeply, the falseness impossible to hear in his voice.

'You honour me with such a grand opportunity, Lord Gutaka.'

'Oh, I'm aware,' the daimyo sighed, unbothered by manners, anxious to return to his temple.

'Fetch Captain Itaro's new sword from the arkinist, then meet Bokao at the stables.'

The daimyo began his ascent, his guards following him closely. Hazukiro turned around. The warden was nowhere to be seen.

No blade poked at his back. His stomach was full, and his skin was warm. After the feeling washed over him, a mixture of uncertainty and bliss, he couldn't help but laugh under his breath.

Even if he could escape, there would be no next step in his journey. Free from the fortress, he'd still be a slave to his own mind, serving himself and his survival across a Blighted island. There would be no honour in that. How long before he helped a village before the night took him? His reckoning would be quick. His service would be cut short either by fang or blade.

Staying meant serving with the Spectors. Leash or no, he could bleed oniku with some force at his own back, the pride and strength of the Academy itself. Though working with dutiful glory hogs constantly breathing down his neck sounded awful.

'*Penance isn't meant to be easy,*' he grumbled.

More could be done this way, he convinced himself, heading for the arkinist.

More can be saved.

CHAPTER X

ARKIN ARTS

THE ARKINIST'S WORKSHOP WAS BULBOUS with plumes of black smoke puffing out of its orifices. The arkinist had supplied the ronin with stave baubles in the past, though he'd never seen him striking up steel in the forge with such bizarre apparatus about. A violet haze of smoke hung in the air as Hazukiro entered the workshop.

Barrels of steel swords littered the corners of the room. Silver smelted beside a forge, connected to funnel and pipes, hissing purple fumes. Arkin arts *and* silvered swords? This was runic majik.

Hazukiro pulled his curious eyes away from the strange apparatus and approached the arkinist.

'Ah, the new recruit!' The man beamed a glorious smile, his cheeks caked in soot, making the white of his smile all the brighter.

Hazukiro recalled far more degrading titles that had been thrown his way in the past. The artisan didn't seem to mind, or at the very least, did not care about the brand on the ronin's forehead.

'Take this.' He handed the ronin a sheathed katana.

The glossed scabbard was black with red spirals winding up to the blade's hilt, a ray skin core which bore the same colours.

'Itaro's new imbued weapon. First of its kind. Worked on it for the past three months. Be sure he gets it. He's been briefed on how to use it. It—' With raised brows, he picked up a ball-peen hammer and proceeded to iron out a hot slot of metal.

'*How* to use it?' Hazukiro pressed.

'Ah,' the arkinist stopped and winced. 'I've seen my mouth run far enough. It isn't my place to say, unfortunately.'

He hammered hot metal. 'I was told to give it to you and for you to give it to him, and nothing more, I'm afraid. Unfortunate. It's worth a discussion or two over some prime saké. It really is a pity. Unfortunate indeed.'

Hazukiro bowed, internally sighing at that tiresome chain of command.

'Of course. Thank you.'

He gently wrapped his fingers around the hilt, admiring the intricacies of its form.

'The details are most impressive,' he whistled. 'Have you given it a name?'

'I appreciate that!' The arkinist beamed again. 'And no. That honour falls to the wielder. After his hand carves through enough demons, of course. I'm sure it will have one before long.'

His hammer struck steel, and with a frantic grin, he waved the ronin off. 'Nightspast, my friend! Much to do. Much indeed. And the Spectors wait for you! An honour. Truly an honour it is.'

Though light in his hand, Hazukiro pondered over the weight

of the weapon's meaning. An imbued weapon? Wars were always won by turned tides. Perhaps successfully harnessing the arkin arts would be that much-needed tide changer. And with kidnappings, deaths, dwindling resources, and an encroaching winter, Hazukiro wasn't sure just how much longer Ijihan could endure without a fresh advantage.

Attaching the sword to his hip, Hazukiro left the workshop and made his way to the stables, pondering still. Itaro would wield this imbued sword before long. Hazukiro could admire and study its strange nature then. If he could fight alongside the Spectors while they wielded such majik against the Night, then perhaps that would be enough for him to reclaim his tarnished soul.

CHAPTER XI

BLOODBOUND

BAKAO GAVE A GRUDGING NOD when the ronin approached the stables. Akumo, however, huffed in delight to see Hazukiro, stomping her hooves when he patted her neck. The mare was adorned with fine leatherwork. The ronin whistled as he ran his fingers along the fresh tack, admiring the soft but sturdy saddle and its rich, dark oak gleam. Buckles, stirrups, the pommel; everything shone silver.

'Fit for a Spector's steed,' Hazukiro stroked the horse's snout.

'Admire it later,' Bakao barked. 'The convoy waits beyond the gate. Head north for the forest.'

Questions flooded the ronin's mind as he mounted Akumo. He knew getting information out of the horsemaster was like drawing silver from a tree, so he simply nodded his thanks while the monstrous gate ascended with a low roar.

Hazukiro squinted at the early morning sun, its shine bathing the desolate land in light. A guard lowered the gate and the ronin nudged Akumo down the stone road. Though barren in every direction, there was no sign of the Spectors. Hazukiro pressed on, the imbued sword sitting in his lap, with his own katana sitting in the fine leather saya. He reached and unsheathed his blade and smirked. Even his old sword had been replaced with silver. He held it high, sun rays dancing along its blade.

'Whatever this is. . .' Hazukiro tapped Akumo's side, '. . .it apparently involves using rare resources for a lowly leashed.'

Though the forests had been cut back every which way, a treeline to the north began to take shape beyond a sloping hill.

'Still no Spectors.' Hazukiro sighed. 'Wait—'

Approaching the hilltop, Hazukiro noticed a man and a horse, but no convoy. The stranger sat cross-legged atop a charred stump. A black steed stood behind him.

Hazukiro cleared his throat and placed a hand on his hilt. 'Nightspast, friend,' he called out, testing the waters with words.

As he drew nearer, the ronin realised who the man was. He wore a robe of deep forest green over bright yellow kesa threads. A jade cuirass poked through from underneath, matching the green greaves and boots he wore. A wooden carving resembling the sun hung from his neck. At his feet, as if carelessly, sat his naginata, while its owner whispered prayers to the wind.

The attire, along with the shaved head, could only mean one thing.

'A sohei?' Hazukiro spoke louder now. 'What's a warrior monk doing beyond the walls?'

The monk opened his eyes, exhaled, and slowly rose to his feet. Hazukiro couldn't help but feel envy. To be approached by an armed stranger on horseback and *not* instinctively reach for a weapon when addressed? No one in Ijihan maintained peace of mind like the pious. And he could hardly fault the Children of

Kesyoka for such beliefs. By her grace, the goddess' light singed demons to ash. This was irrefutable. With such love, power, and grandeur, it took a lot to stir the faith of the Teragaku monks.

'Nightspast,' the monk said softly, offering a bow. 'I was told a prisoner would be joining the excursion.'

He smiled warmly and approached Hazukiro.

'That is one name for me, yes,' the ronin said flatly.

'It seems the daimyo has finally seen that beyond sin can come gainful service.' The monk bowed again. 'I am called Dokshin.'

The ronin lowered his head. 'Hazukiro. You mentioned an excursion. Have you too been summoned to aid the Spectors?'

The monk nodded solemnly and moved towards his horse. 'It seems despite Kesyoka's grace, the Blight continues to ravage every resource in its path. Warriors included.'

He mounted and clicked his tongue, and before long the ronin and the monk were riding side by side, towards the treeline.

'The daimyo requested you join?' the ronin called over stomping hooves.

'I volunteered!' Dokshin called back. 'I didn't expect anything to come from my offer. I offered my aid months past. It seems there is, however, a new quarry to kill. And as rewarding as the temple is, I'd rather serve by getting grime on my hands, truth be told. Chairs, walls, scrolls. . .they keep you from the world sometimes.'

Hazukiro chuckled. 'That may not be so bad.'

He pondered a while as the horses galloped on.

'And so a leashed and a priest join the hunt. I suppose having a ragtag team of warriors who *aren't* Spectors gather at the gate would show the fortressfolk just how desperate the Academy is becoming.'

The monk laughed. 'You appear to know more than I, my friend.'

'I'd wager the opposite, monk.'

Hooves clamoured in concord until the pair reached the forest's border.

'Let's lead the horses from here.' Dokshin dismounted.

A shrill noise came from above. Hazukiro freed his blade and cast his gaze skywards. It was easy to spot behind the cloudless skies. A hawk, slowly circling above the forest.

'Mōkin!' Dokshin pointed. 'Captain Itaro's scout. It is a good omen to be greeted from the sky before noon!'

The monk placed his naginata on his back and led his horse through the untamed shrubland of the woods. Hazukiro led Akumo, watching the skies before the looming treetops blotted out the sun.

'Kesyoka has surely blessed us,' Dokshin beamed. 'Let us hunt!'

CHAPTER XII

THE CRIMSON CONVOY

MŌKIN SWOOPED DOWN AND LANDED on his master's shoulder, perching on the scarlet pauldron. The other four Spectors sat in a half-circle, facing the trees that the ronin and the sohei emerged from.

Dokshin approached the convoy first, a blushing blend of eagerness and humility, grinning and bowing with the profusion of a smitten tea server.

'It is a tremendous honour to be hunting with all of you!'

The seated four gave lacklustre replies. Two nodded, one muttered a greeting, and the other shot daggers at the pair. Itaro set his hawk to the skies and approached Dokshin with a smile grand enough to make up for the other four frowns.

'We are glad to have you!' he turned to Hazukiro. 'Both of you!'

'It's a disgrace. . .' a Spector grumbled.

'Uka.' Itaro's voice was sturdy as steel and deep as graves. 'Was convincing you to meet them here not enough to stroke your ego?'

Hazukiro gave Dokshin a knowing look.

He *was* right after all.

It smelled of desperation for the fortressfolk to have the image of their strong and capable hunters diminished.

'The glory will be yours,' Hazukiro bowed, familiar with the strokes of buttering boastful bread.

'Speak not to me, *leashed*,' Uka stood and spat. 'I've no qualms with aid against the Blight. But *you*?' His voice fell flat. 'I know *exactly* who you are.'

Hazukiro wondered if he could say the same. The man looked to be close to his age, somewhere over fifty winters. His hair was mostly white, tied back in a bun, and time had been unkind to his face. Or perhaps years of war was the culprit? Every other clue hid behind red samurai armour that each of the Spectors wore.

Either way, the ronin could not place the man.

'This is First Lieutenant Uka.' Itaro came between the pair, towering over them both.

'Like you, Uka has seen his share of bloodshed before the Blight. Regardless of how that bloodshed concluded we now share a common enemy in its wake.'

The lieutenant conceded, returning to his seat beside the others, who all sat in silence.

'Come, we're burning daylight. Hazukiro is a scribe. This one is Dokshin, a sohei from the Temple.' Itaro walked over to his men.

'You've already met Uka. The young one over there with his whiskers coming in is Kiyo.'

Hazukiro recognised him; the boy from the barracks who witnessed his whipping.

'Acolyte Kiyo, a pleasure!' The boy stood up, sharp as a sword, and bowed deeply.

'Enough bowing you fool,' Uka chided. 'We're demon hunters, not samurai. Save the ceremonial nonsense for the fortressfolk. Out here you can drop the mask. Stick your hackles up for the dead, not the living.'

Hazukiro held back a smirk as the boy slinked back into his seat. Not one week ago, this sapling had watched as his superior deemed the ronin a traitorous wretch worthy of the lash. Today, it was an apparent pleasure to make acquaintances. The lad didn't know what to think. The sheep mentality of the young, further soured by the bitter old. Hazukiro knew it painfully well.

Itaro concluded the introductions with two tall men. They both looked to be in their mid-thirties, able and supple, itching to kill oniku, but unsure of the new additions to their hunting party.

'And these two hotheads with the silver pikes are Akio and Fura.'

Itaro crossed his arms and sharpened his tone.

'*Help* is not to be scoffed at when we share a common enemy. All of you will do well to remember this. Think twice before sticking knives in backs that are in short supply.'

Hazukiro and Dokshin shared a glance, and Itaro sighed softly.

'It's true. Our numbers dwindle by the day. The oniku are—'

'Smarter,' Hazukiro chimed in. All eyes fell on him.

'Speak freely,' Itaro nodded. Uka rose in protest, and with a silent and firm hand, his captain sat him back down.

Uka was the prime example of a dog begging to be unshackled, snapping at ankles, waiting for the word from his master. And he had the gall to call Hazukiro 'leashed'.

'No matter the mouth, wisdom is wisdom,' Itaro spoke to the company. 'This swordsman scribe has been documenting the attacks for years now, and fresh perspectives benefit us all. They cannot be dismissed.'

Itaro gestured for the ronin to continue.

'Their nature is changing,' Hazukiro took a seat on a stump. 'The first year of the Blight saw the fall of the other four fortresses. The two major towns, and most villages besides. But with these losses came knowledge.'

He paused, half expecting retaliation. To his surprise, they allowed him to continue. For once, his words were worth something.

'Mud covers our scents,' he continued, 'rendering the demons mostly blind. Through the science of our arkinist, we've harnessed the radiance of Kesyoka's light into baubles. Silver cuts through black bones where steel and iron have failed. But even as we've learned to fight back, even after introducing the Blood Spectors, those early nights still saw them coming down on us. Night after night. Mindlessly ambling on, barrelling through the sky in droves, sniffing out food.'

'Blood Spectors are an odd choice to give an oniku history lesson to,' Akio chuckled.

'You see an awful lot from the inside of a prison cell,' Fura mused.

'The daimyo requests I know certain things, for the sake of my scribing. The rest, well, I have a window. And people love to talk.'

'If you've a conclusion, reach it,' Uka scowled.

'Recent attacks have been different,' Hazukiro continued. 'Though swarms still pass through, villager deaths have almost come to a standstill. My last report was that of a kidnapping, as close to the Teragaku as Fushumaka.

'Not uncommon for predators,' Kiyo chimed in, brushing back his hair. 'Many carnivores take their prey to lairs and feed on them there.'

'Of course,' Hazukiro nodded. 'But oniku never have. Their thirst has always been *insatiable*, ever since they first spawned. If they can smell blood, they *will*, without fail, gorge until their victims are hollow husks. The difference now is that while they do still kill to feed, they've started taking people *alive*.'

The Spectors looked to their captain, silent as stones.

'What do you know?' Hazukiro pressed.

'Our destination,' Fura said, swapping glances with the Spectors. 'The survivor mentioned a woman drenched in blood. He was out fishing when it happened. No one was taken. No one was spared. It was a *massacre*. He made for the Academy right away.'

'*Fishing?*' Dokshin uttered in disbelief. 'In the dead of night?'

'The attack,' Itaro shut his eyes and sighed, '. . .it happened in the middle of the day.'

PART II
THE SUNSTRIDER

CHAPTER XIII

QUARRY

DAYLIGHT DANCED THROUGH TREES. A brisk chill took the morning air, declaring the proximate end of autumn. The company set forth in silence, pondering the words of their captain. He'd say no more of the matter, and it was not their place to question why. Instead, they were left wondering while russet leaves tinged by time fell about them.

'We stray far,' Dokshin cut the air. 'Are the wagon roads ruined?'

Akio pulled his horse alongside the monk's. 'Afraid you won't find your way back, sohei?'

'This is the path the survivor took,' Itaro called out.

Akio gestured to the expanse of forest that lay before them. Black pine and birch trees twisted and merged. At their gnarled roots, copses of ferns poked through.

'The village in question is unmarked,' Itaro explained.

'We'll have to take the footpaths through Wisteria Woods.'

'A two-day ride through the thick,' Uka dug heels into his horse. 'We should make haste, Itaro. The woods are largely uncharted. And these old trees could be riddled with hiding places for the burrowers.'

'*Ikari*,' Hazukiro corrected.

'Ha!' Itaro smirked.

Uka snorted as deep as his stallion. 'Kill as many as I have and you may call them what you wish, *leashed*.'

Itaro prodded his horse, setting a quicker pace for the convoy. 'Until then, we should stick to the open wherever possible.'

Hazukiro itched at that.

'Go on, then,' Itaro chuckled, noticing the ronin's frown. 'Feel free to correct the lieutenant.'

'No,' Hazukiro shook his head. 'In this context, he is correct. The notion goes against the grain, that's all.'

Itaro shared a sidelong smile. 'We adapt to different quarry, my friend.'

The captain turned to check on the acolyte. The boy gazed at the clusters of knotted branches around him as if hypnotised by a dance of snakes waiting to strike.

'Kiyo!'

The young Spector gulped, stiff in his saddle.

'The ronin thinks that wandering in the open is safer than sticking to the shroud of the woods. Tell us all why our friend is correct.'

The boy was taken aback.

'Correct, Lord Itaro?'

'*Captain*. And yes.'

Kiyo swallowed. 'He is. . .not.'

Fura laughed. 'You sound unsure, boy!'

Uka clicked his tongue. 'Have you any notion how fast oniku are? I hope to all the gods you're quicker with your blade than you are your tongue.'

'The open exposes us!' Kiyo spluttered out. 'We'd be an easy target for ruffians.'

Kiyo felt his words fumble, his answers treading water under the judgement of his captain. The boy expected either praise or a tongue-lashing, but Itaro simply burst into laughter instead.

'*Ruffians!*' he howled, and the company joined in. Kiyo's eyes darted between the party, feigning laughter.

'Boy, the *Houchou Handbook* is centuries old!' Faru wiped away a tear.

Kiyo cleared a light, chagrin chuckle from his throat.

'*Bandits*, captain.'

Itaro simmered down to a smile. 'Also correct. But *bandits* are predictable, yes? Untrained. Undisciplined. They feel things we've all felt. Greed. Anger. Fear.'

Itaro gave pause, and all hooves halted in echo. He pointed up.

'But in the trees?'

Kiyo cursed under his breath, furious he'd not anticipated the bait.

'But in the trees,' he shook his head, 'the ikari attack quickly and in great numbers.'

'The space gives you freedom,' Itaro lectured. 'Opportunity to manoeuvre. Perceiving the potential gives you options. You'd do well to remember that. Unfortunately, the scholars who wrote the oh-so-renowned handbook did not account for the undead taking flight every—'

A sharp *splat* halted the convoy.

Dokshin gasped. 'What in the hells was *that*?'

Mōkin swooped down to retrieve his prize, caging its corpse in black talons.

'A squirrel!' Itaro held out his hand. 'I'll keep it safe, boy.'

With a shrill cry, the hawk placed the rodent in his master's palm and took to the skies again.

'A silver lining if ever there was one,' Itaro said, pocketing the critter in a saddle pouch.

Fura whistled in agreement. 'Thank the gods the damned demons have no taste for animal blood. I'm not sure I'd be the same man without my meat.'

'I'm sure the monk could attest to *that*.'

The party roared into laughter. Even Dokshin couldn't help but find amusement in the comradery, even if it was at his expense.

Hazukiro growled. 'Does that not frighten any of you?'

'What?' Akio chortled. 'Being a eunuch? Bit late for me, I reckon.'

Fura leaned over and patted his shoulder. 'I'm sure if we asked nicely, the arkinist could whip up a knife small enough.'

The laughter surged then died down when Itaro cast a curious gaze behind him, then back to the shrouded path ahead.

'It sounds like you have some more wisdom to share, ronin?'

Akio looked sidelong, brows baffled. 'Well?'

Hazukiro took in the vista before him. Blood Spectors, fearsome warriors astride their horses, travelling in convoy to hunt their prey. A mysterious enemy that massacred an entire village in the middle of the day. With that image fresh in his mind, the scene before him shifted. Suddenly, these were mere men. Their crimson armour, intricate craftsmanship and all, began to look like painted targets. Beneath all that silver and steel, the Spectors were soft bags of flesh and blood.

To the sparrow, the cat's claws hold dominion. But if a *tiger* invaded that food chain? Control would crumble. Hierarchies would change. The sparrow would be deemed irrelevant, while the simple cat would not be able to comprehend just how blunt his claws were.

'No animal can fight off oniku. The demons could drink the blood of any living creature they wanted to.'

His eyes fell to the imbued sword, still sheathed and unbloodied.

'But for reasons known only to them, we're the only quarry that interests them.'

'Reason?' Uka raised a brow. 'The devils are mindless. They do not see reason. Only my blade before it frees their heads from their bodies.'

Itaro cleared his throat. 'And they've felt that sting for seven years now.' The captain looked up to his hawk, a vicious predator in nature but a summonable servant to him.

'*We adapt to our quarry.*'

CHAPTER XIV

BLACK ICHOR

THE RONIN WATCHED SHADOWS STRETCH across the company's trail, those final slivers of sunlight coating the ground gold. He rode at the rear, studying the body language of his travelling companions.

Kiyo shifted in his saddle, trying to hide his fidgeting. The boy was clearly battling the rising jitters of facing his first demon. Dokshin squinted at the sun between his fingers, holding back nervous words with a wince as if he were squeezing hot coal. The rest of the warriors made no mention of stopping, or of the taunting, setting sun. They simply pressed on, as silent and strong as the war horses that carried them. These were the Blood Spectors, after all. Nights beyond the walls were nothing new to them.

Hazukiro felt the fading sun on his neck and found himself wondering. The hunters seemed so sure of themselves. He wouldn't have been surprised if they'd planned to fight through the night on horseback, baubles flaring and silver slicing. The thought reminded the ronin of his earlier errand at the arkinist.

'Captain Itaro!' he called out. 'I still have your new katana!'

The ronin wondered why he'd not asked for it sooner.

'Thank you, I'll admire it once we're inside the Sanctum.'

Dokshin raised his head. 'Sanctum? There's holy ground out here?'

Itaro nodded. 'Made holy by the bottled light of our grand goddess. We—ah, but we're almost there. You can see for yourself.'

That was enough to soothe the monk's fretting. Hazukiro realised that though the sohei had all bloodied their naginatas during the clan wars, Dokshin would likely be the first of his kin to face oniku.

Uka watched the monk sigh in relief, and disdain crept across the old warrior's face.

He sighed like a disappointed father. 'Goddess illuminate this band of damned *fools.*'

Itaro led the group down several bends beyond the footpaths. The previously packed trees were now spaced and sparse, mushrooms and moss growing over a sea of tree stumps.

'There it is,' Akio pointed out. '*Firefly.*'

Dokshin scratched his chin. 'Firef—'

'*Must* you spew every word that enters your mind?' Uka snapped. He dug heels into his steed and galloped ahead.

'Lieutenant!' Itaro rode off after him.

'Ignore the grumpy old man,' Fura shrugged. 'We know better than to run our mouths around his sensitive ears. And now you know too.'

The Spector gestured to a large mound of boulders, bathing in faint sunlight. 'Our Sanctums are all abandoned silver mines. This one was decommissioned long before Blightfall. We've been clearing them out one by one, and setting up everburn lanterns at the doors. Ones we have to spare, anyway. '*Firefly*' is the name we've given this one. See the marking over there?'

Hazukiro and Dokshin glanced sidelong, noticing the image of an insect carved into the trunk of a black pine. Across the recess, the ronin noticed a second symbol etched into one of the many trees that encircled the glade. At the heart of the clearing, the smattering of stone hillocks merged at the mouth of a cave.

The company dismounted and sent their horses to graze. A large wooden door marked the cave's entrance, a Teragaku lantern hanging at its centre. But as shadows began to creep into the cave, the company noticed that the lamp gave no light.

'Is that—?' Uka stepped gingerly into the dim. He stopped when something crunched underfoot. A faint gleam of shattered glass lay in a puddle of purple. A few feet further in, a trail of red ran towards the door and continued underneath it.

The Spector drew his katana.

'The Sanctum's tarnished,' he whispered back.

Itaro nodded and turned to the ronin. 'I'll take that sword now.'

* * *

With their celestial shield minutes from disappearing, the company moved into the cave, brandishing silver weapons. Each member also wore a bauble that hung from a piece of their armour. Hazukiro opted to hang his from his straw hat. The collective radiance swathed the group in faint lilac light.

Itaro stood at the front, his imbued katana nestled lightly in one hand, and his original sword in the other, stanced in calm akimbo. Uka stood behind him, his own blade poised high and braced. Spread on their flanks, Akio and Fura pointed their polearms. The acolyte stood in his taught stance, blinking rapidly, bracing himself for the worst. Dokshin prayed to Kesyoka for protection, while Hazukiro entered the Hush and cleared his mind of its usual maelstrom.

'Entering,' Itaro whispered. The door creaked open. Its iron latch dangled from it like an eye torn from its socket. The company poured in on shadow feet, casting their collective hue as they stole themselves deeper into the cave.

'Over here,' Uka mouthed softly. He pointed to the blood trail, meandering into a wider pool.

'Still wet,' Akio slotted a bauble into a small iron lamp and shone it on the scene. He cursed behind gritted teeth.

'It's Gerugu.'

Itaro cursed, then sighed deeply. 'I was hoping he'd returned home after we departed. Keep an eye out for Jikabi.'

The dead Spector's body was mangled like a mistreated toy. Limbs, riddled with fang marks, had been torn off and strewn about him. The armour was shredded, his innards splayed out like carmine clothes. Akio moved the lamp closer. Gerugu's skin had been sapped of colour, now ghost-white and crinkled. Even his lifeless eyes were the pallid-grey of a rolling fog.

Kiyo buckled over. It took everything for the acolyte to not relinquish his breakfast.

'Damn it,' Fura grumbled, taking his blade through his fallen hunter's skull. 'We cleared this space last week. They must have already been in a bad way. Fought their way in, but not in time.'

The monk stepped into a pile of viscera with a squelch.

'No, no, no. . .' Dokshin mumbled between sharp breaths. 'Not like this. *Not like this.*'

Hazukiro, deep in the Hush, felt his calmness start to stutter. The uneasiness of the inexperienced among them. Their doubt. Fear.

Weak links break the chain.

'Calm yourselves, all of you!' spat Itaro.

Akio guided the lantern, revealing the blood-speckled cave walls. The sohei took a stammering step back. 'I'm sorry, captain.' Dokshin stammered. 'I—'

'Don't be a fool!' Hazukiro snatched the monk's scruff. 'Night has fallen. We push *in* or not at all.'

'Listen to the ronin,' Uka spat, briefly grateful for his presence.

Itaro huffed, itching to use his blades. 'We press on. They must be cleansed by silver.'

Kiyo pounded a fist to his chest, begging any god listening for a surge of courage. But while battling his mind, he lost focus of his feet. The boy slipped on a blood-slicked stone and fell flat, shattering his bauble. The glass splintered off, tearing into his cheek and eye.

Against all instinct, all former notions of glory, the young acolyte, fresh to the world and its horrors, howled in pain.

And something from the depths howled back.

A pair of eyes tore the veil of dark. They stared the company down, hot-white and sinister, the thing's body still shrouded in shadow.

'Let it approach!' Itaro boomed. 'Hold!'

Dokshin's prayers turned from whispers to cries, spewing scripture as he began to step backwards.

'Hold, damn you,' Hazukiro placed a palm on the monk's back. 'Or you'll get us *all* killed.'

Dokshin held his tongue behind pursed lips. He pointed his naginata toward the dark.

'What do we do?'

The oniku stepped forward, nine feet tall. The demon had a sickly and slender frame that resembled an abominable amalgamation of a dead man and a foam-faced bat. Wrinkled, leathery wings folded at its back. Its tall and pointed ears twitched as it lurched forward on lanky limbs, like the hocks of a hound made upright. Blood-tipped talons as long and sharp as daggers curved at the ends of its gangling arms.

'Closer. . .' Itaro growled through gritted teeth. 'Come on.'

The creature's maw was wide. Overlapping rows of dark razorteeth lined its decaying gums.

'It's carrying something!' Fura bolstered the grip on his pike.

The beast's head swivelled swiftly in a motion that would snap any living man's neck. It ogled the Spector, and lulled its rotting head to the side with curious hunger behind its empty eyes.

In its mouth, protruding over its bevy of black needles, two curved and prominent fangs sat sunken inside deep into the neck of another Spector. The warrior was still alive.

Akio gasped. 'It's Jikabi!'

The victim groaned softly, open-mouthed like a breathless, pale fish.

Hazukiro snarled in disgust, watching as the beast strode forward, chewing on the ensnared body. The victim hung helplessly like a limp rabbit inside a wolf's gob.

Paralysed.

And then the demon grinned, clamping its jaw down into flesh and bone. A carmine fountain spurted with a crunch as the oniku bit the head off. Gobbling it down, it effortlessly flung the heavy headless torso against stone.

Itaro hissed hot.

'*Slaughter* it!'

Blood-soaked fangs bared as the oniku shrieked. A shrill ring reverberated in the cave. It lunged.

Uka was the first to close the gap. With an undulated arc, he swung his blade into the beast's leg. It roared hollow and swiped at the lieutenant. Talons nicked him, but his bauble flared bright and the oniku withdrew with a snort and a hiss.

Itaro leapt in. Katanas akimbo, he bore down, stabbing each of the beast's wings.

'It's grounded!' Akio shouted as he rushed forward with Fura. The two split at the flanks, meeting at the beast's back and pushing their pikes into the creature's calves.

'Floored!' they called in tandem. The lieutenant staggered back, watching as trickles of blood poured through his torn armour.

'Uka?' Itaro called out.

The pinned beast swung its arms wildly, swatting at its back. Akio and Fura pressed their blades down against the strength of the demon, then smashed their baubles against its skin. The oniku howled as its legs began to sizzle lilac smoke.

'Hurry!' Akio cried, hands shaking on the pike's shaft.

The captain snarled and cut both blades free, shredding the wings' sinew like a paper scroll.

Uka coughed up blood and dropped down. His head lolled against the cave wall.

'Quickly, sohei!' Hazukiro shouted. 'Its arms! Let's finish this!'

Dokshin mustered what courage he could and charged ahead with the ronin. Hazukiro slid under a shredded wing, spun on his heel, and came up behind the beast. With measured fury he sliced true, reaping its arms from its body like a sickle to the harvest. Ichor spewed over the company, the beast wailing on its nailed knees as it bled black.

Dokshin yowled and plunged his naginata into the demon's chest. The creature squirmed until Itaro freed his twin blades and sliced again. Blades crossed paths in a perfect cross, two clean cuts through the neck.

The final cry ceased and echoed in the cave for a second like the aftermath of a lightning strike. The oniku finally toppled over, its head rolling deeper into the dark.

'Quickly!' Itaro panted. 'The lieutenant!'

Fura dug into his pouch and produced a vial of ground wasari. He popped the cork off and sprinkled it into the claw marks across Uka's chest. The bleeding stopped almost immediately, and colour returned to the lieutenant's face.

Dokshin gasped with a grin. 'Kesyoka's grace truly knows no bounds.'

Uka gingerly rose to his feet, patting Fura on his shoulder.

'Is it dead?'

Itaro turned to find Kiyo at the mouth of the cave, keeled over and spewing bile.

'Boy!' Itaro called. The boy turned his head, eyes watering, spittle hanging from his mouth.

'You were to strike with the lieutenant.'

The boy looked as if he were ready to speak, but instead, threw up on his boots again.

Itaro sighed. 'He's too inexperienced for this.'

'It's how he learns,' coughed Uka, sheathing his katana. 'He'll receive his lashings when we return to the Academy.'

Akio crouched beside the headless oniku, passing his lamp over the body.

'This was one at least a foot taller than most we've encountered.'

Itaro spat on the demon's corpse. 'It bested two seasoned Spectors. By itself.'

The captain turned to the ronin. 'What do you make of this?'

Hazukiro glanced at the aftermath. Two mangled warriors lay torn to shreds. The oniku's arms lay in a puddle of black ichor. Even with silver, cutting it down was no simple task. Its skin almost felt *tougher*.

'Whatever massacred those villagers could be much worse.' The ronin sighed. 'I think we'll need more men.'

Itaro sheathed his familiar sword, then eyed the new imbued blade. Its intended knack still lay dormant.

'Let's settle in for the night. I have a lot to think over.'

He looked around the cave, faint violet revealing the violence. Limbs littered pools of red and black, man and monster alike.

Itaro unstrapped his armour with a heavy sigh and walked deeper into the dark.

'Akio, take thread and needle to the lieutenant's wounds, then the boy's face. Hazukiro. Dokshin. Bring the horses in. Fura, see that we're fortified. Put every bauble to use.'

Itaro looked around the dim, then paced into the dark.

'Allow me a moment to my thoughts. Lieutenant, when you're on your feet, sanctify this mess.'

CHAPTER XV

DARK DREAMS

AFTER EATING A PORTION of pickled radishes and rice around the cave fire, the company settled their weary bones for the night. It didn't take long for Hazukiro to fall asleep, but with his mind adrift and his subconscious vulnerable, pestering thoughts snaked through and stole themselves inside his dreams.

The usual torment ensued, and again, he dreamed of fire. Of death and destruction. Screams smothered by smoke. Entire bloodlines ended overnight, from the far too young to the helplessly old.

He tossed in his sleep while knots mercilessly weaved in his gut. As cold as the night was, a sweat still swathed him, drying out his lips and dampening his kimono.

'Ronin.'

Hazukiro spun from his sleep and reached for his sword.

Itaro raised his hands with a soft chuckle. 'Easy there.'

The ronin winced with the headrush that took him. He sat up to slow the reeling, and with sluggish and dry eyes, he stared into the campfire. Its embers licked the air like a cruel remnant of his dark dreams.

'You should rest,' Itaro rolled his neck. 'I'll wake you when it's your watch.'

The ronin sighed, glancing over the sleeping company. Envy flooded him.

'I don't think I can,' he sighed in contrition.

Itaro took the tetsubin from the fireplace and poured boiling water into a wooden cup stocked with tea leaves.

'Some ocha, then?'

With the memory of the dream fading, the reality of the late autumn air took hold. Brisk and thin, it began tickling at the sweat on his skin. He took the cup with thanks and sipped away the oncoming chill.

Itaro took a pensive sip, sighing, staring into flame.

'I must apologise, ro—Hazukiro.'

The ronin raised a brow. 'Captain?'

'I've not been kind to you. Back at the Academy.'

Hazukiro shook his head dismissively. 'I deserve nothing less.'

Itaro nodded at that.

'Perhaps,' he said bluntly. 'I know of your past, as much as the daimyo tries to hide it from the rest of the fortressfolk. But I am grateful that your sword arm is here to serve us now. Our people need all the help we can offer them.'

Hazukiro rubbed his throbbing temples, then exhaled deeply.

'That is why it is an honour to serve them,' he stated. 'I don't deserve their forgiveness. But I will regain every scrap of honour I can before my time on this island comes to an end.'

Itaro took a sip of tea and nodded. 'There is *nothing* more important than honour.'

'And what of duty?' Hazukiro prompted, testing the conversational waters. 'And service?'

'Ah.' Itaro refilled his cup and put the pot to rest. 'Both beget honour. When it is time to stand before the radiance of Kesyoka, I wish for my honour to be insurmountable to that of any samurai that has come before. True, we serve no shogun or traditional banner anymore. Save for the law of our Academy. But the people still rely on us to protect them. We must avoid malaise. And there is *nothing* I won't do to maintain that divide between them and the Blight.'

Hazukiro took a thoughtful sip.

'May I ask you something, captain?'

'Speak your mind.'

'Why do you avoid your sword's imbued nature?'

Even then, Itaro's chief sword took favour, resting at his side. The imbued sword lay in its scabbard among the other packs and saddlebags, piled in a corner of the cave.

'You say you hear much from your cell,' Itaro began. 'Tell me. Have you heard of the origin of the Blight?'

'Many theories,' Hazukiro scoffed. 'Most of them outlandish.'

Itaro gave a dark stare then, one that nearly returned the chill to the ronin's old bones.

'As outlandish as the dead taking flight and feasting on our insides?' He put away the thought, undressing his sour mien.

'The most common theory I've heard,' Hazukiro began, 'is that we're being punished.'

'A plausible theory. The scriptures speak of rising hells at the folly of man. Which, incidentally, ties in with a theory of my own.' The captain leaned in. 'Our obsession with mastering majik has led to this grand undoing. The gods have battled, time and time again, over power they can barely divide amongst themselves. And men are no different.' He tossed a stone to the flame. 'We tamper with lives and things beyond our understanding for a taste of power. And tasting power means shedding blood.'

He looked to the imbued sword, nestled and lifeless, but holding a heavy cloud over the captain nonetheless.

'Even in our own hands, I do not trust the very notion of majik.'

Hazukiro brought the tea to his lips.

'And what of the lightflares?' He wiped drops from his beard. 'They've defended the fortress for years now.'

'Yes,' Itaro said. 'I was against that too. But I cannot deny their use. I imagine whatever concoction the arkinist has imbued in that blade will be a great help too. Power *works*. But it also corrupts. I don't want to lose my people to the whims of men meddling with majik.'

He glanced at the sword again, embers floating above it across the fireplace. 'Or perhaps I meddle by doubting power bestowed. Perhaps this *is* the only way.' He placed his cup down and sighed. 'Nothing else has dropped in our laps.' He turned to the ronin.

'Forgive my ramblings. Much has happened since Blightfall. It is a constant gauntlet of navigating next steps. But one truth I can rely on is silver. And my hand wielding it.'

Hazukiro couldn't help but admire the captain's convictions.

'To dismiss something so powerful is an honourable choice.' He smiled. 'It is no easy choice.'

Itaro patted the ronin's shoulder with a grin that masked pain.

'It isn't meant to be easy.'

Hazukiro allowed the resonating sentiment to offer him a moment of mental respite. Hazukiro lay back down, his lids heavy, his mind afire with renewed hope.

Even the honourable captain of the Blood Spectors battled his own mind.

Perhaps he wasn't so alone after all.

CHAPTER XVI

RED MIST

THE SPECTORS PRESSED NORTH, eventually exiting the thick of the black pines around midday. Stopping only at a small stream to drink and bathe, they passed through a stretch of bamboo trees before arriving at the border of the Wisteria Woods.

'Beautiful!' Dokshin exclaimed in awe. 'Everything is in bloom, even out of season. Something holy must have taken root. It is difficult to imagine that evil could taint even this place.'

'Could and has.' Uka passed him, pointing ahead.

Five black-burnt poles huddled at an old signpost beside the path. Hollow remains of victims were tied to each one.

'The Forsaken,' Uka grumbled. 'Mad zealots, the lot of them. They *offer* up people to the night. Gods know why.'

'I hope to never encounter them,' Dokshin swallowed.

The convoy pressed on, holding their mouths and noses shut as they rode past the flies that circled the rotting carrion.

Itaro turned to the hunting party. 'Let us focus on one pestilence at a time. Remember that our quarry doesn't rely on the cover of night to kill. Watch your backs. And watch the skies. The Forsaken are a low priority.'

He waved a hanging curtain of wisteria aside and passed through the forest's purple veil.

Hours passed with little said. Mōkin circled the blanket of purple trees below, scouring for threats and lunch. Itaro and Uka remained stoically silent, focusing wholly on their holy mission. Akio and Fura swapped a few hunting stories from time to time while Dokshin listened with wide ears. Kiyo, likely sulking in shame, wore a scowl and said nothing to anyone. Hazukiro, with no threat of missing a curfew, made the most of the fresh air the forest offered. Though alert, he couldn't help but admire the terrific hues of the wisterias, blowing blue and lilac in the breeze, creating a path of colourful petals.

The company was deep into the heart of the woods when the sun began to set. Half an hour off course to the northwest, Itaro led the group to another Sanctum; a stone-walled space in the mine that used to serve as the dosho's office. This one had been called '*Serow*' after the herds of large backwards-horned antelopes that grazed near the old mine's lake. Fura set about making the fire while Akio fussed over the proper way to brew his tea. The occasional hollow words were swapped over food, but it was clear to everyone that this mysterious oniku was at the forefront of all of their troubled minds. Kiyo, desperate to prove himself, volunteered for first watch.

The desecrated village and the presumable sunstrider that stalked its surroundings were only a few hours north of Serow. For the first time since Blightfall, even the Blood Spectors dreaded the daylight.

***

A small clearing ushered the way to the ruined hamlet.

The settlement had no more than a dozen homes, each covered in mud and claw marks. Hazukiro turned his attention to one razed home. Its shoji doors were torn to shreds. Dried blood blotched the outside walls. The pale corpse of a woodcutter lay in the soil, still clutching a clean axe.

'Such small claw marks,' Fura remarked. 'Too big for ikari, too small for oniku.'

Itaro dismounted and freed his katana, weaving through the ruin with wary feet. Pallid corpses were strewn about. The captain turned to the acolyte.

'Notice anything odd, Kiyo?'

The boy was lost in his mind again, fighting off nerves. He gently prodded at his scarred cheek and studied the scene.

'The necks?'

Itaro nodded grimly. 'The necks.'

Though sucked dry, the bodies all lacked the signature fang marks of a feasting demon. Instead, entire gullets had been ripped from the victims. Wrists too. Shoulders even.

'It's insatiable,' Akio exclaimed. 'More so than the common brute. Almost...inexperienced?'

'We must search these homes,' Itaro commanded.

Hazukiro calmed Akumo and dismounted, sending her off to find some fresh grass. He freed his katana and approached the first house. Its door was ajar. He pushed and peered inside, and lunged back when a corpse flopped at his feet. The throat had been gouged out. Messily, like the others outside. Hazukiro gingerly stepped over the body and stalked further into the shambled home. Shelves had been smashed to splinters. The hearth lay dry and barren, brittle coal crumbling inside it. Inside the kitchen, the sun pierced through a large hole in the ceiling, illuminating two other bodies lying in pools of blood.

'Two more gouged-out throats,' Hazukiro noticed.

One of the victims, a woman, lay on her front, with her clothing shredded at the back. The same oddly small claw marks ran down her spine.

Kiyo stepped into the room, gagging at the decay.

'Did it come in through the roof?' He covered his nose, swallowing vomit and disdain.

'Trees!' Uka shouted.

The company convened outside and looked up. Leaves rustled violently. Then, an inexplicable burst of red mist. Stillness followed.

'What in all the *hells*?' Itaro unsheathed twin blades.

A loud crash drew their attention.

'That came from the tavern!'

Across the hamlet sat the old watering hole. Barrels of sake and blood poured down the tavern's porch steps. The slope of the roof revealed a recent hole, a plume of red smoke billowing from it.

The hunting party approached with caution. A disturbance of mumbled movement came from inside.

'Captain!' Kiyo bowed deeply. 'Please, I ask you for the honour to take lead!'

The boy was still terrified, but his desperation for glory was beginning to still the wobble in his knees.

Hazukiro knew that familiar look of fear. He'd known young men who'd been coaxed to serve at the very mention of honour and praise. At least this boy's war would be one of protecting the island and not one of fighting rival families *over* its prefectures.

'*One cannot be brave without first feeling fear,*' Hazukiro mused, admiring the boy's mettle.

Even if he *was* only after glory.

Itaro fixed his eyes on the odd smoke, now joining the breeze. 'Take the lieutenant with you.'

Kiyo bowed with no further protest. Uka gestured for the acolyte to lead. The boy pounded his chest and swung his sword in an arc, sipping fast breaths.

'Breathe through your mouth,' Hazukiro advised as the boy and lieutenant entered through the tavern's smashed-in doors.

Sour liquor stained the air, hanging on the dissipating mist. The floorboards were so thick with blood that the Spectors' boots splotched as they moved. Uka hastily grabbed Kiyo's shoulder.

The boy froze. 'I heard it too.'

Someone sniffled. And someone else hushed them.

'Survivors?' Kiyo turned a dark corner. A makeshift barricade of aged barrels and storage boxes hid muffled whimpering.

Uka raised sceptical brows, sniffing the air. 'Quickly now, boy. Get them out of there. A foul majik sings on the wind.'

Kiyo sheathed his sword and leapt into action. He shoved crates aside and rolled barrels away, beaming with pride to be wearing the armour of the Blood Spectors. The boy called out with a newfound boldness.

'You don't need to be afraid anymore!' Kiyo rolled away the last barrel. 'The Spectors are here to—'

Two pairs of burning brimstone eyes greeted him. One shimmered with worry, the other hot with fury. Both girls huddled together, kimonos and faces stained from several sinful sanguine feastings.

CHAPTER XVII

A MATTER OF HONOUR

THE BOY STOOD BEWILDERED.

'What is it?' Uka called out, his eyes following the creaking rafters. Kiyo stammered silent words, staring into desperate, panicked eyes.

'Are they alive?' Uka moved in. 'Injured?'

The lieutenant turned the corner and stopped. Stunned. Black eyes met his and a sickening cold throttled his gut.

'Get back, boy.' Uka stepped in, pointing his blade at the huddled pair.

A piece of the ceiling broke free and crashed through the floor, paving the way for a stream of sunlight. The Spectors watched in disbelief as one of the girls screamed. Her skin had caught alight. The other girl panicked, scrambling to move her burning companion back into the shadows.

'Get the others! Go!' Uka shouted over the screams of the girl.

But the boy had made up his mind the moment he'd seen skin sizzle. He saw prey. Some demon trickery. The girl looked human enough, but only oniku would burn in the presence of the goddess' Light. That was enough to convince him to attack.

'Die, demon!'

The acolyte struck true. His silver cut through charred flesh, lopping the girl's screaming head off in one swift cut.

The hunters poured into the tavern when the red mist barrelled through them like a hurricane. Their heads rattled and ears rang as they all fell from the sheer force. Itaro was the first to scramble to his feet.

'Kiyo!' He charged into the inn, both blades braced. 'Uka?!'

The acolyte faced his captain. His face was pale. His expression, horrified. He rose two shaking hands, dripping red, then fell to his knees.

'Help.'

His gut gaped open. Coughing up a small fountain of blood, the boy fumbled at his intestines before dropping dead.

Hazukiro dashed forward to catch him.

'He's gone, ronin!' Itaro yanked Hazukiro's arm.

The captain swallowed the crack in his voice when he glanced down. Uka lay dead. His throat was nothing more than a shredded clump of gnarled flesh.

'Re—regroup!' Itaro swallowed. '*Now!*'

'It's coming back!' Akio shouted.

'Down!' Hazukiro howled and dropped to his belly.

The scarlet wisp burst from the trees like a sudden storm.

It rolled over the ronin and pummelled into Akio.

'*No!*'

The cloud launched the Spector into the air. He tumbled down like a stone.

'Akio!' Fura rushed over to catch him. But a few metres too shy, the falling hunter fell flat and hard. His skull cracked and his neck snapped.

Fura fumed, chasing after the cloud with reckless abandon. The mist tore through another home's wall and settled once more, a muffled cry following it.

'Fura!' Itaro growled. 'Control yourself! Converge outside that house!'

The captain searched the hamlet with angry eyes. 'And where is the *damn* monk?'

Hazukiro straightened his hat and charged for the home, catching up with Fura.

'Come out, demon!' Fura howled.

There was complete silence. The remnants of the hunting party edged closer to the house. Itaro, scrambling to keep his head in the wake of the chaos. Fura, boiling hot for demon blood. Hazukiro, deep in the Hush, moved with measured calm. Dokshin was nowhere to be found.

'Come out. . .' Itaro pleaded to the house and to all the gods.

He produced a shortpear from his pack and primed it for throwing.

A sudden wail let loose, and the red wisp burst through another wall. Itaro hurled his spear as the thing screeched forward. The speartip sliced, going through but not without making a mark. The cloud shrieked and tumbled into a pile of barrels, shattering them. Its haze of red smoke simmered.

'It's down! Surround it! *Don't let it up again!*'

The men formed a half-circle, inching closer to the soaked pile of shattered rain barrels. The shrieks had ceased, but from the cluttered wood came another sound. Whimpering.

'Is that. . .?' Fura stepped closer, urging the others to draw nearer.

Hazukiro followed, his katana outstretched.

Itaro drew nearer on soft feet. 'What is it?'

The men parted their circle, lowering their weapons in what seemed like a show of pity and confusion. Hazukiro pressed on, kneeling, processing.

'It is a child,' he uttered. 'A young girl.'

'A disguise,' muttered Fura. 'The lieutenant wouldn't fall to some child.'

'Some new dark majik,' reasoned Itaro. 'Taking on the vise of our innocent.'

'It does not burn. . .' Itaro moved closer, head tilted like a predator. '*This* is our quarry?'

'The Blight shows no sign of slowing. . .' cursed Fura.

Hazukiro leaned closer to the girl. She sweated profusely, heaving deep breaths as if she'd been treading waters in a never-ending storm at sea.

'Step aside, ronin,' Itaro commanded.

Hazukiro shot him a look of disdain.

'This is a child,' he hissed between clenched teeth. 'She seems ill. Afflicted by the Blight, somehow. The Teragaku could help her.'

'The Teragaku helps the inhabitants of Ijihan by removing these accursed abominations. Whatever trickery this is, it's yet another agent of chaos. Another thing to fear. Look around you.'

Hazukiro soaked in the aftermath. A village torn to shreds. Corpses littering razed homes. Half of the Blood Spectors, dead in an instant. The ronin looked down at the girl.

She looked frightened and confused, fighting her very nature to defend herself. Sweat and blood-matted hair covered her breathless face.

'You're wrong,' Hazukiro said flatly. 'There is no honour in this.'

'You'd reduce this to a matter of honour?' Fura spat. 'There's none to be had here, besides avenging our fallen.'

Itaro lowered his voice. 'He's right. There is only us and the Blight. Life and death. Affliction or purification.' He drew another shortspear. '*Step. Aside.*'

Hazukiro shook his head, disgust bubbling behind his eyes.

'You'd rob a child of life? The very symbol of what it means to be pure in a land of torment, fighting a sickness that it does not understand?'

Itaro held up a hand for Fura to stand back. 'This is no longer a child. It has no life to relieve it of. It's already dead.'

The commander lunged his shortspear forward. Hazukiro spun and deflected, his katana cutting through the spear's shaft, splitting it in two.

'*Heresy!*' growled Fura. 'You'd side with the oniku over the protectors of your own land?'

Itaro raised his brows in utter surprise. He'd seen his share of madness. Fought countless demons of the night. Slaughtered traitorous soldiers and invading Njörkin alike. None had dared to actively defy him like this. He drew his katana.

'Stand back, Fura.' He spat and swished his sword to his side, then pointed its tip at the ronin. 'You. *Up.*'

Hazukiro rose to his feet, steadied his stance, and began circling the captain of the Blood Spectors.

'You've negated any chance of redemption now.' Itaro sounded disappointed, in himself or the ronin, he wasn't certain. 'I was a fool to believe you'd learned the value of duty. Instead, you continue to defy it. You've done nothing but give me an excuse to feed the island's soil with another traitor's head.' He spat the bloodied soil. 'All you've earned is a darker stain to your ledger of dishonour.'

Hazukiro sighed.

'Dishonour begets redemption. I will find it somewhere else, if not at the edge of your blade. But this is no deliberate sedition. I simply will not allow this child to pay the price for acting out of fear.'

CHAPTER XVIII
THE DUEL

'ONCE A TRAITOR...' growled Itaro.

Hazukiro removed his straw hat and tossed it to the wind. 'You would stain your soul before you spat on an order? Because the command came from one who sits above you?'

'Spare your rhetoric.' Itaro kept his eyes and wrists locked, circling the ronin. 'Battles of wit are not the kind that interest me.'

Hazukiro raised his katana high with a terrific gleam.

'Clearly.'

The ronin exhaled and entered the Hush.

The environment washed itself away like silent, crumbling walls. Darkness engulfed the bright colours of the forest. The sounds of birds were the first to fade. The whimpering of the girl died down, merging with the muffled murmurings of Fura as he spewed some choice words for the ronin. Finally, the last of the sounds remained. Itaro's shouting, as he lunged forward to strike.

Half-crouched with a wide stance, Hazukiro propelled himself up with a mighty swing, streaking his sword through the air. Silver met and sang with a sting and a clang. The ronin had seen the captain in action but was yet to feel the weight behind his blows.

Itaro gritted his teeth and bore down, biceps bulging as he pushed their locked blades down. At the point of most pressure, Hazukiro twisted his katana down and slipped free from the embrace. Itaro gasped as he almost toppled forward, exposing the nape of his neck. A fault that the ronin had time to exploit.

He chose not to.

'I need no quarter!' Itaro seethed, regaining his footing. 'Your mercy will only see you *gutted*.'

'That was your first and only grace.' Hazukiro lunged forward with surprising speed behind his steps.

Itaro was forced to block, strike after strike, pushed back by each blow. Each failed parry filled the captain with fury. He couldn't find an opening.

Hazukiro, equally frustrated and unable to pierce Itaro's guard, halted his flurry and took a step back to reassess. Catching his breath and attuning his connection to the Hush, he observed the flustered Spector.

There was no apparent flaw in his defensive techniques, but his emotional guard was cracking. That crack could be shattered into an opening

'Not too different from a demon,' thought Hazukiro.

Hungry to end his life. Seeing red. Driving out the fresh failure of losing his men. Each passing second and each ineffective strike only boiled his anger over.

People were not all that different from monsters, the ronin had found. The minds of men had stronger barriers, but beneath those emotional walls, they could be reduced to their primal instincts. The ronin had known this to be true of himself as well. It was one of the reasons he practised the Hush daily. It was the only thing preventing his own walls from crumbling into madness. Sometimes, the crack became a broken barricade because it was thought of as only a crack. That was the folly of men. Everything appeared strong until it broke.

'Come on, then,' Itaro hissed, not even bothering to regain his composure anymore.

'I cannot imagine a more embarrassing situation,' the ronin began, as he circled Itaro again.

'Your men are dead,' Hazukiro coaxed, hiding the distaste for his own tactic. 'And you live, having failed them, only to battle and *lose* to a traitor.'

Itaro's eyes twitched.

'Against a lowly prisoner,' Hazukiro pressed.

Itaro twisted his hilt but maintained the pace of circling. He shot a glance at the last Spector of his hunting party. Fura's eyes begged his captain to allow him to join the fight. Itaro shook his head. This was to be *his* victory.

The ronin subtly lowered his stance as he prepared his next taunt.

'Against an old man...'

Itaro lunged once more, spittle fleeing from his snarling mien. The ronin dug one foot into the ground. He pushed up and twirled, rolling like a curtain as the breeze of Itaro's blade swooshed behind him. Hazukiro reset his stance, hunkered down, and thrust his blade behind him. The tip drove through Itaro's armour. The captain spat and coughed, his torso pierced, silver sticking into his ribcage. Hazukiro followed the motion through. He swirled with the embedded blade and tore through the Spector's stomach.

Hazukiro turned to the child, half-expecting her to lunge at the spillage, but she kept still, sobbing to herself. The ronin turned to Fura.

He'd barely removed the blade from the gut when Fura charged him. He yelled and swung, leaving a small opening near his chest. The ronin swung up instead to block the strike. He raised his foot and kicked Fura's chest back.

'Go home,' Hazukiro boomed. 'I didn't want any of this!'

Fura steadied himself and thumped his chest.

'A traitor must pay with blood,' Fura recited in anger. He swirled his pike and lunged at the ronin, a spinning flurry of anger and grief.

'You don't have to do this!' shouted Hazukiro, blocking blows. He grunted and flicked his katana in an upward arc, deflecting the silver tip of Fura's polearm.

'Stop this!' Hazukiro ducked under another hasty swing.

And another. Fura howled as he thrust the pike again. The ronin leapt backwards, quick enough to avoid a fatal blow, but not fast enough to prevent the blade from making contact entirely. The silver tore through his kimono and into his midriff.

'You defend *demons*?' Fura tore his weapon free and primed another jab. This time it nicked the ronin's hand, sending his sword sailing into the air.

Hazukiro improvised. He rolled away, groaning at the fresh cut, and snatched up the nearest weapon. The arkinist's majik blade.

Freeing it from its home, the runic silver blade sang in the sunlight. Fura was quickly upon him, blind with rage.

Hazukiro hurriedly parried a strike, then sidestepped another. But not before the blade tore across his cheek. He hissed at the sting, panting from both exhaustion and pain.

There was no way out of this. For Itaro's death alone, he'd be captured and strapped to the pyres. The burden of age began to hinder him. He felt his strength and stamina wane. Something inside of him, something stronger than his doubt, encouraged him to push through it all.

He bore forward, sidestepping another strike while splitting open Fura's leg. An artery tore in two. Blood splattered across the ronin.

Before Hazukiro could turn back, another searing sting tore open his back. The sheer force behind it was enough to buckle his knees. It cut deep. His shredded kimono clung about cuts that pooled the cloth in dark red.

He tried to steady himself once more, but a swift kick commanded him to stay down. Hazukiro stumbled until his head struck a stone. The sight of Fura lunging, blurry as a dream, was the last thing he saw before he blacked out.

CHAPTER XIX

IMBUED

THE YOUNG GIRL SQUINTED into the late afternoon sun, unaffected by its glow. She had clambered up a tall tree and sat on a sturdy branch veiled by flowers. Perched like a bird, she peered through with caution, overlooking the carnage of the village below her. Heart in her throat, she began to cry, frantically wiping away tears with blood-crusted hands. Her burning eyes fell on the wrecked tavern. She sat with a swirl of twisted knots in her belly. That sharp and demanding pain of knowing that her sister lay inside, reduced to nothing but a pile of ashes.

The girl tried to tear her eyes away from it all. But the macabre of the massacre seeped deep into her heart, and she could only stare and cry while fighting off wave after wave of rippling migraines.

The bloody vista stared back. Destroyed homes, emptied corpses and disarrayed limbs, and in the midst of the dead Blood Spectors, a ronin who'd come to her aid. She wiped at stained cheeks while studying him, curiously.

Hazukiro twitched, startling the girl. She heard the muffled groan of him rolling over. Wincing, the ronin forced himself to his feet, fiercely fluttering heavy eyelids. Stray rays of golden light slithered through his blurred vision. That familiar threat of an ending afternoon and an encroaching evening.

'*Of course.*' Grunting and clutching his side, Hazukiro whistled for his mare.

'Where are you, girl?'

The ronin tripped over Fura. A fresh blood pool skirted the Spector's snapped neck.

'*Girl?* We need to go now!'

The pain made it difficult to enter the Hush. Where did the sohei disappear to? And the Spectors' steeds? Scattered?

'Mōkin must be flying home. He'll arrive without his master.'

There was far too much to process in the fading hours of light. All that mattered was that Hazukiro found a horse and made his way to the nearest *standing* settlement. The ronin repeated these words in his mind's eye, while his weary voice called for Akumo.

'Horse!' bellowed Hazukiro, folding over, feeling the exertion. He whistled to the wind while he searched the ground for his katana.

The girl with bloodshot eyes watched the ronin from her perch as he scurried about like a broken-winged bat.

She drowned in a plethora of emotions.

Grievance, mostly. Curiosity, second of all.

But niggling at the back of a pale, parched throat, she *thirsted.*

Fixing the final notch around his waist, Hazukiro tested the heft of the katana. As he swung, his sides ached, and he cursed the still-absent horse. As he began to sheath the blade, sunlight caught the steel and glinted as sharply as its black edge. The brief light revealed along the blade's ridge line, and more along the grain.

He chuckled lightly. If the shogun had discovered the daimyo was beginning to arm his Spectors using the forbidden arkin arts, he'd be left for the pyres without remorse. But the shogun and all that ruled under his thumb on the mainland had long since turned their backs on Ijihan. For all he knew, the rest of the world could think Ijihan a desolate wasteland. A cautionary tale told to children.

The ronin examined the finer details of the imbued katana. The shaft's braid was midnight black, the ray skin underneath a deep purple. The end cap bore the Blood Spectors' sigil. Steel collars held the glinting guard in place; two bat-like wings met to form its round shape.

His eyes followed the length of the silver blade in awe until his gaze fell on the etchings the sun had revealed. The symbols felt familiar. They weren't from the creed of the Blood Spectors. No mantra of the smithing guild verses either.

The memory clicked and flooded his mind. An old translation of the original scriptures, an excerpt from the Book of the Daystar. He spoke the words in their original tongue.

'*Make ashes of them all, you, true cleanser of the night.*'

He scoffed, then flipped the blade over to find a smaller rune, etched just above the crossguard, gleaming white.

'Another excerpt. *Soot and cinder?*'

The katana answered to the words let loose. A terrific violet hue chased the blade's length like a lavender flood. The low hum and violent reckoning of a tower bell shivered in the ronin's grip. When the weapon's tip gleamed, the hum dimmed and softened. Hazukiro squinted at its glow, holding it at a distance from his face. Its abrasive light slowly dimmed, and in a moment, only the runes and its razored edge still glowed in vibrant regality.

A snap of twigs caught the ronin's glare. Instinctively, he white-knuckle gripped the sword as if it had been his for years. The point shone as waves of sun warped along its violet edge.

Akumo burst through the bush, swaying her mane and blowing air as she whinnied. Frustrated that she had disappeared in the first place, Hazukiro sighed in relief as he sheathed the blade.

'Better late than never, old friend.'

He swept up his hat from the floor, now matted with dirt and blood and placed it firmly on his throbbing head. Grabbing whatever satchels and packs he could find, he loaded them onto his mare and searched for his water gourd. He struggled into his saddle and patted Akumo's neck. While the grey mare snorted and settled, the ronin looked over the hamlet one last time.

'Oh, Hana,' he whispered to memories in his mind. 'What have I done?'

Taking a swig of water, Hazukiro dug his heels in and the pair set off. The young girl watched as her saviour rode off. His departure stirred up dark feelings of anger that she could not explain. Before she could decide whether or not to follow him into the night, her hollow hunger throttled her inhibitions instead, sending her scurrying down the tree towards the beckoning blood feast below.

Exiting the hamlet north, through miles of trees and petals, Hazukiro eventually merged with the remains of a main road that ran through the Wisteria Woods with under an hour of daylight left at best.

There was no time for secure paths or back routes. The closest town he was aware of was Hog's Bristle, a fishing settlement located further north, near the headwaters of Tsujia River. Running through acres of the Wisteria Woods, the main road ran parallel to it. Though without upkeep, that was the ronin's path. Akumo charged on, Hazukiro wincing at every little bump as the sun neared its routine retreat.

He cursed himself for being caught out near dusk a second time. His sense of caution was something deeply ingrained, and something he *usually* took pride in. Although the actions of the girl were out of his control, he'd still felt like a foolish and naked slice of meat flailing in the open as the dark drew nearer.

***

Hazukiro hoped to all the gods that his memory of the town was serving him correctly. That Hog's Bristle was close enough to reach before sunset. Apologetically, he pushed Akumo harder, desperate for the town to come into view as the road rolled over baregreen hills beside Tsujia River.

'At least two more miles,' he groaned, holding his side.

He scoured the environment for other options in case it came to that in a painful pinch.

The trees grew sparse along the river. A few scattered rocky outcrops lay about, likely only harbouring shallow caves. Barring and baubling an entrance might have to do. But Akumo would not fit inside.

If it wasn't a bloodstained ruin, the town would be the only option.

Now miles north of the massacre, Akumo's breaths sharpened. Trees grasping the road's edges grew fewer, dotting portions of the wilderness in between stumps. Further along nearer the river's headwaters, the thickness of the pink-coated forest dwindled.

'Hya!' The ronin bore down ankles, shirking the shadows enveloping the land.

Akumo whisked past a wooden signpost ravaged by rot, the etchings faded but still legible.

'Hog's Bristle'.

CHAPTER XX

SANCTUM

THE MAIN ROAD RAN through the village with thatched-roof farmhouses and shops on either side, their plaster walls caked in fresh mud. The residents had done away with the traditional shoji doors, replacing them with sturdier, thicker, wooden doors that could be barred shut. Not that this would make a lick of a difference, the ronin sighed.

Even newly formed oniku in their infancy, which the Teragaku had come to call 'callows', still boasted enough strength in their mindlessness to tear through wood to satiate their thirst.

A sharp wind nipped through the early evening air. Hazukiro shuddered as it hit him. He'd not realised just how much blood had accumulated at his side, and the breeze against the wet was an icy sting.

Akumo halted at the arched gate of Hog's Bristle.

'Not as big as I remember. But it's still standing.'

Hazukiro gingerly dismounted, whispered thanks to his mare, and led her towards the town.

He felt foolish, stumbling headlong into a residential area minutes before sundown, spruced with red like a bloodied serving. Until he had to rely on his own two feet, he hadn't realised just how sluggish he was. He rubbed his eyes and searched for a stable. A child pointed at him and gasped before a parent snatched him up and shut their door, staring daggers at the ronin. Hazukiro ignored the glares, something he was used to for one reason or another. He stumbled on, passing a wooden statue of

Kesyoka, the goddess of the sun. Flowers and offerings were gathered at the deity's oaken feet.

Only two or three townsfolk were still outside, desperately splashing buckets of mud over their walls, exchanging hurried arguments before shutting themselves inside.

The slamming doors startled a horse, and Hazukiro followed the sound to a small barn with a steep, thatched roof. Mustering the last of his strength, he propped himself against one of the doors and heaved it open. Two horses and a mule were grazing inside.

'Get,' Hazukiro managed, tapping Akumo's hind. She snorted and joined in the hayfeast. Scrambling out the door, the ronin felt the cold damp of his clothes clutching to his skin.

'Bleeding again,' he groaned, forcing the barn door shut. He leaned against, breathless, licking crusted lips before trudging back to the street, searching for shelter and, potentially, a healer.

'Sanctum,' he choked out, cursing out how broken and soft his voice was.

'*Sanctum!*' he cried, folding over. Hog's Bristle stood as quiet and dormant as the dead. The last trickles of sun chased the road into the dark of the hills around the village.

'S-sanc...' Hazukiro dropped to the dirt, his weary body spread out in the centre of the street. The houses and their residents stayed deaf to his pleas. With his cheek pressed to mud, Hazukiro squinted at the golden-orange hues blanketing the street. The colours drooped with his eyelids.

He groaned and lifted his head at the loud bang of a door bursting open.

'Gods in heavens, how can you all be so heartless!'

An old woman sprinted to the ronin, cursing as she moved, hindered by sixty or seventy winters in her joints. Hazukiro feebly glanced up at the woman's wrinkled face, plastered in anger and mud.

'You're heavier than you look. Curse you, traveller.'

Hazukiro smirked as he felt his arm flop over the woman's shoulder.

'I can't do everything. Now get up. No time to waste. Up. Up. *Up!*'

She yanked the ronin's arm, and he winced at the woman's strength. Finding his balance, he managed to bring himself to his feet, leaning most of his weight on the small woman.

'Don't make me regret this. Gods, shift your weight!'

The last speck of orange had faded from the sky, and distant and dead voices screeched into the night sky. The woman had no time to be delicate. As she approached her home, she swung her weight and tossed the ronin onto her floor before slamming and bolting her door.

'Mud, in the corner.' She commanded, but the ronin was still fumbling on the floor. She cursed and dashed to the bucket herself. With one hand she tore at the ronin's kimono, and with the other, she smacked a dollop of mud over the gash. Hazukiro cried out. The woman slapped his mouth shut with her muddied hand. The ronin winced but managed a weak nod, gripping her wrist and pulling her hand away.

'Thank you for this,' Hazukiro wheezed.

'Quiet,' the old woman pressed a finger to her lips. 'They approach.'

CHAPTER XXI
THE HUSH OF NIGHT

'WE HAVE TO SEAL that up. . .' the woman said. 'A trickle of blood is enough to drive them mad. An open wound, even one covered in mud, will eventually permeate the air thicker than a gas swamp.'

Hazukiro nodded, being no stranger to the truth of the matter, and the need to stay silent while enduring pain.

The woman muttered something to a wicker basket. A soft voice responded, and the basket's lid popped off, revealing a small child. The boy crawled out of the basket and along the floor to a cabinet where he began digging through its contents.

Hazukiro eased himself onto his back, still clutching his blood-soaked side. The boy scampered back to the old woman and handed her a small box. She whispered thanks and gestured to the basket. He nodded, scurried off, and climbed back inside.

'Yours?' Hazukiro asked as the woman lifted his clothing. The gash was wider than expected, and as she placed her hands around it, the blood inside rose and trickled down his ribs. She reached for a small bottle on a nearby shelf and bit the cork off, pouring the contents of spirit and water into the wound. She turned to the box the boy had retrieved and unlatched it.

'No,' she stated, unwinding a spool of fishing gut. 'I knew his parents.'

Hazukiro paused as he felt the cold sting of the needle pierce his skin.

'Something to bite down on?' the woman offered without stopping, her eyes and hands focused on the motion of her threading.

'No,' Hazukiro breathed sharply. He tensed and clenched his fists while the needle wound to and from his skin like a sadistic snake with an unforgiving bite.

'The boy looks to be four, maybe five winters?' Hazukiro pursed his lips as the shredded flesh embraced in a bitter greeting.

The woman squinted and slowly tugged the line through its patterns. 'Could be.'

Hazukiro relaxed his hands. 'Foolish to knowingly have children after Blightfall.'

The woman took shears to the thread and tidied it before dabbing the area with another cloth. Without looking up, she pointed to her bookshelf.

'They're over there.' She was pointing to an urn. 'If you'd like to take it up with them.'

The woman took to her feet and wiped her hands.

'You're the town healer?' Hazukiro asked.

'Yes. And that's the best I can do for now. We'll have to have a proper look in the morning. For now, keep quiet.'

* * *

They came in the hush of night, washing over the town like cold and dark spirits. Like the leathery vermin they partially resembled, the oniku relied on sound and smell over sight. The mud masked their prey, dulling their aura that made them possible morsels.

The old woman silently raised a finger to her lips, then raised her head skywards. A thud on the roof shook dust free. Soft whimpering came from the wicker basket. Through the thatch, Hazukiro could hear the low rumble of a lone oniku, tasting the air. It dug its monstrous talons into the roof as it scampered across.

A shriek iced the ronin's blood. Another bat-like corpse dug into the roof, followed by growls and commotion.

Bickering over food.

It was impossible to say how many oniku were stalking the town, street by street, rooftop by rooftop, likely growing in frustration at the lack of food.

Minutes that felt like hours washed over Hazukiro's sweating brow. The old woman exuded calm, save for her lips, offering silent prayers with her hands clasped. The boy in the basket continued to whimper.

The calm was cut by a blood-curdling cry. A woman. Hazukiro crawled over to the boarded-up window and gently pressed his forehead against it to peer through a crack.

An oniku had found an opening. A rotting plank board just below the roof's edge of a house across the way. The wood had no doubt weakened under the constant wet of rain and slathered mud. These people had no means of fortifying themselves day in and day out. Things were bound to waste away.

The oniku wrapped a wrinkled hand around the wood and squeezed, crumpling it like soggy paper. The woman inside the home screamed again.

'*Foolish*,' Hazukiro couldn't help but think. The mud may have masked her enough before the beast lost interest.

But fear exists because we cannot justify frightening truths, Hazukiro admitted to his more pessimistic side. And when we come face to face with these fears, all snarling teeth and hideous with hungry intent, we cannot always control its icy grip that clutches our hearts.

The demon thrust a clawed hand through the hole and leapt from the roof, tearing the wall asunder with its talons as it slid down. It grinned black fangs as it strode into the dark of the home.

Two cries sounded off this time. Even across the way behind sealed walls, the ronin could hear the sinister crunch. The oniku emerged from the house with the woman in its razored maw. As pleased as a starved leopard, its bloodshot eyes sang celebrations.

Hazukiro's stomach still spun at the sight of them, and the way they slaughtered humans with such merciless ease. He'd seen enough death to last a lastime.

A second oniku landed beside the first, lanky arms and claws outstretched. The ronin recoiled slightly, expecting a fight. Instead, it sniffed at the woman and growled. She was petrified, but alive. Her mouth gaped like a fish pulled from water, reminding the ronin of the Spector in the mine. The second demon exhaled like a bull and leapt into the house. The other spread its gristly wings and took flight with the woman's neck between its teeth.

The second demon emerged from the home with a second woman. She was also alive, shaking in a feverish sweat. Talons impaled her, and the night demon, carrying his morsel half his size, flung her to the ground and bit into her vertebrae. Unhooking its fangs, it let out a wail like a choir of sobbing souls.

The healer looked to Hazukiro and raised her hands and brows in question, silently asking him what was happening. The ronin shook his head, discouraging the sordid answer.

'Avert your gaze,' he whispered.

Scowling with pursed lips, his stomach turning, he couldn't help but look on.

'What comes next is never pretty.'

The demon's cry summoned more of its kin. Through the crack in the wood Hazukiro peered through, flashes of wings whizzed past, presumably seeking more food, while three broke off and landed beside the crier. This was the most coordinated Hazukiro had ever known oniku to be. He'd seen the demons tear each other limb from wing over prey in the past.

Their feeding process was gruesome. With her spine snapped, the woman could only lie on the ground, bleeding and motionless. The four oniku lowered themselves, slowly swarming her, crawling forward on haunched arms and legs like starving gargoyles. Their maws gaped wide to reveal those razored vortexes.

Biting down onto one limb each, they began to gorge on their victim. Locking their jaws over flesh, they sank their teeth and drank their fill, draining the woman of her lifeblood in moments. After a minute, they each receded from the body. The body was nothing but a pale corpse with shrivelled weeds where limbs once were.

And with blood-splattered mouths and glowing eyes, the oniku shrieked, satisfied, and absconded into the night.

The turning never took long. A scratch from a claw could take a few days, sometimes a week, to take effect. Even then it meant nothing more than the victim's demise. An excruciating but definitive death.

A feed meant worse. You died and came back, still dead but not yourself; a thrall of whichever demon lord had brought upon the Blight, or so that theory went.

First, the withered limbs fell off the body like a snake shedding skin. Next, the woman's hair and nails slid off like melting ice, as if the corpse was thawing itself free of its humanity. The corpse growled and lurched upright like a puppet. Its bones cracked, up its spine and along its neck. The jaw fell off to make room for its wider, sinewy, tooth-filled gob.

New bones sprouted from the sockets of missing limbs. Longer, more rancid arms and legs ending in claws and talons grew from bursts of black ichor. As the creature crawled on all fours, it cried in agony and thirst, the remnants of the woman it once was, now completely gone. Monstrous, sticky wings ruptured forth like some hellish cocoon shedding its chrysalis. Goo dripped when the wings started to flap. The rest of the oniku swarm, now departing, summoned their newest addition. With a final cry, the demon took off into the night and rejoined its swarm.

CHAPTER XXII

PALE FACES

THE VILLAGERS GREETED THE sun as a long-sought friend. They began to trickle from their homes to begin their day.

A few stopped by the ruined home to offer their prayers to the two sisters who'd lived there. Most people averted their gaze, painfully aware of the nightmare they lived in, wanting nothing more than to ensure that their own survival was met by the morning sun.

Hazukiro stayed with the healer for several days after that, mostly sleeping and eating, and having his wounds tended to in between with odd herbs that the woman mixed with mortar and pestle. Herbs he'd never seen sprout on the island, but he had no reason to question the old woman's methods.

The townsfolk took mud and barricades to their homes each night without fail, fearing a breech, but the evening came and went quietly, allowing the ronin some much-needed sleep in a soft bed.

On the fifth morning, Hazukiro sat crossed-legged on the floor, gently patting the bandages across his waist. The healer, who was yet to divulge her name, sat across from him with the child, pouring steaming soup from a pot into their bowls. Hazukiro thanked the woman before eating the hot food, going down smoothly and warming him against the nip in the early morning air.

'I feel my strength returning. Thank you,' Hazukiro wiped his beard. 'For your hospitality. And for the risk you've taken. Especially for one such as myself.'

The healer waved her hand dismissively and gulped down more soup. Expecting her to say more, Hazukiro paused. Instead, she simply scooped up another serving from the pot and gestured towards the ronin's empty bowl. He hesitated, and she took that to mean he was too polite to ask for more. He exhaled and thanked her again.

The healer gestured to the boy, who had still not spoken a single word. The child quickly nodded and stood to gather the empty bowls, before disappearing into another room. Hazukiro noticed a beautifully carved wooden bow resting against a corner with a leather quiver at its base.

'Please,' Hazukiro motioned to the bow and quiver. 'Allow me to bring you some game, for your troubles. I'm no stranger to the way of the bow. I could bring something substantial for you and the boy.'

The woman stood and brushed off her clothes. 'That would be fine. Now is a good time. If it's all the same to you, I'd rather not house a leashed longer than I have to.'

She pointed to the ronin's branded forehead. 'I've a responsibility to these people. I won't be able to help them much if I'm tried for helping a wanted man.'

She smirked. 'That being said, they've not much daylight to do their own chores, let alone waste it stringing you up. Gives you enough time to kill and skin something for us.'

'Of course,' Hazukiro stood and bowed. 'I will return with something, collect my horse, and be on my way.'

'Don't let those bandages come loose.'

The woman disappeared into the other room and the little boy followed her. Hazukiro moved to the bow and admired it. It was recently restrung, he noticed. Taught and strong. The wood itself had a new polish over it too; she clearly knew how to use and keep the weapon.

'I suppose she has to know.'

* * *

The ronin wandered passed sour gazes until he reached the far end of Hog's Bristle. He followed the rising sun rays over a bridge to the east, across dried fields and stump-scattered patches of grass before reaching some shrubbery that preceded a forest. The trees varied, with several remnants of pink and purple wisteria petals blowing about the cool breeze, sailing through clusters of ancient moss-covered trees that contorted and wrangled skyward. The birdsong returned, a strong contrast from the barren fields closest to the town. He followed the tunes to the beginning trickles of a stream.

Though Hazukiro wore vigilance like armour, he couldn't help his mind from drifting. He would find a deer. Return to the healer. Give his thanks. And after that? He'd had time to ponder over the past few days, but it seemed as if his mind had begged him to simply accept the rest he needed.

'I cannot stay here.' He sighed, his thoughts stirring again. *'I cannot stay anywhere.'*

The Teragaku was no doubt reeling at the loss of their greatest protector. Itaro was gone, and his hawk would have returned without him. His body was rotting somewhere, either into the ground or perhaps as a callow demon at this point.

Hazukiro wrestled with the notion that anyone would believe that an old man, a lanky prisoner even, could have bested the great captain of the Blood Spectors. That the Teragaku would place the blame on a demon attack, with no way of verifying anything. But it was not enough to shake what he knew about the Teragaku.

He'd seen what punishments they were capable of for harbouring criminals. And for one thought dead, roaming the island unafflicted while their Blood Spectors lay as stains on grass, meant anyone harbouring him would risk retribution. He sighed at the only conclusion he could conjure.

He would have to wander, as he did in his youth, though his stomach turned at the memories. A snapped twig brought him back.

A serow strode gracefully towards the stream, fluttering its ears. Hazukiro crouched slowly, retrieving and nocking a feathered arrow. It soared and met its mark. A clean kill. The action once again threw his mind to the days of his youth, and he forced himself back to the present.

Returning the bow to his shoulder, the ronin began to cross the stream.

A swift wind knocked him flat.

He shuddered at the water's chill and scrambled to his feet, searching the trees. His eyes widened as they fell on the deer carcass.

Is that...?

The girl had sunken her teeth into the animal's neck, drawing blood like a starved fiend. With each gulp, her eyes grew brighter and redder. The veins along her face and neck pulsed across her pale face, like a web of rushing rivers flowing through snowy mountains.

The ronin kept still but firmly clasped the hilt of his sword. His training took hold. Reasoning took the forefront of his mind. But when the girl looked up from her food, something else stirred inside of Hazukiro. He even surprised himself when he spoke.

'Can you understand me?'

He let go of his sword and raised two open palms. The girl seemed just as surprised, unclenching her toothy death grip. By most means, she still appeared human. Hazukiro saw through the blood-covered face to that of a young and scared girl. And she sat, hunched over the carcass, while the sun washed over her like it was nothing.

Her shimmering red stare began to dissipate, and the whites and true hazel brown of her eyes returned. She nodded gently. Hazukiro nodded back, then took a cautious step forward. The girl recoiled, her claws reducing to nails and retracting from the deer.

Hazukiro stopped. 'I'll do no harm if you can promise me the same?'

He tilted his head, his hands still up. The girl broke eye contact but nodded again.

'This water chills the bone,' Hazukiro said. 'Would you allow this old man to place his feet on dry land?'

She gave another shy and cautious nod.

'My thanks.'

He gave a bow before striding through the water, diagonally, so that he didn't step too close to the girl. He reached the bank and shook his feet out.

'Your bow,' the girl said.

Taken aback, Hazukiro looked to see her standing closer, gesturing to a flat rock, a stern look on her face, her chest heaving. Hazukiro nodded and removed the weapon from his shoulder. She kept her finger pointed until the bow sat on the rock.

'And your katana.'

Hesitant, but without much choice, the ronin nodded and complied, holding the sword by its blade with two hands in good faith. The girl winced at the sight of the silver, but quickly forced her composure and restored her hard look. She flicked her fingers backwards, motioning for the ronin to back away. Again, he complied. She stood in silence, seemingly as unsure of the situation as Hazukiro.

He used the pause to study her.

Her kimono was once-white, now a blend of dirty and dried blood. The pink flower pattern came through the filth in patches. The cloth was frayed at her legs and arms as if she'd been crawling through a battlefield for days.

Her flushed face reminded him of war too. The youthful dying young, the fear of those still living, a victory or a defeat, the only certainty of war were the hard-to-forget seas of pale faces.

Hazukiro decided to speak first.

'Who are you?' The ronin lowered his hands.

The girl wiped the red from her face, almost ashamedly.

'Thank you for not using *'what'*.'

Hazukiro continued to assess her and the distance to his katana. She'd dissolve into a wisp and slice through his gullet before the second step. Words, as he had come to learn, were often the best way forward, and she seemed comfortable enough to exchange some.

'I am called Taiyō.'

A myriad of questions amassed in the ronin's mind. He sifted through them, but before he could settle on some wise words, a jarring horn sounded.

'Damn it,' Hazukiro moved towards his weapons but the girl stepped in front of them.

'Step aside, girl,' Hazukiro commanded.

His tone surprised Taiyō.

'If I wished you harm I wouldn't have stood against my own—against those hunters.'

The girl mulled over the words, then solemnly stepped aside. He swiftly sheathed his sword and threw the bow over his shoulder. Crossing the stream in a sprint, he noticed that the girl had chosen to follow him.

'Stay here!' he called out, picking up his pace. 'They won't hesitate to cut you down!'

She stopped at that, and her blood-soaked figure disappeared into the trees as the ronin sprinted on.

Hazukiro reached the forest's border and crouched to peer through some shrubbery. A convoy of guards from the Tergaku had dispersed themselves through Hog's Bristle, searching door to door. Two Blood Spectors were with them, standing beside an emissary, an older man donning emerald-green robes. They were too far away to make out the words.

'I can hear them.'

Startled, Hazukiro looked up to find Taiyō perched on a branch.

'They're looking for a prisoner with a branded forehead,' she continued, unprompted. 'They've found your horse, so they know you were there.'

Hazukiro cursed under his breath and watched as two guards led Akumo out of the barn by her reins.

'They'll take her back to the fortress,' he sighed, slight relief in his voice. The thought of potentially keeping her alive in the wilds night after night had weighed heavily on him.

A voice cried out, loud enough for Hazukiro to hear.

'That's MY horse!'

Hazukiro made out the figure of the healer, exiting her home with the little boy tucked behind her. Silent words were exchanged. Hazukiro looked to Taiyō.

'If you would?' He softened his voice. 'Please.'

Taiyō nodded and shut her eyes. An ear poked through her long, black hair, and the ronin noticed that they weren't pointed like the oniku, another human trait left untarnished. That, and the fangs that had receded into regular teeth after feasting.

Her pale ears twitched.

'The guards are saying that they know she is lying. That the horse belongs to the. . .' She looked down at the ronin. 'To the Blood Spectors.'

'She belongs to the Teragaku,' Hazukiro admitted. 'But she was only saddled for me. Too old and misbehaved for a soldier's horse, apparently.'

Taiyō continued. 'The old woman is saying you were there, but were gravely injured, and that the *oniku* came and made quick work of you. What are oniku?'

'I will explain later,' Hazukiro said irately, 'Please, the conversation.'

'They seem to believe her. They're. . .laughing about it.'

Hazukiro noticed the emissary raise his hand and make a gesture.

'He's telling them to regroup,' Taiyō continued, repeating what she heard word for word this time.

'*What about the horse? Help an old woman, kind sirs. The Teragaku has provided us with nothing.*'

One of the guards raised the back of his hand and the old woman recoiled. A Blood Spector clasped the raised wrist.

'Taiyō.' Hazukiro found the girl watching, as if studious about the interaction. She snapped out of it.

'The one in red armour,' she continued. 'He said the horse is useless to them. *Let the old hag have it.*'

Hazukiro breathed in relief. The barn in the village seemed more secure than the homes, clearly a priority before the Blight, when the farm had no doubt thrived on livestock.

'Perhaps she can help them sow the fields,' Hazukiro told himself. 'A more honourable final chapter than most of us can ask for.'

'Do you often speak to yourself?'

Hazukiro looked up at the girl who stared back at him with a roguish grin.

'I suppose I do,' he caught himself, realising he was sharing musings with a bloodthirsty predator.

'They're arguing. . .' Hazukiro shot his glance back to the town. The two Blood Spectors were having heated words with the emissary. The robed man conceded, nodding, and the Spectors drew their swords and took off across the fields towards the forest.

'Damn it, what happened?' Hazukiro took to his feet and ran. From tree to tree, the girl sprung like a weightless bird, dissolving into a red mist as she travelled.

'They said they wanted to make sure!' she shouted.

She returned to her physical form and ran alongside the ronin. 'Wait!'

'Move!' Hazukiro ran, breathless. 'Hide yourself!'

'There's only two of them,' she breathed effortlessly, not breaking a sweat as she traversed roots and rocks.

'*No*,' he shouted. 'No one else needs to die.'

'Someone always needs to die.'

She burst into a mist and crossed the stream.

The Spectors approached the forest's edge. One of them dismounted and studied the ground profusely for tracks, while the other searched the trees for movement.

'These woods are thick,' the one still mounted commented. 'Could be ikari about.'

'And a jaguar.' The other stood back up and pointed to a faded print. He stood for a moment, scratching his chin.

'Lieutenant,' the other sighed. 'Even if he survived the night, he won't endure another. He's old. Weak. Without his horse. At best he finds shelter in the cave of this sleeping cat.'

The Spector sighed and mounted his horse, turning it about.

'Come,' he conceded. 'Afternoon duties await.'

The other looked back to the forest. 'Are you certain?'

Hazukiro was still sprinting, deeper into the forest. The girl trailed him, treetop to treetop, sometimes returning to her human form to run behind him, repeating the distant words back to the ronin as they moved. Whether she was toying with new prey, or simply curious about him, Hazukiro didn't yet know. There was only one thing he knew for certain.

This was the point of no return.

CHAPTER XXIII
DEAD ANSWERS

HEART THUMPING HARD, the ronin stopped running and pressed his back to a tree. He breathed deeply, placing his hands on his hips. With the aura of red mist close behind, he felt like a wounded hare evading an enclosing wolf pack.

He told his legs to press on, but one of his knees buckled him to the ground. He hissed at the sudden tweak, still sucking air rapidly through his teeth.

Looking up, he was startled yet again to see Taiyō looking him over. His senses had never felt so dull.

He waited for her to speak but she simply stared.

'I've no doubt you've sniffed this out?' He gestured to his wounded side. 'I can't outrun you. Make it quick, if you must.'

She gave an amused grin, which soon dissolved as her canines grew two inches. The whites of her eyes merged with her pupils to form shimmering pools of ink-black voids. Hazukiro reached for his katana. Before he could free it, she collapsed, falling from the tree, heavy as a steel shield.

Hazukiro ambled to his feet and drew his silver. He pressed the blade's tip against the nape of her neck. If she decided to move, a swift pierce and an utterance of the sword's mantra would end her.

He assumed.

There was no contingency for a demon that could walk in the day. There were no known weaknesses for this...sunstrider.

Taiyō stayed still, breathing sharply, but unconscious.

For the better, Hazukiro told himself.

He decided to keep his sword drawn, vigilant for any demonic tricks. With his gaze locked on the girl, he carefully backed away.

Another horn sounded in a melody he recognised. One short chime, followed by one long blare.

'PREY.'

The deer carcass.

They'd be on him before long. The density of the forest would prevent them from continuing on horseback, buying the ronin moments more. He looked down at the girl, her blood-smudged face, her soaked kimono.

They'd behead her outright.

Emotions were running rampant and loud. Hazukiro exhaled and entered the Hush. The enveloping trees melted into puddles of green and pink. The world blurred and darkened, until the ronin stood, calm and collected. Before him, in the shadow of his silent mind, the girl lay, a large red thought. Intrusive and impossible to ignore.

He returned to the world, sheathed his sword, and cursed under his breath.

Taiyō was far heavier than she looked. Slung over the ronin's shoulders, Hazukiro took off into the woods, scanning the surroundings for somewhere safe to hole up.

'The mine.' Taiyō coughed, her words weak, her sight blurred.

Hazukiro didn't stop running.

'The mines are all sealed off or infested with oniku.'

Taiyō lilted her head to get a bearing of her shaking surroundings. As if jilted from a nightmare, her vision returned, accompanied by a tremendous wave of energy.

She dissolved into mist and materialised again beside the ronin.

'This way!' She ran off. 'Keep up!'.

Hazukiro rushed past a signpost riddled with vines.

Jina Mine North.

'Have you lost your senses?' Hazukiro leapt over large roots. 'This mine was closed *before* the Blight. It'll be festering!'

'It isn't,' she pushed through shrubs. 'I made sure of it.'

Taiyō pushed through a curtain of moss and disappeared. Hazukiro, once again limited with options, followed her in.

Rows of hanging moss receded into the mouth of a large cave. It widened, dim even in the day, turning pitch-black as the pair proceeded deeper.

Hazukiro drew the imbued sword.

'Soot and cinder.'

A terrific light eddied up the blade, washing the cave's walls in violet. Taiyō stopped running and turned to the blinding light, her glowing eyes peering through the dark.

'It's not for you,' Hazukiro growled. 'Unless you've lured me here for nefarious reasons.'

'It's that dark in here?' she replied, seemingly astonished.

The ronin furrowed his brows. 'You cannot tell?'

'My eyes adjust immediately. Come, it's safe.' She paused for a moment. 'Watch your step though.'

Hazukiro cautiously lowered his bright blade towards his feet as he followed the girl. The light revealed three separate piles of bones. The ronin crouched to examine them more carefully. They were black as coal, and picking one up revealed its immense weight. Lifting a femur was like lifting an iron battleaxe.

'These belonged to oniku?'

'The demons? Oniku, you call them? I've heard them called *'thralls'*. They ignore me for the most part. But when I entered this cave, these three almost took my head off. Probably because I interrupted a feed. Luckily, the rest of the mine is blocked off by collapsed stone walls.'

She gestured vaguely to the piles. 'Only these three nestled at the cave mouth.'

Hazukiro had never seen the bones of a demon. There were no traces of the human skeleton that once was. He picked up a wing bone, running his fingers along its jagged surface. This was a whole and complete creature. The only dead oniku he'd seen had all turned to ash come morning. Skin and bone and everything grotesque in between.

He walked around the bones, still curious. '*You* were heavy to carry.'

'Is this your first time speaking to a young lady?'

Taiyō examined the ronin. He seemed genuinely curious, a trait she preferred over aggression, but the dulled glow of his silver blade did not exactly put her mind at ease. She also knew he would not trust her in the dark of a cave.

Among the remains of *her* kills.

'You must have questions.'

'Many. I've collected information for years for the Academy, and this is a discovery of note on its own. But the dead rarely speak.'

'And here you have before you something dead who can provide answers,' the girl folded her arms.

'So you are *dead*?' He lowered the blade and she flinched.

'Calm yourself,' he said, placing the sword down. 'I imagine why you'd not be forthcoming, but as I mentioned outside, I've no intention of gutting down a child.'

'I'm nineteen.'

Hazukiro scoffed. 'As you like it. A nineteen-year-old with the naivety of a child, then.'

Taiyō ignored the jab. Fixing her eyes on the blade laid bare, a feeling overcame her. *Trust*, she would like to have believed. Or perhaps it was just the absence of threat for the briefest of respite.

'Twice you've saved me at the risk of your own life.' She paced back and forth. 'You'd not kill me. Unless I attack, that much is clear.' She nodded towards the katana.

'Defending myself is natural. Earlier your eyes sparked at the mere mention of me as a morsel.'

'I will not deny that it is challenging to control. The thirst; it's no small thing being parched. To bring light of it in the midst of a craving doesn't make it any easier.'

'Yet you can drink animal blood.' Hazukiro chose his words carefully. 'The others cannot stomach the stuff.'

'I am *not* them!' she spat, and the red glow of her eyes competed for colour against the sword.

'Clearly.' Hazukiro remained calm. 'So then. . .' He trailed off, hoping she'd continue.

'So what am I?'

'If you'd be so blunt. Or you could tell me *how* you came to be afflicted? Who that girl at the hamlet was, and what you two were doing there? How is it that you can walk in the sun and look as you do? As I said. Many questions. And the dead do not so idly offer answers.'

He sat down, placing the katana further away from him, casting a glow to creep and arch against the cave's ceiling, illuminating the pair in purple.

Taiyō edged closer, appreciating the gesture. She sat down and crossed her legs. The red of her eyes thawed back to hazel brown.

'I am only what I am because of what he made me.'

Hazukiro recognised the bitter look simmering behind her eyes.

Disgust.

'And who is *he*?'

Taiyō's exhale fluttered. She closed her brimming eyes.

'He made us address him by his chosen moniker.'

She shuddered as wounds too fresh tore open.

'He called himself The Foremost.'

Hazukiro did not prod. Taiyō was teeming, clearly burdened with weight with no one to share it with.

He waited for her to continue.

'I hope, with all that's left in my black bones, that those who Become do not suffer as I did. As I do, daily. I can recall it all. My entire life, in agonising detail. Things I've repressed. Including the year I spent imprisoned in the temple of Mount Shinok. That was where it happened. Where I Became.'

Taiyō wiped away trickling tears.

'This man *made* you?' Hazukiro began. 'Is he responsible for the Blight?'

Two clear streams ran down the girl's pale face. She felt her eyes burn as she forgot to blink, fixing her gaze on the cave wall but looking only at her stained mind.

'He said he was.' Her breath shivered when she exhaled. 'And he was *proud* of it. Like a father that's spawned a sinister offspring.'

Hazukiro had come to know the burden of memory. He saw a scared child, suffering from a past she was forced to endure. His humanity told him not to press her.

'This is something no one on this entire island knows,' he thought.

'Most memories are blurred. Some, far too vivid,' she continued. 'Strong in a vicious way. *Heavy.*'

'Relieving that weight may lighten your mind.'

Taiyō smirked. 'Is that something you picked up from the Scriptures?'

Hazukiro offered a small smile. 'No.'

CHAPTER XXIV

THE CRUCIBLE

'I LIVED IN GOMOHAN, a village just south of the foot of Mount Shinok. Four years into Blightfall, when I was sixteen, two main towns and a few of the smaller surrounding settlements had been bled dry. Only corpses and empty homes. The demons grew in number over time, and we'd never seen any of these 'Blood Spectors' so far north.

'Soshihan Village was a day's walk to the north of us. Hearing of their downfall sent everyone into a panic. Gomohan was expected to fall next.

'Some folk fled, ignoring the fact that the nearest shelter would take longer than a day to reach. No one had horses to make the journey. They thought caves and mud would be enough. Despite the warnings, at least half of the villagers fled regardless.

'Some, like myself, stayed. Not that I had much choice. My parents were already dead, and a bitter man had taken me in, along with four other orphaned girls.

'Baru, he was called. A stubborn wheat farmer who made us earn our keep by tending to his fields for measly meals. He spat on the idea of abandoning his home, spouting often how he feared no devils.

'His neighbours implored him to join their trek south.

"Let them come!" Baru spat. "I'll not leave my life's work out of *fear*!"

"*Your* life's work," I mumbled under my breath. One of the other girls, Simaro, chuckled lightly. Baru cast a mad gaze her way. We all felt it like the sneering start of sunset and promptly returned to our tasks. The youngest girl, Jira, would simply laugh, thinking everything was a game. That poor girl.

'I was the newest addition to his posse of workers. All of us were either orphans of the Blight or the Clan Wars. Desperate for food and shelter, but not enough to strip down for it. And Baru, as vile as he was, saw us only as mules with opposable thumbs. A part of me was grateful for that.

'One morning, he finished arguing with a neighbour who threw her hands up in defeat, gathered her two children, and ushered them ahead of her. Those little ones wore packs on their backs that were far too big for them. They were young. Too small to understand the scale of their journey. And likely far too small to have made it somewhere safe in time. I remember their faces when they waved at me and disappeared into the woods.'

"That'll be enough for today," Baru commanded as the sky turned orange. "Gatherings!"

'As ordered, the five of us gathered our wheat stalks and tossed them into our wicker baskets. Long shadows stretched over the fields by the time we were carrying our harvest into Baru's barn. Simaro and I exchanged smiles as often as we could. We'd developed a sisterly bond in those three gruelling years. There wasn't much to keep ourselves happy. All the five of us had were each other.

'But Simaro was special. Unbreakable. She'd once received a solid lashing for accidentally damaging a vase, and returned to us with a torn tunic and a flippant grin. She'd only wink when we checked in on her, producing all manner of shiny trinkets she'd stolen from Baru's property when he wasn't looking. We don't know where she hid them, but she hid them well. The old farmer hadn't a clue where his things had disappeared to.

'That evening, Baru laid out a small pot of gruel, and three cast iron bowls for us to share. No spoons. We were certain his hounds ate better than us. There were no animals in the barn which means they probably slept in the main house. It was just the five of us, a pot of porridge, and itchy hay piles that we all huddled atop to keep warm through bitter-cold nights.

'Simaro often hummed lullabies for us until the sun went down. She would stroke our hair, searching for any knots to unravel, as if she were our mother, though she couldn't have been older than eighteen herself. We assumed she must have had younger siblings at some point, the way she cared for us. The way she cheered us up. The way she brought us shiny trinkets and kept them safe for us. But she never spoke about herself. Never mentioned any family. And we never pried.

'We only had each other.

'After scoffing down our dinner, Baru locked us in the barn as he did. We sat quietly waiting for the night devils to pass over. It began to rain, and the rhythm of the drops, and the waiting, put me to sleep.

'When I awoke, the girls were whispering, wondering why they'd not heard a single beast outside. Their voices grew heated. Louder.

'I was about to shush them when three loud knocks came at the barn door.

"Girls?" Baru called. "O-open up. Would you please?"

'There was something odd about Baru's voice. Besides sudden manners. It had a new inflexion to it.

'He was afraid.

'Simaro leapt up first, gesturing for us to stay back. She approached the doors and slowly swung them open, trickles of rain dancing in with the wind.

'Baru stood hunched over, shaking like a wet dog with its tail between its legs. A figure stood beside him, still masked by the night.

"Good evening, ladies."

'His voice was dark and heavy, like an echo inside your mind, but somehow also as smooth as melting butter.

"May I come in?"

'Simaro looked Baru over. The farmer's glazed eyes were fixed on the floor. His teeth chattered in between incoherent mumblings. His face was pale and slick with sweat.

'Simaro turned her attention to the man smothered in shadows. He was tall, traipsed in fine red and black silks, the kind the shogun might wear for a ceremony, but slimmer, fit to outline his slender physique. His hair was black, soft and long, as sleek and beautiful as his attire. He looked to be around sixty winters.

'I had many questions, as I'm sure you do now, ronin. But unlike you, I couldn't find the words.

"Do as he asks, child!" Baru spat. "I apologise for them. Sincerely!" he spewed, trembling, dropping to his belly to show the lowest bow he could muster.

'Who was this man that the fearless farmer would buckle so easily? I felt a strange and cold cauldron of fear, curiosity, and admiration bubble inside me.

'Simaro narrowed her eyes but conceded.

"You may," she said.

The man grinned a glistening smile as if the words were the key to his rusting cell. He placed one foot in, closed boots gilded gold, then sighed with delight. Placing hands behind his back, he circled us while callously licking his lips. He stopped in front of me, glancing me up and down. I stared at my feet while his glare cut like katanas. Placing a pointed nail to my chin, he forced our eyes to meet. That icy gaze hit me like an avalanche.

Sudden and cold and *powerful*.

'You will all come with me,' his eyes commanded.

* * *

Taiyō looked to the ronin, her eyes filling with regret. The memories were too fresh, too painful to share.

'What happened next, child?' Hazukiro pressed.

She cast dark eyes his way, brimming with tears.

'I don't remember.'

Hazukiro sighed. 'I cannot help, then.'

'You don't sound like you want to.'

'I *don't*,' he spat. 'You've cost me all hope of redemption now. I'll never cross Kesyoka's Threshold with a plethora of dead Spectors under my obi, a fortress I can never return to, on top of the fact that I—' He squeezed the ridge of his nose and squinted hard. Taking a deep breath, he sighed and stood up.

'Ignore me,' he finally said, pacing the cave. 'I must take hold of my senses. Give me a moment.'

'I don't remember because he *made* me forget,' she continued regardless, a scowl washing over her frustrated face.

'After we left that barn, our *home*, as rough as it was, he muddled our minds. I don't remember the journey to the mountain. I don't remember him placing those silver chains on me.'

She thrust her wrists up. Her kimono sleeves rolled down and revealed scorch marks.

'Silverburn doesn't heal. And it hurts more than the hunger. The thirst. That's all I remember. The burn of chains and the pangs of a hollow stomach. Everything else was a blurred dream stained red. I was both hot and cold. In between groggy months, all I heard was the constant choir of screaming. I never knew agony could sound so sinister. I called for Simaro. For the other girls.'

Hazukiro nodded in understanding, a weight of guilt digging into his shoulders. 'You don't need to continue.'

'All you need to know is. . .that *monster*, the man who calls himself The Foremost? He turned me into *this*. I don't know how. Just that it was painful. I had to *die* for this to happen. That he made clear on more than one occasion.'

She placed a pale hand on her chest, shaking her head with pursed lips. 'No heartbeat. And he probably killed my sisters too. The girl I managed to escape with? That was Zia. Another girl the Foremost found gods know where after taking us. I'd known her for a few months. But my sisters? If any of my sisters are still alive. . .' she choked back tears. 'I left them. I don't even remember *leaving* the temple. I was running and then I was. . .mist. Then I was running. Starving. Parched. Confused. Scared. I—'

'You are only a child,' Hazukiro stopped her.

'Please,' she continued. 'I cannot return on my own. Those girls need to be set free.' She hung her head. 'One way or another.'

Hazukiro looked at the pleading girl, seeing her desperation and regret.

'I was about ready to cut you down for costing me my redemption, girl. The Blood Spectors serve this island. To rid it of the Blight. And I stopped them from killing an accursed.'

'You regret this?'

'I hope not to.'

Hazukiro picked up the katana and shone it toward the cave entrance. The girl waited on his next words.

'The oniku that are taking women. . .'

'His *thralls*,' Taiyō spat. 'They do his bidding. They are all tethered to him. To his *will*.'

The ronin frowned, sceptical. 'But you aren't?'

Taiyō shook her head. 'I would never have escaped.'

Hazukiro nodded, coming to a decision. 'You will lead me to this man, and I will end him.'

Taiyō shot her head up. 'You'll go back with me?' She wiped away tears, standing, eyes wide with disbelief.

'I wish to pardon my past,' he hung his head. 'There's nowhere else for me in Ijihan anymore. So I hope to all the gods you aren't lying to me.'

'Thank you, and I'm not!' she whimpered, wrapping bloodied arms around the ronin. He recoiled.

'Keep your distance, girl. No matter your intentions, I've seen what you can do to people.'

'Those *people* provoked me,' she thrust bawled fists down.

'And I'll keep that in mind around you.' He sheathed the sword, diminishing its glow as it nestled in.

'Let's go.'

CHAPTER XXV
SHRINES REMEMBER

AKUMO SNORTED IN DELIGHT to see the ronin approach the barn at Hog's Bristle. Thanking the healer profusely for everything, Hazukiro handed over her hunting bow.

'I'm sorry I couldn't find any game, but please take these.'

He handed her a pouch of valuable medicinals, and another small bag containing pieces of silver, both items scavenged from the felled Spectors.

'Dare I ask where a branded prisoner came by such rarities?'

'You daren't.' Hazukiro shared a smile with the woman and led his horse into the woods away from prying eyes.

'You can come out now,' Hazukiro spoke to the trees. Taiyō leapt with a rustle and landed beside Akumo, startling the mare.

'Easy, girl!' Hazukiro tugged on her reins. 'Friend.'

Taiyō hunched her shoulders and slowly approached the mare.

'That's right,' she said softly. 'Friend.'

Akumo rolled her head and stomped a hoof, but slowly regained her composure.

'Let me get on first.' Hazukiro mounted the mare and held out his hand. 'Slowly, now.'

Taiyō clasped his hand and nestled herself in the saddle behind the ronin.

'I still don't know the way,' she said as the horse trotted on.

'You mentioned a temple in the mountains,' Hazukiro said. 'We head north for Mount Shinok. Though most bridges and many roads have been blocked off. We should pass through Shiburiki, but we'll have to make a detour to the east first. We'll find Sanctum for the night at Sun's Embrace.'

'The Site of Shrines?'

'Yes.'

***

Dusk set in when the pair exited the Wisteria Woods. Roads petered out into grasslands sloping east towards the coastal cliffs of Sun's Embrace.

'Here we are,' Hazukiro breathed in relief, dismounting Akumo and helping Taiyō off.

A large stretch of shrines to fallen warriors of Ijihan rolled out over the grassland before them. The site was dead silent; not even crows crooned over the mass grave.

Passing through pointed stone structures, Hazukiro led the way to the pagoda tower that overlooked the Eastern Sea. Clouds bellowed and crashed over the horizon, mirroring the weightless waves at sea that lapped against the cliffside below them. Though the sight of shimmering sun on a turquoise blanket was something serene to behold, Hazukiro noticed that the girl looked only to the graves. The fading sun coated the stone slabs, illuminating the memory of honourable men and women.

Taiyō stared, as silent as the stones about her.

'Someone you knew?' Hazukiro finally asked.

'My parents,' Taiyō admitted in a broken whisper.

Hazukiro lowered his head and removed his straw hat.

'I am sorry.'

'They were both soldiers, but that's not how they died.' Taiyō's tone was bitter. 'Blightfall struck, and the sanctity of tall, stone walls made people desperate. Dishonourable.'

She forced her trembling fists to soften. 'My parents were trampled to death by people they were trying to escort to safety.' She looked to the sky, squinting at the fading golden rays.

'Are we safe out here?'

'I cannot say for certain,' Hazukiro began. 'But the Sun's Embrace has never seen a single thrall cross its threshold without bursting into embers. Perhaps Kesyoka has declared the dead be left unbothered. Or perhaps the service of these people spoke to the monsters' black hearts?'

'You mock,' Taiyō said. 'But here I sit, accursed, beyond the threshold.'

Hazukiro looked at the pagoda near the cliff's edge.

'I will never know the pride my parents felt. . .' Taiyō sighed. 'To be a part of such an honourable cause, before the Blight. Fending off the Njörkin invaders for years.'

'There is nothing honourable about killing, or war, for that matter,' Hazukiro stated. 'Not ones determined by others forcing your hand.'

He took in the sight of thousands upon thousands of shrines.

'A horde of demons. An army of invaders. They're all the same. A mass of enemies whose names you know not. All to come home with a wet blade and a tale for the taverns. But when everyone has had their fill of food and drink. And gone home. And you're left with the taste of the day and bitter sake. Your ceiling mocks your need to sleep. And you see those faces without names. And their fear. And suddenly your bravado melts into guilt. And that guilt pins you to your sheets in a cold sweat until the sun rises again.'

'Parents never want to burden their children with the demons they fight within,' Taiyō said softly. 'At least their inner turmoil died with them. And the shrines can remember, leave everything else they did for us here on blessed ground.'

Hazukiro held back a scoff. 'Or so they say. Come, the tower is our best bet for the night.'

To his surprise, the girl produced a wooden flute from inside her kimono. Kneeling between the shrines of her mother and father, she turned to the ronin.

'I'll meet you there.'

Hazukiro hesitated. When he looked at Taiyō he saw a girl mourning her parents. But she was more than that, and that harsh truth was something he couldn't idly ignore. It had cost the Blood Spectors their lives.

'Can I turn my back on you, girl?' he finally said, a hand on his hilt.

She raised her flute to quivering, dry lips. 'I don't know.'

A lone tear broke free and flowed like a river with the note she blew from the instrument. Dancing fingers with finesse, she strung together note after sorrowful note, the symphony on her lips filling the silent stones with harmonic repose.

Hazukiro felt the urge to cry rise up and quickly fall. He couldn't explain it. The craving to express and repress. Deciding it was easier to repress, he turned Akumo away and made his way to the pagoda.

'Ronin,' she said softly, stopping her own song. 'I'd like to think music means nothing to monsters.'

The universal truth of life made known by the dead. The ronin turned to the girl and nodded.

'Call me Hazukiro.'

* * *

Taiyō stood at the door to the temple. A large spherical window took up most of the cliff-facing wall, streams of sunset light shining onto a stone altar of long-dead flower offerings. Hazukiro sat on the altar steps, laying out the packs and satchels. Akumo lay in the corner, thankful for the load to be off her back.

Hazukiro looked up and saw the girl standing there, hesitant.

'Finished your performance, then?' he said, unfastening buckles.

'Yes,' Taiyō sighed. 'I'm grateful for a captive audience but that lot were very quiet. Not so much as a pity applause.'

Hazukiro shot his head up. The girl swayed side to side, uncomfortably holding back a grin.

'You've a strange sense of humour, girl.' He shook his head and rolled out the leather of a hunter's toolkit.

'Why are you still standing there?'

'I won't—I won't burst into flame, will I?'

Hazukiro stopped his task, looking around as if she'd made mention of some fiery trap.

'You said these grounds were blessed,' Taiyō continued.

'We've long passed the threshold. The temple's no more sacred than the shrines. Come inside.'

Gingerly, the girl moved in and sat herself on the altar steps.

'What are you doing?'

'Taking inventory,' he explained, eyes moving from item to item. He stood with a sigh.

'Rations for a few days. Five functional baubles. Three silver kunai. One silver wakizashi. A vial of ground wasari. Two small pouches of coin for trading. And in this one...' He pulled out a rolled-up piece of fabric and shook it out. 'A cloak.'

He looked at the girl, then sighed. 'Here. You'll get cold.'

'I won't,' she said matter-of-factly.

Hazukiro nodded and donned the large cotton cape. Deep red with black edges, it flowed over his torso, front and back. Placing his straw hat down, he pulled the hood up, shrouding his forehead.

'Do you like it?' Taiyō asked.

'It'll cover the brand and keep me warm,' he lowered the hood. 'It will do.'

Her eyes hid the question. She'd ask about the brand. And if he answered, she'd only ask more.

'We should get some rest. Stay away from the windows.'

He moved to close the temple doors, then curled up in the

corner against Akumo's back, lowered his head, and tried to catch that which always eluded him.

Peaceful sleep.

CHAPTER XXVI

RUMBLE OF TIDES

THE HONEYED HORIZON BARED the morning sun. While the girl slept, Hazukiro walked outside to the cliff's edge and took it all in. The salt of the sea breeze tickling his nose. The glinting of gold rays shimmering atop the vast azure canvas of the Eastern Sea. Amber clouds cascaded across the early sun, and distant gulls squawked against that marigold vista while rumbling waves rolled in with the tide.

A kunai cut the silence. It whizzed over the ronin's head. He spun around and drew his katana.

'You're alive,' Hazukiro sounded genuinely surprised.

Dokshin threw a second kunai. The ronin deflected it with the clang of his silver blade, sending it reeling over the cliff.

Dokshin scowled. 'And you aren't supposed to be.'

He threw a third blade, and it sliced free a small patch of straw from the rim of the ronin's hat.

'What is this?' Hazukiro called out. 'You followed me all this way, for what? Because you think I betrayed the Spectors?'

Dokshin spat, and slammed the hilt of his naginata into the ground. 'To hells with those fools. The Blight will take this island long before any kind of dent can be made in thinning the oniku numbers.'

'Why join them then?' Hazukiro steadied his stance. 'And what of your service to Kesyoka?'

Dokshin smirked and raised his naginata, spinning the hoku as he edged closer to the cliff.

'Look around you. These graves were filled long before the Blight. Kesyoka has abandoned us. We're nothing but lost souls grasping at holy rhetoric. But I, at the very least, wanted to see you die with my own eyes. When I heard rumours around the Academy of the Spectors' needing warriors, and that even the damned *leashed* may be helping, I had no choice but to volunteer.'

He held his weapon forward, sizing up his opponent and his own proximity to the cliff. The tide drew nearer, crashing cold white spray against the cliff.

'I don't know you,' Hazukiro finally said.

'But I know you. My family *knew* you. Though I'm certain all those faces blurred into one at some point?' He laughed from his belly. 'And now you defend an *actual* demon! Perhaps the rumours were true all along.'

Fury doused the sohei's face.

'Maybe you *are* a demon.'

He lunged without another word. The naginata blade skewered the air inches from the ronin's ear. Hazukiro launched into the air, spinning with silver in hand like a swift cyclone. The blade came down and shattered the naginata in two.

Dokshin cursed, flung aside the bottom half, and swung the bladed end like a large butcher's axe.

'Stop this!' Hazukiro growled, recoiling side to side like a snake, avoiding fatal blows.

'You deny nothing!' Dokshin panted, mad with enmity, stealing himself inside the ronin's reach. 'You watched them all *burn*!

He stepped back, regaining his footing and breath. 'And for what?'

'You won't win this fight,' Hazukiro said assuredly. The warrior monk ignored the warning. He raised his arms and dashed forward with blind contempt.

'Damn you. . .' Hazukiro whispered as he swiped in time with the salt-kissed wave that crashed over them.

Dokshin screamed as his hands flew into the air.

'I'm sorry,' Hazukiro flicked his blade to the sea breeze, then sheathed the sword solemnly. The monk wailed to the wind, and as he stammered in shock at his bloody stumps, he lost his footing and tumbled off the cliff.

There was only a cry, a crack and a splash, then nothing but the wash of waves. Hazukiro offered a silent prayer as the tide took the sohei.

Turning around, he saw Taiyō standing among the shrines, looking on at the aftermath of the brief duel.

No words were shared. No glances, even. Hazukiro shouldered past the girl and whistled Akumo over.

Taiyō stared at the horizon, listening to the waves roll in, unsure of what she would say even if she did feel like speaking. All she felt were abrasive memories of worse things she'd done, surfacing in number the longer she remained in her mind.

'Come.' Hazukiro fastened the last strap and climbed into the saddle. 'We make for Shiburiki.'

CHAPTER XXVII
SILENT VOICES

WINTER GREW EVER NEARER. Leaving behind the barren cliffs of Sun's Embrace, the ronin and the girl headed north. But as the day drew to an end, Hazukiro worried about the lack of shelter along the way.

'We should reach Shiburiki tomorrow,' Hazukiro said, eyes scanning the rolling grasslands ahead. 'But we'll need something for tonight. I could have sworn there was an old watchtower somewhere along these roads.'

When the shadows grew long, Akumo's anxious nature started to simmer, neighing and rolling her head.

'It's alright, girl,' Hazukiro patted her neck. 'We'll find something.'

'There aren't any around,' Taiyō said.

Hazukiro turned his head and raised a brow. 'You're tethered to them after all?'

'No,' she crossed her arms. 'But I can smell...blood. Yours. The horse's. And theirs. Though it's not the same, it's more like—'

'Black ichor,' Hazukiro said.

'Yes,' Taiyō said, lifting her hand and examining the dark veins that ran under her pale skin. 'I have no heartbeat. Just strange pulsing that sets my black blood flowing. Dead but alive. Or perhaps neither?' She shook her head. 'But there are none nearby. I'd smell that shared scent a mile off.'

Hazukiro retorted without a moment's hesitation. 'Meaning they can smell you too?'

'I assume so,' she shrugged. 'But they ignore me.'

Silence returned and Akumo trotted on, still restless with her braying.

'Probably appreciate something a little fresher,' Hazukiro finally said. Taiyō was not amused.

'Is that supposed to be funny?'

Hazukiro shrugged. 'You've a strange sense of humour.'

* * *

The cobblestoned road revealed the remnants of a signpost that Hazukiro recognised. After passing over a grassy weald, they shifted through wild shrubland and overgrowth, eventually finding the old stone watchtower, walls and roof still intact.

A wide road spiralled up and around the tower to its tip, originally made big enough for heavy transport wagons that would carry weapons and equipment.

'There you go, Akumo,' Hazukiro said. 'No stairs for you.'

The mare moved through thick grass and ate her fill. Taiyō scavenged the bush for winterberries, collecting them in a bundle in her sleeve. Hazukiro managed to snag a wild hare, and before the sun had set, they had settled at the top of the tower with their collective bounties. The ronin pulled old and rusted spears from the wall, cutting down their shafts to kindle the fire.

He set about skewering the skinned meat, rotating it as he stoked the flames. The crackling sizzle of its charring body rattled inside Taiyō's head like a den of hissing snakes. She hugged her knees but couldn't pull her eyes away.

'I take it you still eat food, then?' Hazukiro said, tossing more wood to the fire.

'Yes,' Taiyō said softly. 'Though it's the thirst that throttles me the most. If I divulge I can be sustained for a few days. Not to mention the strength it gives me.'

Hazukiro examined the girl. She trembled as if she were cold, and sweated from her brow as if stepping out of a steamed room.

'It *has* been a few days,' he said, 'You've eaten only berries.'

'The meat will help,' she said, rubbing her shins.

'I'm not serving it raw, girl.'

She shook her head. 'Don't let it concern you. This is my problem.'

Hazukiro pointed to his katana that lay beside him. 'Until it becomes mine.'

'Like you said,' she sneered. 'I'd prefer something *fresh*, you old goat.'

Hazukiro left out a hefty laugh, a sound he'd not heard from himself for what felt like aeons.

'You're probably right,' he chuckled. 'You're likely to get a mouthful of dust.'

Taiyō's own mien shattered, and she grinned like a maniac, stifling a laugh. As her stomach tensed it stung with a rumble.

Hazukiro thought for a moment, staring out the watchtower window at the blanket of stars in the night sky.

'Since the oniku ignore you,' he twisted the skewering stick. 'Perhaps you should find another hare to draw from.'

She licked dry lips. They stayed dry.

'I fear I may have to.'

She pushed herself up and immediately fell back down.

'I fear so too.' Hazukiro retrieved his wakizashi and cut some meat from the carcass, then tossed it her way.

'Eat something first.'

* * *

Taiyō returned in a red mist, startling Hazukiro. He sighed and eased himself back down. Akumo slept through the sudden cloudburst.

The girl wiped a trickle of blood away from her mouth and sat beside the fire.

'I'm sure that *form* you take must sap your energy,' Hazukiro warned.

'It does,' Taiyō said. 'But I was in no mood to walk all the way back up that road in the cold.'

Hazukiro chewed on some charred meat. 'The thirst you feel. I'd like to know more about it.'

She thought on the words, rocking back and forth, clasping her feet together.

'You've been thirsty?'

'Of course,' Hazukiro shrugged.

'And hungry?'

'Yes...'

'Imagine a culmination of both hunger and thirst, and then the splice of a knife to the gut, all the while your head pounds like a thousand drums, you shiver and you sweat, and your own mind tells you to give in with what feels like a literal painful push. You're exhausted but can't rest. You're weak but can't stop tensing your muscles. You're stagnant but your mind is on the move. Have you ever felt something like that?'

Hazukiro smirked. 'Perhaps not to that extent,' he admitted. 'But I've some experience in the hushing of such loudness.'

'Would you be willing to impart such wisdom?'

Hazukiro shrugged. 'If you're willing to learn.'

The Hush was simple in premise. One had to clear one's mind of all distractions in order to focus their mental energy on one task.

'Putting it into practice is the tricky part,' Hazukiro began explaining. 'Clearing your mind is no small task, even in a quiet room atop a silk cushion. I use it when I feel that some measure of calm would suit me better than reckless words, and when I need to maintain composure in the face of death, either by fang or blade. But I imagine you could use it to help stave off your thirst.'

'It's a lot harder to control than a burst of anger or the need to cry,' Taiyō said, deadpan.

'Of course. But that intrusive tongue lapping against your itchy brain? Your mind will make sense of it by latching a feeling to it. If you feel anger simmering, the irritating voice inside you will only fuel it like oil to flame. The purpose of the Hush is to wash that flame back, allowing you the quiet patience to focus wholly on what you need to in the midst of chaos. It's no permanent solution. It serves to get you through moments of panic or danger.'

Hazukiro sighed, thinking of dark days past. 'It's a difficult thing, battling your own mind. You're essentially fighting yourself, and whichever flame you stoke *will* win.'

He tossed wood to the fire illustratively.

'It will become easier, and faster, with practice. There will come a point when the sinister voice in your head will make the most sense. A silent voice. One you'll *feel* rather than hear. It will actively defy your reasoning. Your logic. And when you can silence that, you'll have mastered the Hush.'

The ronin smiled. 'And you'll have to master it all over again the next day.'

* * *

While the ronin slept, the girl went over the principles of the Hush. Drowning out the dark voices that demanded blood felt impossible. Though she had just consumed, her mind rattled red with the pleasure of quenched thirst. She searched her head for something to latch onto, something that went against her nature. All she could find was the human side of her that felt immense guilt at the need to feed, and those emotions felt feeble in relation to the powerful pull of demon blood.

'I'll try again in the morning,' she told herself as she lay down.

A cold hole filled her gut as she closed her eyes, and a silent but sinister voice echoed whispers behind her fluttering eyelids.

'*Try all you want.*'

CHAPTER XXVIII
A WORLD IN RUIN

FROST CRUSTED THE GRASSLANDS north of the old watchtower. Hazukiro walked on foot to warm his joints, leading Akumo with Taiyō nestled in her saddle. He wrapped his cloak over his kimono, grateful for the extra layer. A light fog hung on the bitterthin air, faded shrubbery barely visible ahead.

Each day brought them closer to winter, and to those snow-tipped peaks of Northern Ijihan, beyond the shadow of the mountain and into the maw of the enemy.

'Even I can feel this cold.' Taiyō looked about, seeing only blurred outlines of distant trees, shrouded in grey.

One of her many thoughts made its way to her mouth. 'Surely there are good people who would fight with us?' she asked, leaning back on the saddle.

Hazukiro sighed a cold cloud. 'People are unreliable.'

Taiyō rubbed her pale hands together, expecting more. The ronin gave nothing, only the sight of a tired old man, growing wearier with each passing day.

'If we were to explain—' she began.

'*No,*' spat Hazukiro. He exhaled and lowered his voice.

'The people of Ijihan are convinced the Blight is a punishment. That centuries of civil war, of spitting in the face of the gods, who blessed us with a bountiful and beautiful land, is the reason we're facing the consequences of our hubris. Some say the hells opened up and swallowed us whole without us realising, and that this domain is now another realm of the Underworld.'

He scoffed. 'There may be some truth to that. The way we were headed, Ijihan was one war away from crumbling into a nation of corpses. If divinity intervened, we'd likely have been deaf to it over the constant clash of battle.'

A soft breeze whistled through the tall grass, carrying a bite on its edge.

'They won't understand *you*,' Hazukiro concluded, rubbing his eyes. 'Instead of seeing you as the curse, they'll see you as *cursed*. Either way, you won't be 'them'. You'll be regarded as something incapable of receiving blessings. Tainted.' Hazukiro grunted in disgust.

'You'll find no help from *people*. No matter your plea.'

The winds swirled again, flicking Taiyō's hair up into her face. It felt as it did when she was alive. Just another orphan of war, trying to survive, matted in labour-induced sweat. She now felt the sticky substance of crusted blood, and the sensation of being dead struck like a reckoning bell with each minute her heart didn't beat. Brushing strands away, her eyes fell on the ronin. He'd stopped to massage a throbbing knee.

'You're helping me,' she offered to the breeze.

Hazukiro froze at that, before finally standing up straight and rolling his shoulders.

'That doesn't make me *good people*.' He pushed forward with a sudden aggression in his step.

'It just means that I'm desperate to forget the bad.'

Taiyō chewed the words carefully before her next.

'So a man cannot change? He cannot pursue good deeds and become virtuous?'

'Only to the world,' Hazukiro lamented. 'Not to himself. *Never* to himself.'

'He can try.'

'That he can. But it does not suture the wounds of misdeeds.'

'Trying should matter. . .' Taiyō steered Akumo, overtaking the ronin '. . .or there'd be no point to anything.'

She stopped, offering him the courtesy of keeping pace.

'The stonebridge to Shiburiki should be a few hours away.' Hazukiro conceded, masking his thoughts. 'Let's push on.'

* * *

The dead meadows grew wider. Small trees were scattered about, growing stunted and slanted towards the canyon that prefaced the village. The first tattered sign poked through the morning fog that was slowly lifting. Hazukiro kept a cautious eye on the dark clouds that had begun crawling overhead.

'We're almost there. You're certain Shiburiki is abandoned?'

'Yes,' Taiyō explained. 'The dead bled that area dry years ago.'

'So the accounts say,' the ronin retorted. 'But you've passed through it. Recently. And are no threat to them. You could've stepped over a sleeping oniku and not known about it. Or perhaps you even encountered a few and forgot.'

'I'd remember that. It's directions and details that elude me. Kia and I were moving fast, expecting fangs in our neck at any given moment. Besides, I can still smell when they're near, if it comes to that.'

'Keep your nose sharp then. The streets of Shiburiki wind like a serpent. Best if we can—'

The foot of the stone bridge halted Hazukiro. Though it once arched in the middle, the rise was gone, jagged at its end like a terribly cut loin.

'No...'

Hazukiro burst into a sprint along the cliff's edge, desperate for a fresh perspective, until the fate of the bridge was painfully clear.

'Destroyed,' growled Hazukiro. 'It's completely destroyed. Crumbled down into the valley below.'

Taiyō took tentative steps behind him, looking ahead to the ruined structure.

'It wasn't when I crossed it,' she said softly. Hazukiro swung around sharply and Taiyō flinched.

'How is that possible?' he barked. 'Not a soul lives here! Oniku aren't strong enough to tear down *stone*!'

He caught his breath, sharp with frustration. Taiyō stepped back, her tongue slipping loose with what she felt was the right thing to say.

'Control yourself,' she said flatly.

Hazukiro looked up at that. Taiyō swallowed, clenching her fists, her stance unwavering. The ronin fluttered his eyelids, exhaling deeply and the girl braced herself, squeezing white-knuckled fists.

'You are right,' he said. 'Nothing can be done about it, and daylight wanes.'

Taiyō let out stiff air in relief, but quietly.

She could dissipate into a mist. Embody the strength of five men. Outpace them in a blink. And while she hated what she'd become, it was the only weapon she had against the world. Against the ronin even, she felt the strange absence of a familiar feeling. A pounding heart at the familiar outburst of anger from a bitter man.

'I apologise,' Hazukiro said softly.

Taiyō released a sharp gasp at that.

'I. . .I am tired.'

'We can rest a while,' Taiyō said assuredly. 'There's no whiff of dead on the wind. We've time.'

'No, no,' Hazukiro began moving back to the foot of the bridge. 'Tired of all of this. The Blight. The night. A world in ruin.'

When the ronin looked at the girl, she offered a warm smile. For a brief moment, Hazukiro thought of his wife.

Hana.

She always called him out on his tangents with her soft smile.

The memory grated like a cold, rusted blade plunged deep into his chest. He clasped its grisly edges and pulled it free from his heart and mind, leaving many unspoken words on his tongue, extinguished by the only words he was willing to say.

'Let's keep moving.'

Taiyō looked at the broken bridge. 'Where to, then?'

Hazukiro hid the hesitance in his voice. 'We must pass through Fujima Falls.'

The name meant nothing to Taiyō. His excursions as a scribe had clearly taught him something she didn't know. Before she could ask, he breathed deeply, tapping his fingers on his hilt.

'We'll have to hug the canyon wall. Below the bridge, near those mooring stones.'

He gestured to the deep drop below, the rush of cold rivers pummelling through the narrow.

'Watch your step as we go.'

CHAPTER XXIX
FUJIMA FALLS

BENEATH THE RUINED BRIDGE, precarious scaffolding lined the canyon wall.

'Before the Blight, workers moved along those narrow ridges for the upkeep of the support beams,' Hazukiro explained, pointing out their rickety route.

'That plank path will eventually widen out and lead to a solid footpath. An old trail that folk often visited in the springtime.'

Hazukiro carefully walked down the rockface.

'Then we can go through the falls to the end of this canyon. It'll eventually merge close enough for us to get across. Then we can loop back around to Shiburiki.'

He placed firm feet on a protruding ledge. 'The detour back will take too much time. We'll have to find a cave in the falls to spend the night.'

'And Akumo?' Taiyō stroked the mare's mane. 'Will that path support her?'

The ronin sighed, patting her neck with affection. 'It will have to. We can't leave her out here.'

Hazukiro and Taiyō approached the first plank of the platform. The ronin pressed a cautious foot to the wood. A crack revealed the river below.

'This does not exactly fill me with confidence,' Taiyō looked down. 'And I—'

She dropped to her knees, clutching at her reeling head. She groaned and fell to her side, a single foot slipping off the edge.

'Careful!' Hazukiro shouted, clutching her kimono with one hand and Akumo's pommel with the other. He grunted and pulled her to her feet.

'Careful?' she groaned. 'The thought hadn't occurred, thank you for—' She winced, pressing a palm to her burning eyes.

'You need to feed,' Hazukiro said, placing a hand behind her back as she staggered on weak knees.

'I ate. . .*yesterday*.'

Taiyō rolled her eyes back, suddenly breathless.

'*Hey!* Focus, or you'll send us *all* over.' He grabbed her shoulders. 'I'm not in the mood for a swim.'

She feigned a smile, rolling a heavy head.

'You fed on a small animal,' Hazukiro said, stroking his beard. 'When did you last feed on. . .' he exhaled, then softened his voice. 'On human blood?'

She shook her head, blinking fast. 'Not since the Spectors.'

A cold wind licked the air. The wood below their feet croaked and creaked, swaying slightly.

'It will rain soon,' Hazukiro said. 'Get on the horse, if you're unable to walk.'

'No,' she said softly. 'Heavy black bones.'

An icy gush slapped Hazukiro's face. He reached to secure his hat, squinting at the gathering grey above.

He rolled up his sleeve and thrust his arm out, revealing soft, succulent flesh. 'Drink.'

Taiyō slapped his hand away. Hazukiro recoiled and winced. The girl's fast fingers stung like a wasp.

'Keep going,' she shook her head. 'It's passing.'

Hazukiro knew there was no time to argue. 'Stay close to the cliff wall.'

He tugged at Akumo's reins. Taiyō nodded and followed the ronin, gingerly stepping where he and his horse stepped.

'How are you faring?' Hazukiro asked when they reached their halfway mark, lower into the canyon.

'I'm alright,' she said flatly.

'The falls have patches of pools as it descends,' Hazukiro gestured ahead.

'Flat outcrops with some shrubbery, too. A few trees. Should be ripe with animals, at the very least.'

'I'm fine, really,' Taiyō insisted, leaping over a questionable plank. She stumbled and clutched the ronin to brace herself.

'I can't risk you passing out up here. These paths twist and turn for a while. I need to lead Akumo' He pointed down, stone-faced. 'And it's a long fall.'

Taiyō hung her head, squinting hard.

'A drink, then,' she conceded. 'Keep moving. I'll listen for an animal. To sustain me. Gods, how do I have such a throbbing headache with no heart?'

'You did not choose this curse.' Hazukiro knew the look of shame that crept over the girl's face.

'Do not blame yourself. You're using the only means available to you to survive. No one can blame you for that.'

She looked up at the ronin, searching her mind for the last time someone gave a damn.

Hazukiro placed a gentle hand on her shoulder. 'I certainly don't.'

* * *

The pair breathed in relief when the last of the shoddy steps were behind them. Akumo trotted off in search of some green. Now lower into the canyon, outcrops and paths grew wide and vegetated. Near-bare trees and evergreen bushes surrounded wide, shallow pools of water. The roar of Fujima Falls hissed white behind them.

Taiyō tasted the cold air, but couldn't sniff out a single animal.

She listened instead, the ronin attempting the same.

Hearing anything beyond the thunder of the falls proved impossible. Taiyō, however, had found that when it came to feeding, she could separate the living from the inanimate.

But even then, there was no birdsong. No squirrels scampered up trees. The pool was vast and ankle-deep, not deep enough for fish worth eating. Above them, more outcrops poked along the cliff face, lining the towering rockface like mushroom flats along a rugged oak.

'Nothing,' she dropped her shoulders, defeated. A sharp pain returned, ringing around her head like hammered bells.

The feeling pulsed downwards like twin blades, stopping at her gut to stab at it.

'There has to be *something*,' she spat with a sudden hoarseness to her voice. The colour ran from her cheeks. Her fangs glistened and grew.

'The Hush,' Hazukiro calmly commanded.

A sinister look washed over Taiyō's eyes as she choked down spit in between snarls.

'It's too. . .*sudden*, I—'

She dropped to her knees and slammed a fist into the ground with such might that she cracked rock.

'I'm burning up!' Her cries muffled as she curled up. Wrists contorted and fingers twitched.

'I need—' She forced herself to her feet, then threw up black ichor.

'I'll find something. Sit back down.' The ronin approached her as she stumbled about like a newborn calf.

'I think I'm going to—'

She keeled over, splashing face-first into the shallow water. Hazukiro quickly pulled her face from the pool.

'Girl?' He shook her shoulders. '*Taiyō!*'

She fluttered heavy lids, revealing pallid pupils.

Concern washed over her milky-white face. A soft croak escaped her mouth, lips quivering as she tried to speak again. The ronin reached to calm her shaking hands.

'You're alright,' Hazukiro assured her.

She managed to mutter one soft word before fainting.

'*Up.*'

A silent figure descended.

Without thinking, Hazukiro clutched Taiyō and rolled, scrambling to his feet and unsheathing his sword.

A young woman stood before him. Her hair was long and dark, bound in a ponytail and drenched in water. She wore flowing navy-blue silks in between studded light leather greaves, gauntlets and boots. Smaller kunai blades and potions pouched in bandoliers were strapped across her chest and slim waist. A larger pack hung at her hip.

A Silkspinner.

'How did the Teragaku get an assassin from the mainland?' Hazukiro shouted over the hissing water. 'Shouldn't you be off somewhere thinning the ranks of kings?'

The woman said nothing, but cast her dark eyes to Taiyō. The girl lay drenched and unconscious, still pale as a corpse at sea.

The assassin moved an inch forward but was met with the swish of Hazukiro's blade. She stopped to stare him down.

'Do not *touch* her!' the ronin roared.

The woman huffed through her nose like a taunted bull. She produced a coil of rope from her hip pouch and unravelled it with ferocious finesse.

Hazukiro moved over to shield Taiyō.

The assassin's fingers moved fast, swinging her weapon.

'*A rope dart.*' Hazukiro examined it.

Its blade resembled a hooked dagger, and the coarse rope it hung from hummed red like threaded blood. Both the blade and the cord gleamed as she rolled her wrist.

'*Silver*,' Hazukiro noticed. '*It's even stitched into the rope. Who is this woman?*'

She stepped back into the wide, shallow pool, swinging the blade in slow, perfect arcs. Had she been smirking, Hazukiro might have mistaken the casual bravado as a taunt. But the Silkspinner's face remained sourly serious. The ronin, to her, was seemingly nothing but an obstacle. Something she'd need to dispatch so she could reach her true mark.

When she reached the pool's centre she stopped and beckoned him.

'Will you not reason with me?' Hazukiro shouted. 'Will you not hear what I have to say, at the very least?'

The woman's silence was her answer.

'I gave you the courtesy,' Hazukiro stepped into the waters, katana poised.

'What follows is on you.'

CHAPTER XXX

THE SILKSPINNER

THE RONIN STUDIED THE ASSASSIN.

An opponent with a raised or lowered sword could be anticipated quickly. The woman stood stall, straight and disciplined, swinging the blade without giving anything away. Hazukiro would have to make the first move, and a position that allowed him to strike from several angles was the best move.

The *hasso no kamae* stance.

He knew he would have to pay close attention to her movements, but after a full minute, the woman had only moved her weapon in its consistent arc. Knees stayed unbent, her mien still stern.

The open stance almost beckoned. She was wide open.

With his katana pointing true, Hazukiro splashed through the waters and leapt to the woman's side, striking left.

She spun to avoid it, gracefully turning on the spot, before returning with the full force of her whirling blade. It shrieked through the air and tore through the straw of Hazukiro's tengai, knocking the hat from his head.

The blade continued its path and struck the waters, rippling the surface and sending the rope into a frenzied coil. The woman yanked the rope and clasped its end, flinging it from her hand again like a striking snake.

Hazukiro regained his balance and swished his head to the side. The silver hook sliced through his cheek. He cried out, blood splattering into his eye.

Finding his resolve, he grunted and looked for an opening.

The rope coiled back and lashed out again.

Hazukiro struck up, aiming for the outstretched rope, but the Silkspinner was too fast. She summoned the blade back.

'Gah!'

The ronin rolled aside before it embedded the back of his skull along its return journey.

Hazukiro returned to his feet and created some distance. He looked at his opponent's face. To the movement of her hands, her footwork. For something he could use against her. But the Silkspinner remained stubbornly obscure.

The waters settled again, reflecting her calmness. It was as if this woman was the Hush made manifest, while the ronin could feel the ripples of frustration toil inside of him.

He tried to slow his laboured breathing and enter the Hush.

His eyes fell on Taiyō. She was still unconscious, clenching her fists and breathing rapidly, drenched head to toe. Something stirred inside the ronin.

'*Focus*,' he commanded his mind. '*Or she dies.*'

The trees disappeared first. Then small shrubbery. The rocks fell away next. In the void-like vista of his mind, Taiyō remained illuminated

A bright, nascent seed in the endless, rolling dark.

Routine and discipline, the two masters of the Hush, told Hazukiro to eliminate *all* distractions. He cursed at those voices. Banished them like holy light to grim spirits.

How could he dispense what he was defending?

The thunder of Fujima Falls was the hardest to drown out. Water hissed and howled in his ears. The persistent spray of the mist shower was cold. It trickled down his head, picking up sweat and blood with it.

Taiyō's light shone brighter still. The eminence of Taiyō's fate stressed its own importance, and with a final push of focus, the sounds of the falls began to soften.

The red rope struck like lightning.

It came from above this time, like a crimson whip ready to punish. The ronin sidestepped and used the momentum to give himself more distance.

He only had a moment. The blade would come barrelling back. Driven by the Hush, the ronin dashed forward, blade high. Before the Silkspinner's brow could rise, the shine of the ronin's katana came down.

It sliced through her bandolier and into her shoulder. The pouches split and tore from her chest, soaring over the edge into the rushing waters below.

The Silkspinner grasped her shoulder, then pulled away a bloodied hand. She gritted her teeth and shook the drops from her hand. With a soft wince she summoned her blade back.

'This sword can cut through demon bone,' Hazukiro said, panting. 'Leave us. She's a victim of the Blight, same as you. Same as all of us, one way or another.'

Dark clouds huddled, rumbling with rain.

'No.' The Silkspinner spat. 'It's a demon.'

The bruised black sky began to shower the outcrop with heavy rain.

'Have you ever *seen* oniku not burn under the sun?' Hazukiro lowered his sword in a show of good grace.

'There's more to this.' He held out a hand. 'A skilled blade at our side could make all the difference.'

The woman looked to Taiyō, still lying on the rocks, masked by filth and rain.

Sighing, she lowered her rope.

'Let's get somewhere dry!' Hazukiro offered. 'We can still speak of this.'

'I have nothing against you,' the assassin said.

Hazukiro stepped closer, his hand still held out. 'Are you not tired of being on someone's leash?'

'I'm no one's prisoner,' she spat.

The woman reached into her remaining bandolier and produced a throwing star, then cast her gaze back to Taiyō.

Hazukiro leapt forward. '*No!*'

His cry was met with several in return. Monstrous screams, louder than the rushing falls or the unrelenting downpour.

The shrillness grew as a horde of thralls poured through the falls, talons and fangs itching.

They swarmed and swirled through the rain, flapping water off their leathery wings, attempting to sniff through the rain.

They turned their burning gaze to the two warriors. The ronin, dripping crimson nirvana. The Silkspinner, oozing ecstasy.

'Put that weapon to good use,' Hazukiro raised his katana. 'Aid me in ridding the world of *these* demons. After that, Silkspinner, you may die.'

The assassin grunted, pacing to pair her back with the ronin's.

Hazukiro raised his katana. 'Soot and cinder!'

The violet of the blade burst forth, and the swarm dived in like a crashing wave of hurricane claws.

The Silkspinner was the first to strike. She gripped the heft of the dart and sent the rope sailing through the rain. The silver pierced a thrall's wing. It shrieked, hooked like a baited fish. Tugging down, the assassin shredded the wing into two useless flaps. The oniku screamed and spiralled over the edge.

'Let's hope this is a passing downpour,' Hazukiro squinted upwards. The clouds stubbornly shielded the sun.

Another oniku swooped its claws at Hazukiro. He thrust his bright blade into the beast's belly. The ronin braced, allowing the momentum of the falling creature to tear itself open on his sword. Skins, innards, talons and everything black in between ignited in a flash of orange embers. Before its body pummelled the ground, it smouldered into ash and splashed across the water's surface in a haze of powdered grey.

The Silkspinner launched her blade again. Its tip missed, but on the recoil, she angled it to wrap around the neck of another swooping oniku. With fierce focus, she wiggled her elbow, spun around, and pulled. As the rope constricted, the silver of its threads ate into the beast's neck, severing its slobbering face from its corpse.

The headless body landed at Hazukiro's feet, still splashing about in desperation. The ronin plunged his katana into its heart, shredding the body down to speckles.

'What are they doing?' Hazukiro glanced up.

A dozen thralls in flight circled before settling themselves amongst the outcrops above. They sat on their haunches, drooling, their gazes still fixed on the bleeders below. Perched like gangly gargoyles.

Not one of them paid any attention to Taiyō.

Digging claws into rock, one of the oniku thrust his head back and screeched so loudly that both warriors fell to their knees and clasped their ears.

'No. . .' Hazukiro looked at the falls.

Another dozen oniku burst out through the water curtain.

Sharing calls and cries, they all took flight, unified and numerous.

'We cannot keep this up for much longer,' Hazukiro spat away water. He looked to Taiyō. Rain still pummelled her as she slept.

'Wake up, child,' he hissed through teeth.

The Silkspinner swatted the ronin's shoulder and pointed up. Returning to the fight, Hazukiro entered a lower stance, ready to strike up. As the cool air brushed his hair back, he closed his eyes and reattuned himself with the Hush.

The assassin pierced a demon's chest. It kept going, folding its wings backwards and diving towards her.

'Get ready,' she grunted.

Enduring the sting in her shoulder, she tensed and swung the cord with all her strength. The oniku's path faltered, diving over her and towards Hazukiro. As the rope arced, bringing the beast with it, Hazukiro cut the thrall in two. The rope dart flung free and returned to its master's hand.

'Behind!'

The Silkspinner ducked before claws could tear her throat out. Hazukiro's katana slashed the thrall's forearm off. It wailed while embers engulfed its helpless body.

Returning the favour, the woman swung her blade over the ronin's head to hook the maw of another demon. She slammed its jaw into the pool.

'There's too many of them!' Hazukiro roared.

The woman tugged her blade back, poised to thrust it, when she felt the violent clutch of talons around her arm.

The oniku took flight. She scrambled, reaching for her throwing kunai, sticking the small blades into the creature's foot, chest, and wing. When one blade met its eye, the demon shrieked and dropped her.

It crashed beside the ronin. He lobbed its head off and looked over the edge, barely catching a glimpse of the Silkspinner as she sailed silently into the depths.

'Damn it,' Hazukiro growled.

Off-guard, a claw clasped his shoulder, digging into flesh. He cried out, swinging his katana in a violet arc that tore the monstrous hand free.

The beast screamed and fell forward, its weight knocking the ronin off-balance. He stumbled, battling the pain of his shoulder, the blinding rain, and the slippery rocks he stumbled on as he scrambled for solid footing.

One misstep took him from stone to air, sending him over.

He grunted, straining muscles to hold onto the slippery ledge. He watched as his katana fell, its light growing fainter and smaller before it disappeared into the dark.

Pain shot up and down his arms. Trembling fingers fumbled desperately.

'*Akumo!*' He shouted, his energy fading fast. He whistled sharply, garnering the attention of several oniku.

The mare thundered through the trees, whinnying as she stomped across the pool. She braved through a pair of oniku that swooped down over her.

'Hurry, girl!' Hazukiro felt a finger slip free. '*Hurry!*'

Akumo stopped at the ledge with a snort. The ronin reached out a hand, swiping at her bridle just out of reach. The mare moved in a panic, rolling her head in the wet as demons screamed above. Hazukiro felt the leather of the stirrup and snatched it.

'*Yah!*'

Akumo galloped. The ronin cried out. His side scraped against the cliff as he was pulled up.

'*Stop, Akumo!*' His shoulder felt like it was ready to tear itself free.

The horse halted, still flustered. A shadowy figure from the rain drew nearer, wings spread wide. Hazukiro reached for a kunai and flung it, hoping to hit something.

'*Turn!*' He kicked Akumo's side. '*Please*, girl! Turn!'

He yanked on her reins, wrestling with the strength of the panicked mare, pleading for her to veer towards Taiyō.

'*Move!*'

Talons sank into Akumo. Flapping wings furiously, the oniku began to lift the horse and the ronin. It managed a few measly feet before it retracted its grip in defeat and flew off.

Hazukiro and Akumo fell.

They plummeted through cold kisses of rain towards the waters below.

CHAPTER XXXI

MA

THE CONCEPT OF 'MA' often eluded Hazukiro. Or at least, the perception Hana had of it, and how she often encouraged him to perceive it. She would ask him to try it the way one would recommend their favourite food, share a song that spoke to them, or point out a shooting star before it vanished.

The ronin always regretted how quickly he dismissed what it meant to his wife. How she wished he too could appreciate those indisputably necessary 'moments of mundane', as she'd called them.

The silent reflection of a full and satisfied belly. The space after the last chord struck in a song. The unspoken pause after making a wish.

'Not that wish,' Hana whispered like a petal-laden wind. 'Not yet.'

'Hana?'

Hazukiro found himself standing outside their cottage. That familiar, soothing voice, soft as silk, carried harmonies on the evening breeze.

The sounds warmed the cosy stone home under a garden of stars. Escorted by the tender pluckings of her biwa, the songstress sang a tale of kodama in treetop homes.

Hazukiro stepped forward, his eyes brimming.

The cottage door creaked open to a field of white poppies and a woman in pink silk. She cradled her instrument like a broken soldier, soothing it and igniting its joys harnessed beneath its wooden exterior.

The moment he stepped closer to admire his wife's talents, the fields lit up in waves of fire. Song turned to harrowing cries. The ronin felt himself sinking. A sea of burnt corpses swallowed him, slowly drowning him under pleas for help.

* * *

Hazukiro awoke underwater, bubbling and swirling about the rapids. He broke through the surface, desperate for air. The pummelling falls had pushed him downriver, and the stream was steep and haphazard. Shivering and fatigued, the river eventually calmed, as if subsiding from a barrage of punishment. It spat Hazukiro against a reed bank. The ronin clutched at the plants, dragging himself onto shore. He sputtered up a storm when he staggered to his feet.

He looked around and a cold panic set in. He'd been unconscious, and night had already fallen. Searching his clothes, he retrieved his last vial of wasari, still intact. He poured the contents of the scratch wounds, wincing as it stung. Relieved that his wakizashi was still attached to him, he drew the smaller blade and began searching the dark gloom along the bank.

'Akumo!' he cried, clutching his side.

The old wound was still sensitive, and the battering he'd taken along the river made him ache all over when he walked.

'Akumo! Girl!' He mustered the strength to whistle. 'Where are you?'

He pushed out the thoughts that told him the obvious.

'No.' He whistled again. 'She's fine. She's luckier than an iris gard—'

Along the bank, a figure of grey lay. Small noises puffed out with each rapid breath.

'No. . .' Hazukiro dashed over and dropped to his knees beside Akumo. He reached out with a trembling hand, stroking her snout.

The wounds from the oniku's talons were deep, and one of her legs had broken in the fall.

'*No!*' Hazukiro cursed. 'Please don't let me do this. . .'

The mare's dark eyes moved up and down her master, searching for comfort. Hazukiro realised this, and that he was giving her nothing but panic.

'I'm sorry, girl,' he said, softly this time. She snorted gingerly.

He tousled her mane.

He patted her neck.

He bore down his blade and freed her from her suffering.

Hazukiro placed his forehead to Akumo's, and tears finally flooded forth. He'd only allowed himself such a feeling for one other loss. And sending a request to the heavens, he gently laid her head down and bowed deeper than he had for any lord.

'Please see to her.'

Silently, he reflected on the noble acts of Akumo.

Then in prayer, he whispered his wish. '*Please see to her.*'

The words left his lips, and he allowed the pause to last longer. He swore he could feel Hana's smile warm his heart.

'*I've prepared a place,*' she said.

CHAPTER XXXII

TRIBUTE

THE RIVER RAN THIN and slow now, and the shrubbery along its banks grew thick with green. But even now, Hazukiro hadn't seen or heard any signs of life, no matter how far north he walked. No owls sat perched in the trees. No fireflies danced across the river's surface. No critter scurried about. Even the often vocal cicadas were gone. And no visible path back to Taiyō. Nothing but the sheer steepness of the Fujima cliffs that seemed to wind on forever.

Hazukiro staved off dark thoughts and instead fought the need to stay warm. He was drenched, head to toe. The wound at his side still stung, and his cheek seared fiercely. He prodded himself, feeling fresh bruises forming, perhaps even fractures. Chilled bones and throbbing pain all over made it difficult to pinpoint much.

His katana was gone as well, lost to the falls, and the eerie silence of the deadwood unsettled him to his core. It wasn't until he approached an old road and brushed back a branch that he realised where he was. Six charred poles lined the path.

Prowler's Rest.

It was, to his knowledge, the most oniku-invested locale in all of Ijihan. No survivor in the Academy had met or heard of anyone who had made it out since Blightfall.

In his cell, Hazukiro had heard fortressfolk whisper of this wasteland. Some believed it to be a circle of hell itself, with a god at its centre that judged damned souls. Others had murmured that it was a kind of crucible, where oniku would spawn from a larger, mother demon before taking flight for the night. He'd even heard a Blood Spector make mention of the island's zealots who worshipped something sinister there.

As wild as all the theories may have sounded, one thing permeated through the conjecture.

Something large prowled at its heart.

Prowler's Rest. Down below the falls, among the abandoned temples and hamlets in the shadowed reach of the island.

Even the animals had had the sense to leave.

Hazukiro looked up at the pyres as he passed them. Skeletons hung, tied at the wrists and ankles by fraying ropes. Each pole had a wooden board at its base, all of them with the same word spelt out in faded blood.

TRIBUTE.

These poor souls had been tied and left as offerings.

Hazukiro swallowed his disgust. The oniku must have swarmed these people like flies to a honey-stick.

Hazukiro proceeded down the dark road, rubbing the chill from his hands. He looked back at the cliffs to the south.

Taiyō wouldn't make it on her own, he worried. No one would take her in, with her blood-soaked clothes and her deathly pale face.

They wouldn't understand her and her turmoil.

He didn't.

The universal truth across all realms is that people outright *shun* that which they don't understand with either sword or spittle.

Hazukiro wasn't convinced he could fit the role himself. But just because her path wasn't his, it didn't mean she deserved to be abandoned to walk her way.

Who was he to deny her that?

He knew the way of the sword and she didn't.

He had to get back to Taiyō.

If not for her, then at least for the sake of his own damned soul.

* * *

Thunder rolled its tongue and Hazukiro looked to the sky.

Dark clouds still hung overhead, masking the moon and stars. As he traipsed through the dead silent scape, he felt the cold drizzle of another onset of rain.

He considered climbing a tree to get a better lay of the land. But while he heard no birds, he couldn't eliminate the possibility of nesting ikari.

He had no choice but to press on. His wounds were a double-edged sword, throbbing and burning, but forcing him to stay awake and alert.

Another silent hour into the night, Hazukiro finally spotted something in a large lake beside the road.

A slanted bell tower sat half-submerged. One side of its stone wall still stood strong, and the other had crumbled away, forming a pile of rubble that bedded a rusted, cracked bell. Its foundations hid beneath dark, stagnant waters. A wall of carmine vines encrusted the building's facade, but the ronin recognized the architecture.

Fujima Temple.

Straying off the road, his steps became staggered, and he found himself catching his footing as the ground grew steeper. Passing through the bush in a stealthy slouch, Hazukiro saw what had befallen the once-sacred temple.

Years of rain and rain had seen its bearings weaken. It must have crumbled and settled into the lake. Beneath its red creepers, algae had formed along its rim and reeds had sprouted out, swathing it in a cradle of green.

Portions of the temple, entire rooms and pillars even, poked out of the waters around it like the shattered remnants of dropped glass.

The temple's red hall and adjoining black tower lay slanted and faded amid the ruins.

When the clouds dispersed, the moon cast a generous glow across the shallow lake. The waters seemed to extend far beyond a simple swim, though the distant darkness made it difficult to be certain.

The walls of the hall seemed solid enough, and the consistent silence did nothing to soothe the ronin. He needed to rinse his wounds. And to rest, above all.

This would have to do for the night.

* * *

Wading through the water, Hazukiro approached the first protruding piece of rubble. Wary of sudden dips, the ronin clambered up the structure and cautiously leapt from stone to stone. The belfry appeared more unstable up close, its stature and slant intimidating.

Hazukiro closed the final gap between the pillars and the temple's entrance steps. Two large doors stood ajar, wet with rot, keeping nothing in or out for some time.

Stepping into the silence, Hazukiro entered a wide hall. It was rich with acoustics, made known only by his steps and the occasional water drop. The ends of the area were diverted into other hallways and rooms. Some were sealed off by rubble, others half-drowned.

Hazukiro shut his eyes and listened.

Even the lake was devoid of the usual ring of frogs and crickets. Any sound would have been a relief at this point. Anything from outside of the temple, at least.

But no sound came from either.

Hazukiro pressed on.

The hall was dark, with only speckles of moonlight filtering through the debilitating ceiling.

'Damn it...'

Though the odds of finding decent weapons in a temple were slim, he hugged the walls and brushed his hand along their dusty, cold exteriors, hoping for a mounted polearm of some esteemed temple guard, or the naginata of a sohei, perhaps.

He felt only the mould of tattered banners, the once proud Ijihan flag reduced to shreds as if to mirror or mock its current state.

As the ronin strode deeper into the dark, one sound became prevalent. Dripping water. It did not surprise him, but the amount of torn floorboards, piles of rock, and stagnant puddles made him cautious of his steps. He chuckled to himself for a moment. Perhaps being crushed to death by the literal destruction of his faith would be an end befitting a man of his misdeeds.

With some floor still solid, and some banners thick enough to keep him warm, Hazukiro managed to find a spot that would allow him to rest until daybreak.

He tore one banner down and dried himself with it. Sitting in his trousers, he wrung out his cloak and kimono as best he could, laid them out, and wrapped himself in the less tattered banner.

With heavy lids, he shivered himself to sleep.

* * *

The light was sudden and fierce.

A gust of wind flooded the hall, licking lanterns along the walls as it passed, igniting all of them in green flame. The force behind it was cold. It stung Hazukiro's skin and surged him from his slumber, dagger in hand.

He scrambled to his feet, looking up and down the hall at its strange new hue. Illuminated now, the sheen of a spear lodged in rubble caught his eye. Hazukiro dashed over to it, pulled it free, and assumed a defensive stance. The entrance doors had been bolted shut.

From the inside.

'What is this?'

Across the length of the hall, where the altar would have been, he noticed a crater in the ground, sieving in water. Beyond it, where the back wall had been, a massive hole now arched, opening further into the temple.

The same green aura beckoned beyond it.

Tired and cold, he marched over to the entrance doors in nothing but his pants, trying it first. He heard the rattle of chains on the other end.

He groaned and turned back to snatch up his wet clothes, but gave pause when a voice rang around the acoustic hall.

'This way.'

The lantern lights surged in unison as if agreeing with the command. Hazukiro swung the polearm in his hands and pressed on.

'Fine,' he grumbled, moving forward, scouring the ceiling.

'This better be worth losing sleep over.'

When he stepped through the hole in the wall, the next section of the temple's lanterns lit up with the same emerald aura.

This room was wider with a rounded ceiling, mostly desecrated, the sky and moon visible. Hazukiro turned to the walls and swallowed hard when the stench of decay slipped up his nose.

Carcasses.

Shrivelled carcasses, burnt black, tied to all manner of makeshift contraptions. Some bodies were impaled and plastered against crude platforms. Many were piled into pyramids at the corners of the room. But most of the bodies hung from their feet.

They adorned the walls to the ceiling like decaying decor. A long pile of bones, almost resembling a wall, stretched out against the back of the room.

'Tribute!' a man's voice cried out.

'Tribute!' another cry followed, this time a woman's.

The word was uttered repeatedly, staggered, each time with more voices joining it.

The calls came from above, and the ronin grit his teeth, searching the ceiling. Behind curtains of corpses, he could make out small balconies. Though mostly shrouded in darkness, rows of hooded heads stood out like a graveyard audience, chanting that incessant word.

'TRIBUTE.'

'It's them...' he scowled, readying his spear.

The Forsaken Sons and Daughters.

Their voices bounced and echoed across the walls like a hellish choir. Hazukiro tried to slow his breathing to enter the Hush. The consistent cries prattled on, louder each second, making it increasingly difficult.

'How did the rhyme go?' He turned back, circling the room, checking and rechecking his blindspots.

On the east wall, a blood-covered message masked an epitaph of Kesyoka's journey across the realms.

'Man has done much that cannot be undone
No hands of grace reached out to save us
So we embrace our state, spit in the light's face
And absolve our sin by feeding the decided fate.'

'*Tribute!*'

The tone behind the cry turned from word to instruction, then, from an instruction into a desperate plea.

Their wails soon dissolved into pitiful cries, moaning the word any which way, thrusting arms into the air. Hazukiro could see their skin now. Sickly and grey, as if they'd bathed in ash. Gaunt and bony as if they'd lived past a century or two. They no longer sounded human, only husks of their former selves. So when one voice broke through the wailing, it stirred Hazukiro's stomach.

'Forsaken sons and daughters!'

The voice belonged to a man. His baritone was broken and unsettling.

'A tribute has come. Of his own accord!'

The croons of the followers continued in ghoulish harmony.

'Do you see, my brothers? My sisters? The mark that shapes this man's visage?'

Hazukiro looked around the ceiling to pinpoint the crier. The voices were many, bouncing across the acoustics like clambering ants about a mound.

'He has been shunned! Cast out! His past is *tainted*!'

The voices shifted, some still chanting, others groaning in agreement with the speaker.

'As have we all. . .' The crier's voice fell dark and pitiful. 'As we deserve.'

Hazukiro leapt back as something fell and rattled at his feet. It was a solid, black skull, embossed in some strange substance that had prevented it from smashing to bits.

'Step forward and receive your punishment!' The crier continued. 'And do so with vigour, for no reward is received sweetly without first sweating for it!'

The crier cleared his throat. 'Now, greet death as you would an old friend. Kiss the skull.'

Voices clamoured again. '*Yes! Tribute! Death! Greet death!*'

The ronin cast his eyes back to the balconies. He scoffed and tossed the skull to the rubble.

'I'm losing my patience,' the ronin growled, raising the spear. 'Unbar the doors. Now.'

The voices halted as one, leaving a sharp echo, and then silence.

The wall of bones stirred. A pained groan followed.

The speaker howled one final word.

'*Chastiser!*'

His steps receded. Dozens more followed, pattering away from their podiums.

Hazukiro's eyes roamed the room before falling on the bone wall. He stood with fettered feet as the mound of rumbling ivory moved.

CHAPTER XXXIII
THE LIGHTLESS LEECH

THE APPARENT EMINENCE OF the temple emerged. Musty bones rose and fell as the beast stood up, roused from a deep sleep.

Hazukiro ran for the open wall behind him. A crank rattled and a makeshift iron barricade lowered to block it. The ronin caught a glimpse of the followers behind it. A sea of manic grins and withered rags bade him farewell before he was sealed in.

He'd surveyed the room while the criers were nattering on. That was his only exit, and beyond there, he'd still have to get through the barred entrance.

'You are no morsel.' The beast's voice carried across the hall. Its pitch snatched at Hazukiro's chest, dense and laden with power.

'It speaks?'

Hazukiro slowly turned around to face the monstrosity.

'It does,' it replied.

The oniku lumbered forward, fixing itself upright to nearly twenty feet tall. As it rose, its four curved horns rattled against the skeletal remains that garnished its lair.

Hazukiro studied the looming thing a moment longer.

Leathery wings remained folded at its back. Its legs were as sturdy as a warrior's, not hackled and curved like its lesser kin. The arms were long and sleek, ornamented with bangles of gold, and its hooked fingers were wrapped in rubied rings. Its maw still resembled that of a thrall, wide and razored, but the most unsettling features were that its face mostly resembled a man. White beard hairs ran along its face and down to its chin, twisted and bundled in yet more jewellery. Between pointed ears, four emblazoned eyes stared the ronin down.

The beast tilted its head and lowered it towards Hazukiro.

'You are wise, it would seem. Too wise to be scraps.'

It reeked of mould and damp death.

'And why is that, demon?'

Hazukiro moved about inside the Hush, fighting off the innate desire to shatter the illusion of calm in the face of this overwhelmingly grotesque and inexplicable entity.

'You seek reprieve for your soul.' The thing's voice boomed around the room. 'I can smell your blood, tribute.'

It rolled a black tongue across its fangs. 'I smell *guilt*.'

Something seized Hazukiro then.

The creature did not move, but the swirl of its eyes turned from molten red to warm gold. A soothing sensation tickled the ronin's skin. The aches of his body lifted. The Hush, the technique he had spent decades perfecting, swallowed in a sea of gold in a single moment.

'I do not deserve to live,' Hazukiro found himself saying. The words echoed warmly, alleviating his mind of great pain.

'I must be absolved of this pain.'

This time his voice was a whisper, almost a whimper.

'There is no greater sacrifice,' the oniku rumbled. 'There is nothing more for you in this withered world of yours.'

'There is nothing.' Hazukiro said, again hearing the words as if a stranger had been speaking.

'There is nothing,' he repeated.

He tasted the words, bitter and unnatural, and fought to counter the security he felt. A part of him knew it was a false feeling.

His arms hung at his sides now, but one still clutched the spear. His fingers stirred.

'Use it,' the oniku's inviting eyes pleaded. 'Tear yourself free of your torment forever.'

Perhaps it was the ambiguity of the statement. Or perhaps it was the ronin's lifelong accumulation of defiance. Maybe pure stubbornness? Be it divine intervention or an innate desire to finish what he started, a myriad of resistance swirled inside Hazukiro. Stronger than the chaos inside his head.

Taiyō. The name struck his mind like a hammer.

'*Tear yourself free of your torment,*' the words rumbled again, the beast leaning closer.

'As you command.'

Hazukiro thrust the spear through the beast's eye.

It wailed backwards, clutching its spewing wound.

'Blasphemous *bastard*!' the oniku spat.

Its iron steps rattled the hanging corpses, and it lunged out wildly with a clenched fist.

'Look to me, filth!' it commanded. 'Abide my gaze!'

Hazukiro exhaled swiftly, shutting his eyes. Even through his lids, he felt the violent pull of the demon's magma glare. He heard the beast step back, skulls crunching underneath its feet. The ronin took the moment to bring the speartip to his hakama, tearing a piece off at the shin and wrapping it tightly over his eyes.

'I will not.' Hazukiro's voice was firm. 'Grant me an audience.'

He heard the beast's step falter, followed by silence.

'You dare...'

'I do not wish to die without answers,' he continued. 'I will bend to your will thereafter. Grant me this peace. Who is your master?'

The footsteps grew louder. Faster.

'I rule this domain!' it cursed, rattling steel contraptions. 'As is promised! And *you*. You *will* submit!'

Blind but focused, Hazukiro listened for the jingle of arm jewellery, then darted underneath the giant's swing. He thrust the spear upwards, scraping against thick hide but piercing nothing. The oniku swatted behind it.

'Submit!'

The beast paused, then swung with its other hand. Again, its bangles betrayed it. Hazukiro dropped to avoid the crushing blow and swung the spear up again. But the beast's hide was thick. The futility of the task became apparent soon enough. The ronin wasn't entirely certain if even a well-oiled silver sword could cut through this monstrosity. He wished to all the gods that he had his imbued katana with him, and that the Academy had more information on this *'chastiser'*. They'd only known of the nefarious affairs of the cultists feeding it. And the only other people likely to have even seen this behemoth now hung from the walls.

The ronin choked on musty air, hoping for a second to catch his breath. He evaded another fierce swing. The enraged beast fumbled in fury. Hazukiro knew he could not keep this up. His muscles pulsed tighter. His lungs began to burn. He knew the truth of the matter, and that it was that nothing he wielded could cut down this demon.

But he knew what distant, unattainable weapon could.

Sunlight.

He tried to discern how long he'd manage to sleep before the surge of green lights had woken him. But he was also unconscious for a spell in the river.

One option was to tear off his blindfold and look to the moon while risking the beast seizing his mind. Either way, the temple seemed small in relation to the size of the demon, and he'd have to be outside. There was no exit, but there was a means of making one.

Hazukiro listened for the murmurs of the Forsaken, humming behind the barricade. He dashed for it, and the beast howled after him.

'Get back here, you squirming worm!' Strings of drool whipped the air.

'This way, you unholy cur...'

The beast stopped its frenzy short, tilted its head to the side, and morphed its maw into a dark grin.

'You think me mindless as the rabble beneath me, tribute?'

It took a step towards Hazukiro, chiming dangling bones like a noren curtain.

'You think me some vermin born of blasphemy?' Its laugh furled out like a rumbling rock. 'Perhaps in the Blight's infancy.'

The beast took another step forward, sliding bangles further up its bony arms. It flared fangs, four scarlet eyes swarming with want.

'Not anymore.' It stalked forward, grinning. 'Not with the bounty of gallons upon gallons of blood.'

It stopped before Hazukiro. 'Blood teeming with divine fear.'

'You'll find that lacking,' Hazukiro spat. 'If you're finished spitting hot air, then?'

The beast threw a fist down, splintering the floor beside the ronin. Checking his footing, Hazukiro thought of the best way to encourage a strike capable of demolishing the barricade.

'Stand still!' The beast roared and thrust another fist down.

'You'll have to be—'

The ground gave way, crumbling beneath them.

The sudden gap plunged the ronin into a pool of darkness. The water was frigid, its envelopment harsh and sudden against his bare skin. Hazukiro tore off his blindfold and opened his eyes under the murky waters. Only a shimmer of moonlight percolated through. He squinted into the dark, gently swimming forward.

Something deeper caught his attention.

A chain of bubbles, squeezing out of a gap in sunken rubble. The ronin moved closer, carefully reserving his breath to reach it. After some manoeuvring, he was able to free some of the stuck stone and create a small opening that was just big enough for him to swim through.

The trail of bubbles led to an air pocket. Relieved, he ascended, wary of the ripples he'd create.

His head breached the surface, slowly. He breathed in the musty air, glancing around a different room. It had to have been close to where he fell. He could still hear the beast stalking the hall.

He dove back down, swimming through the dark to discover a different escape, one with some distance to the oniku.

Swimming through more murk, he surfaced inside a dark corridor. It was quiet, but trumped the alternative of being crushed to death.

With the spear sunken somewhere, he silently stalked the waterlogged corridor.

Unarmed.

CHAPTER XXXIV

DARK CORRIDORS

BARE FEET SPLOTCHED AHEAD. The steps were slow, cautious almost, drawing nearer from the dark. Hazukiro inched closer to the wall and crouched, squinting ahead. The steps splashed louder, accompanied by a faint rattle of chains. A familiar green glow tickled the end of the corridor. When the two kyokushi turned the corner their lanterns lit up the passage.

The ronin acted swiftly. He sprinted through the shallows and pounced. Slow to react, one of the robed men received a fierce kick to the head. His skull smacked against the stone wall. Quicker than his cabal, the other man tore a knife from his belt. He thrust the blade. Hazukiro letched forward and snatched the man's extended arm. With a suppressed grunt, Hazukiro pressed his flat palm on the man's elbow and forced the bone free.

The grisly crunch rippled down the corridor. Hazukiro braced for a giveaway cry, reaching for the knife to end it quickly. But the man did not call out. He stood, vapid and hollow, head tilted, torn arm dangling like a snapped branch.

'It would be wise to surrender your soul,' he whispered. 'Why invoke the ire of the Caeldriic?'

The kyokushi cackled so softly it sounded like he was choking. His grin grew. His eyes were wide and empty.

'Who are the Caeldriic?' Hazukiro pressed on the man's wound.

The man cackled, licking crusted lips, without so much as a wince. 'You've still time. Before the Blood Moon. Here at the unfolding of the *Grand Epoch*.'

The zealot's eyes watered as if he'd borne witness to some grand design. His throaty laugh rumbled relentlessly.

Grimacing, Hazukiro planted the knife in the man's neck. His back fell against the corridor wall, and as he slid down, gurgling, his ghostly face still grinned.

'Brothers?' another voice called from around the corner. Hazukiro pressed himself against the wall, watching for the glow. When the other zealot approached, he moved quickly, diving in for a gut stab. He tore the knife free and weaved it into the third kyokushi's throat.

Hazukiro picked up one of their lanterns, noticing it had a chain link in place of a handle. He placed it around his neck and searched the bodies for more weapons. Better weapons. He only found another knife, smaller than the last.

Hugging the wall, Hazukiro kept low and ventured deeper into the dark gauntlet, stalking the corridors like a cat in the night. After turning three more corners, he came across a room.

The door was splintered down the middle, and a faint candlelight came from beyond. He peered through the gap, but could only see sodden shelves.

Knives in both hands, Hazukiro gingerly stepped into the room. A dead end. If the other zealots found their dead brethren, he'd have only backed himself into a corner. As odd as it felt leaving the security of four stone walls in the middle of the night, the ronin exited the room and proceeded down the winding dark corridors.

Wary of every step, Hazukiro couldn't help but let his mind ponder on the cultist's strange words.

'Caeldriic? Why does that sound familiar?'

Delving any further into memory would have to wait for another time. A time of sun and dry clothes.

'Curse this damned place...' He smirked at the redundancy of that thought, then more voices pulled his attention. Another three men.

'Brothers!' one called out down the dark. 'Any news of the tribute?'

Hazukiro hugged the wall, wriggling his fingers on the hilts of his knives.

'Come and see, already,' Hazukiro mumbled in his mind.

'Brothers?' another called. 'Why do you not respond?'

Hazukiro wheeled around the corner, knives coming down.

'It's *him*!'

The three zealots flashed macabre grins and cried out, lunging forward, each brandishing a small blade.

'*No!*'

The beast's fist razed the wall, slamming the Forsaken into stone, crushing them under the rubble. Hazukiro fell forward as the behemoth hand swooped over him. He tossed his lantern behind him and darted ahead, over the rubble and bodies, and back into the dark.

The beast tore its way into the narrow corridor, and, feeling foolish at the diversion, smashed the lantern and turned around. Its shoulders and horned scraped stone, and it began barrelling on all fours down the dark after the ronin, water rising with it as it tore open the ground.

'I offer my strength. . .' a weak voice called to the beast. The dying kyokushi extended a bloody, trembling hand.

The demon grunted, tearing the broken body from the rubble and shredding the man in its maw. Blood trickled down its jewelled beard. Its eyes burst scarlet. It screeched, more banshee than beast as it rampaged through the rubble, four orbs burning in the dark like comets across the sky.

Hazukiro pressed on, sprinting, his shoulder tweaking, his breathing laboured. Clusters of stone and wood toppled around him. The water continued to rise and slosh about the rumbling floors. He could hear the growing wail of the angered demon as it thundered through the passage, swooping up the ronin's kills and devouring them. With no corners to turn or exits to use, the ronin's options dwindled.

Finally giving in to the turmoil inside the temple, the bell tower collapsed. The monstrous brass bell crashed through the ceiling behind Hazukiro. He heard a pained growl and an ear-piercing gong. A haze of stone and wood sang all around like a storm. When the ronin looked up for an escape, a wave of water knocked him off his feet. He scrambled to swim as the water and wood battered him against a wall.

Carnage swished him about like a ragdoll swept up in an underwater cyclone.

CHAPTER XXXV

SILVERBURN

THE RONIN WASHED UP outside with ringing in his ears. He rubbed groggy eyes, fending off waves of pain from throbbing temples. Standing up with a groan, he looked to the sky and praised the sight that signalled the soft hues of twilight.

The sprawled remains of the temple settled, more decrepit than ever. At the foot of the scree, the brass bell lay half-sunken. Hazukiro cursed when he realised he'd lost the knives. The sunrise was not far off. The grass banks were only a swim away.

He turned to make his way shoreside, but his stubborn feet would not move.

There was no fear behind their stillness. To leave felt like disobeying an order. But not to any master.

Only to himself.

'*I cannot let this lie.*'

It made no sense. He was weary. Injured. Unarmed. But turning away felt like an unscratched itch, one he knew would torment him to no end the further he distanced himself.

'Where are you?' he found himself calling out. 'Come and take your tribute, devil!'

A muffled groan came from the ruin. Wading through the water, the ronin turned a corner to find the temple bell, resting atop a pile of debris. A dark arm lined with bangles poked out. The limb quivered, emitting strands of steam. Hazukiro recalled why the bell had seemed familiar, or rather, relevant. He'd dismissed the story behind it as a distraction, something trivial from before the Blight.

The bell had been a gift to the temple, on behalf of the mining consortium. Sodai had taken in a crew of injured workers one winter, housed and healed them, and charged them nothing, accepting only prayers as thanks. The consortium forged a symbol of gratitude regardless and had the architectural gem fixed into the temple's tower to replace the rusted original.

From the ornate lip down to the clapper itself, it was made of *pure silver*.

The beast thrashed about, its groans reverberating inside the bell. It swatted its protruding but pinned arm to no avail. Hazukiro looked to the east and realised he had no reason to push the matter further. And that made him shake with an itching anger. His hackles were already up like a wolf.

While the skin of the demon limb sizzled, Hazukiro's fists clenched.

Entering the Hush became a passing thought that tumbled into the back of his mind. He didn't *want* to control himself. Not this time.

The feeling was difficult to understand, and he prided himself in mastering what he felt. Keeping it under wraps to avoid a repeat of his past.

What made it stir? He'd felt fatigue like this before, and been injured far worse. And although he'd never faced this particular manner of monstrosity, he was no stranger to the stench of silverburn.

Another question entered his mind.

'*Why bother trying to understand?*'

He allowed that thought to stay, convincing himself that it didn't matter *why* he boiled with rage.

It demanded to be felt.

His ears pricked up. Wailing Forsaken survivors began emerging from the ruins, gathering around the tragedy of their lord. Some were limping, others bleeding, all were drenched in water and filth.

Hazukiro fumed at the sight of them for one simple reason.

They reminded him of himself.

Hazukiro picked up a large stone from the lake's bed.

'*You will all pay for the innocents you've slaughtered.*'

The Forsaken huddled around the bell. One zealot clutched the beast's hand, burning himself as it writhed. As if to soothe it, or to share in its suffering.

He was the first to die.

Hazukiro softened his skull with the stone, painting his face with blood. Roaring with a blinding fury, he struck again.

The ronin forged a path of blood and stone, striking and shouting, tainting the lake red. The criers lunged at him, their own fury at the desecration of their beloved rising within. Knives, scythes, and hammers plunged at the ronin. A knife sliced his arm. A hammer strike bruised his back.

But nothing stopped him.

After hurling the stone at a zealot's head, he snatched up the bearer's scythe. He used it to tear through the crowd like a farmer at harvest.

'Stop!'

The cries meant nothing. They melted into a storm of sound, The muffled clanging and groans from the beast, the splash of shallow water, and the shredding of cloth and skin.

The chaos *held* him.

The scythe tore into a gut and held firm. He released it and snatched a hammer, swivelling its iron end against jaws. When the tool finally snapped, he tore a knife from someone's hands and plunged it into throats.

Body upon body splashed dead.

Hazukiro swirled like death dancing, snatching lives without bias, and like death, he couldn't be avoided or stopped.

'*Stop it! Please!*'

Spittle flew from his snarl. He didn't *want* to stop.

'*Hazuki—*' The fury left the ronin's eyes.

His stomach churned cold. Weapons dropped. Hands trembled.

'Taiyō?'

She gasped, clasping at the blade in her side.

'Where did you—how?' Hazukiro heaved, watching the girl breathe sharply.

'D-don't take it out yet, I'll...'

He didn't know the end of that thought.

Now that a sense of reality had washed over him, he stood in the present in utter disbelief. Denial. *Disgust.*

'It's not silver,' she winced, pulling the knife free. She gently dabbed the wound with her palm. Black ichor and skin overlapped, shrinking the gash each second.

Hazukiro retched, then licked dry lips. He caught his breath and watched as the wound closed completely.

A scared voice, soft as petals, whispered in his mind.

'What have you done?'

The words bounced around the ronin's head repeatedly. He tore himself away from her and laid his eyes on the red lake. The sight shook his core and sent his forehead drumming. When he pinched his eyes they flashed tormenting visions of the past.

Ruins, bodies, blood, and fire.

He forced his eyes away from it all. The Forsaken bodies that surrounded him. The surreal memories that flashed in front of him.

Every sin blended and surged along ice veins, awash with guilt and regret.

'I cannot explain it.' He could find no other words. 'I cannot explain it.'

Taiyō stared at the bodies, each corpse oozing red delight.

'We have to go,' she said, grabbing his bloodied arm.

'H-how did you get here?' Hazukiro asked.

Taiyō hung her head, then shot it back up to avoid fixing her hungry eyes on the corpses.

'A thrall,' she said, disgust in her voice. 'I woke up to one biting my neck. I bit down and I. . .I fed on its ichor. Sapped it until it was still.'

She spat at the thought. 'It gave me enough strength to mist down the falls. My head's still reeling and it was the most vile thing I've ever tasted but. . .'

She started leading him away by the hand. '. . .I had to find you.'

A shrivelling cry cut the cold air. Taiyō hadn't noticed the bell or the writhing thing within. It had been quiet for some time.

Even at the strange noise, Taiyō's stomach, and the violent voice in her head forced her to look back to the waters at her feet.

The lake was layered in blood. Corpses oozed red honey. It was distracting enough, setting her tastebuds afire, her chest pounding. It was almost as if she had her heart back, as if the ichor pulsing through her was begging her to remember how *alive* she could feel with the taste of human blood.

She exhaled deeply and searched for a way to enter the Hush.

But another cry from the beast in the bell broke her focus.

'What is that?'

'Don't.' Hazukiro clutched her arm and pulled her back. 'It's no ordinary thrall. The sun will take care of it soon enough.'

Taiyō tore her arm free and sprinted to the bell.

'What are you doing?' Hazukiro stormed after her.

'That band on its arm...' Taiyō splashed down in front of the arm, tears welling. 'That's Simaro's ring!'

Taiyō dug her nails into the beast's monstrous wrist, twisting it. 'What did you do to her?' she screamed. 'What have you done with my sister?'

Filled with strength, she clasped the base of the bell to try to uncover the monster, but the silver sent stings like needles up her wrists. She hissed and leapt back.

'Get back!' Hazukiro commanded, staggering over.

'*You abomination! What happened to her?*' Taiyō roared. 'Get out here and face me!'

She clasped the bell again. White flame scorched her palms, shooting up her wrists. With sizzling strain and a gurgling cry, she tipped the bell backwards. It rumbled and rolled down the debris. The beast underneath lay huddled in a steaming ball.

'*WHERE IS SHE?*'

The first rays of day burst forth. They latched onto the beast's skin like golden whips, lacerating burning flesh. It roared in agony. Hazukiro grabbed Taiyō and stepped back, squinting at the bright storm of embers. Taiyō clutched the ronin's arm, looking at the monster as it tapered down.

'It can't hurt anyone now, child,' Hazukiro repeated, stroking her back as the oniku continued to wail.

'Wait—' Taiyō stumbled back. 'What's happening to it?'

A strange sound tore free from beyond the beast's moans. A voice far less monstrous.

'Hazukiro?' Taiyō turned to him for answers.

He had none to give, but kept her back with his hand.

Flames danced off the beast, tearing its body down to ash and bone. But beneath the leathery layer of singed flesh, something softer and paler seeped through.

Skin. *Human* skin.

Down to bone and embers now, Taiyō looked at the shrinking thing and locked eyes with what screamed underneath.

A young girl. Only half her face peered back at her, drowning in fire.

Taiyō gasped sharply.

'Simaro?'

The girl, licked by flames, shed black tears.

'I wasn't in—in control,' she whimpered. 'It wasn't me, T-Taiyō. I would never h-hurt any— Listen, I–I lov—'

The sun snuffed out her tears. Her bones brittled down into a flock of embers and the wind carried her ashes away.

Taiyō collapsed in stunned silence. There was nothing she could do. No way she could have known.

Pieces of tarnished jewellery rained down into the lake of blood and ash.

Hazukiro placed a hand on Taiyō's shoulder. The touch crumbled her to tears. The ronin quickly caught her as she trembled and melted into herself.

He rocked her back and forth while she screamed herself hoarse, pleading and bargaining and cursing at deaf gods.

CHAPTER XXXVI
ANOTHER DAY

TAIYŌ TORE HERSELF AWAY from the floating morsels, fighting off confusing waves of emotion. She felt the pang of hunger claw at her stomach, begging for blood, marring all else. At the same time, she stifled tears at the intrusive image of Simaro's charred face. Possibly more overwhelming than the hunger itself, was the underlying question she didn't want to address. The question of what this meant for *her*. She felt selfish for thinking it though she knew she would have to confront it sooner or later.

'Drink,' Hazukiro said, walking behind her.

She spun on her heel. 'What?'

'From one of the bodies,' he said. 'You need it.'

'I don't *want* to—'

'It's a need for you,' Hazukiro said. 'Like eating or sleeping. And you do *need* it.'

It was difficult enough to fight off her own inner voices encouraging her to divulge. Now the ronin was saying it. It all but drowned out her voice of reason.

' You've been strong,' Hazukiro continued. 'But now is not the time.'

He gestured to one of the cultists.

'In fact, sustaining the oniku with their blood just about sums up their entire doctrine.' He walked past her. 'Drink. We can face our sins another day.'

Hazukiro gave a final glance to his handiwork. A familiar feeling soured his mind. These people were not soldiers, and they had fallen to his rage. They had fallen by his hand, one by one, dropping like flies torn to shreds. At the same time, he couldn't rightly recall killing them, or how. Just that they were now dead.

The inner demon of denial, forever present. Always preventing him from finding peace.

* * *

While Taiyō abated her thirst in shame, Hazukiro found a secluded spot across the lake and gingerly lowered himself into it.

The water crept into his ears and silenced the world as he squinted into the morning sky. Thickened blood trailed off of his body from too many cuts to count, and the cold constricted his tired muscles. Part of him wanted to fall asleep there, and let the water bubble over his nose until he was nothing but another corpse in the lake.

'*Not yet,*' he heard his wife whisper.

* * *

Hazukiro found Taiyō in the woods beyond the shore. She sat in front of a fire she'd prepared. The ronin noticed his cloak and kimono had been laid out to dry on a rock beside it. Resting beside the attire, his imbued katana shimmered in the sun.

'You found my clothes,' he smiled. 'And my katana.'

Taiyō breathed deeply and nodded. 'The clothes washed up while I was—yes. I found them. And I found the sword at the bottom of the falls with one ration pack. It just had the flint and rice in it.' She pointed to the pot above the fire.

'And. . .I saw Akumo.'

Hazukiro felt cold clutch him.

'I'm sorry you lost her,' Taiyō said softly.

Hazukiro sat down slowly, hissing at a dozen aches. 'So am I.' He looked to Taiyō with concern.

When he'd first found her, she was huddled in a ball, devoid of warmth, drenched in fear. Now, she embodied the weariness he'd seen countless times after the haze of battle. Tear-stained faces, burning eyes, alive but dead, victorious but defeated.

She lay down on her back and stared at the sun as if wishing it would rip her skin from her bones and be done with it.

'Why does Kesyoka spare me?' she whispered.

Hazukiro nodded slowly. 'I often ask myself the same question.'

'Why not rid me from this place, along with the curse that clutches me?' she continued.

The ronin sighed knowingly and moved to sit beside the girl.

'To feel undeserving of life is more common than you might think.'

The words resonated, but Taiyō kept quiet.

'We wander under Her light, still, while the best of us wither below us.' He chewed his next words. 'It isn't fair.'

Taiyō's eyes welled with worry, picturing Simaro's pleading, burning face.

'But let me ask you this,' Hazukiro continued. 'When we think of those who've left us, who've been *taken* from us too soon, do we not wish we'd done something to stop it?'

'Of course,' Taiyō choked.

'Of course,' Hazukiro echoed. 'Most of the time, we blame ourselves for not doing all we could have, even if it was beyond our control. We find ourselves fixating on other outcomes. Wishing someone would have helped.'

He placed a hand on her shoulder, squeezing it gently.

'You can be that for others.'

Taiyō sat up, and Hazukiro's fingers trailed off. She wiped her cheeks, sniffled, and looked to the ronin.

'You mean *we*?'

'Though you are endless, child, my time is limited.'

She shrugged and forced a small smile. 'I could turn you.'

Hazukiro scoffed.

'I can't think of anything worse than living forever.' He smiled back. 'You'll live a thousand lifetimes without me, and I'll fade into memory. At the very least, try and remember what I have taught you.'

'The yellow snow tastes bad.'

They shared a laugh, then sat in the first comfortable silence that followed it. Hazukiro told himself to remember that feeling. And to appreciate the moment of brief calm that followed it.

Ma.

'Back at the lake. . .' Taiyō trailed off, unsure if she wished to continue.

'I lost my temper because they reminded me of *me*, and I wanted them dead because of it.'

He exhaled deeply, shook his head, then turned to the girl.

'You've come this far with me.' Hazukiro said, thinking of the blade he'd thrust into her side. 'And I intend to see this through with you. To the end. So it's only fair that you know who you're travelling with.'

His sigh was painful and long, and Taiyō could tell that he hadn't shared his tale with anyone.

'I was once a Hatamoto. The Hand of the shogun. And that title carried immense weight. And dread.'

CHAPTER XXXVII

GHOSTS OF THE PAST

'I WAS ONCE MARRIED. Her name was Hana. She was the daughter of a noble lord, and only ever graced my path because of my service to the shogun. Being a cruel man, Shogun Tenjao required protection at battlefields and banquets alike from many enemies.

Hana performed for him one evening after a civil skirmish. She sang songs of heroes and victory, plucking at her biwa for war-weary men. I remember thinking how strange it was to hear songs of death coming from the lips of such a delicate lotus flower. That was when I met my Hana.

'With the shogun's blessing, it was easy to convince her father to allow us to wed within the year, and we were granted a generous land in Southern Maija, the mainland. We had a stone cottage constructed at the edge of a lush forest that bordered white fields of heather and wildflowers. It was the most heavenly sight, and it made it that much worse every time I had to leave for battle.

'Whenever I returned home, sticky with blood and sweat, she would unfasten my armour, massage and bathe me, and hum beautiful melodies. And each time I returned, I felt less deserving of her. The excursions weighed heavily on my soul. But I was young and foolish. I saw duty as my lady first and foremost. I regret that, maybe more than anything. I was pushing her away. In her eyes, I could see she was only happy to see me safe.

'Killing Njörkin invaders was one thing. Their attacks on our shores persisted for a decade, and by the time their final defeat was at hand, I'd lost count of the battles, let alone how many men I'd killed. I'd become numb to it.

'And I was good at it, and I improved with each skirmish. The shogun provided me with resources to train in between battles. Scholars who taught me strategy. Veterans who knew ancient techniques. The Hush was one such technique, in order to clear my young and clouded mind. As I aged, I became a seasoned warrior as well as a trusted advisor. Such is the responsibility of the Hatamoto.

'The Shogun's tactics were always brutal, but they worked. He sent me off with a small army at my back, along with his most trusted generals, and eventually, the Njörkins stopped invading.

'It wasn't until ten years after their final attack that civil war broke out among the continent, spreading even to Ijihan. And now we were killing our own because *they* opposed the continued cruelty of Tenjao, and his 'leashed' hound.

'*Hatamoto Hazukiro.*

'I had been killing for decades at this point, but this was different. Age and disease had clutched Tengao's mind, and he refused to let his legacy die. He insisted on shows of strength, to quelch any uprisings in their infancy. This meant. . .culling the doubtful. *His* dark words.

'Ijihan had always produced a lot for Maija, and many questioned his warpath for the sake of setting an example. But none stood up to him. How could they? They feared retaliation. They feared *me*.

'The shogun's campaign to silence those who claimed him a tyrant lasted two years. And for those two years, I did my duty. I set torch and sword to villages who'd dispersed rumours of rebellion. Sometimes I was sent out with a samurai cohort. But as my name grew it became enough to hear that the Hatamoto alone was on his way.

'I didn't return home once for those years. Hana was informed that I was serving the shogun honourably, carrying out tasks for the sake of preserving Maija.

'All I could think of was her waiting for me in our little cottage, but a part of me did not want to return to her. She was the softest part of me. And my duty had no room for softness.

'I closed my heart to all of it. The pleading of burning villagers. Their *screams*. This was the will of the shogun, and it was all I'd ever known.

'Hana wouldn't understand that.

'One winter morning, I rode through yet another town. Alone. The fogs were thick, and though I couldn't see them, I could hear people whimpering in their hiding places. And after I had taken a torch to half of their homes, black smoke shrouded the roads, rolling in with the heavy fog. I dismounted my horse to get a better view of the path.

'I didn't see the farmboy until he'd already run his father's sword through me. He let go of the hilt, and with tears streaming down his young face, he cursed for me to know only a life of torment.

'That is one face I do remember. The anger that seethed from his spittle-laced screams. I retrieved the shallow sword and tossed it aside. He screamed at my stubbornness to die, and reached for the sword again. I ran my blade through that boy's gut. I watched the anger drain from his face, turning to shivering fear. He went pale, and I watched the cold of his last breath taint the air.

'I heard a cry from beyond the fog, a woman calling for the boy. For the first time in my life, I ran. I left my horse behind and sprinted for the woods nearby. I stopped only to retch, and eventually, fell on my back, writhing in regret.

'Like the rising fog around me, the veil was starting to lift. Golden sunshine warmed my face, and I felt the immense weight of my life crash down on me all at once. I'd believed that the honourable thing to do was to blindly follow my superiors. But as I pictured the shogun, I felt only malice and disgust. The ghosts of the past tore at my mind. Relentlessly.

'I knew then that I would never be able to undo anything. All I *could* do was the unthinkable. Something no one but lowly traitors, criminals and foreigners had ever attempted. Except I knew that I could actually do it.

'I could kill Shogun Tenjao, and end his madness. After that, I would rid the lands of its other affliction. Myself.'

***

Taiyō sat in silence, unsure of how to process the tale. Hazukiro half expected her to flee.

'If anyone is undeserving of life, it is me, child.'

The surfacing of his story began to tear away at him. He found that he was unable to look at Taiyō, though she could hear by the tickle in his throat, he was weeping.

Quickly dismissing the brief moment of catharsis, he wiped his face and continued his retelling.

***

'It was easy to get close to the shogun.

'When I wasn't killing and when I wasn't home, I was by his side. He even watched me train at his palace dojo, where it wouldn't be odd for me to have a weapon in my hand. It was easy enough to put an end to him.

'I was in the middle of sparring with a spear when I feigned an attack on my opponent and hurled the polearm into Tengao's chest instead.

'The strike was bittersweet, ending what I'd known for my entire adult life. I was already around fifty at that point. I signed my own death sentence there, but at the same time, putting an end to the real threat to Maija and Ijihan.

'Once Tengao's fell from his seat, I raised my hands in surrender. I considered this my first act of penance to Maija. To Ijihan. To Hana.

'The palace guards seized me immediately, and the dojo was closed off. I was given a solid beating before being carted off and imprisoned at the Teragaku Fortress. I was to await the severity of my trial. It was obvious what would become of me in the end, but I knew I would face torture before I met that fate. And because I felt that I deserved it, I never resisted any of it.

'A year passed with no trial. I'd only gained new scars and time to reflect on my misdeeds. And while I withered away in my cell, Blightfall began.

'I seethed at the irony of me being protected within the fortress walls, while more innocents died beyond the walls, night after night. Eventually, the daimyo decided to put my experience to use. I saw it as an opportunity to atone for my sins. Those that put me to work thought I was seeking redemption for my betrayal of the shogun. But my atonement was to the people.'

Hazukiro sighed.

'I know there's no undoing what I've done. But all I could think to do was to strive for redemption. If that meant facing bandits, angry villagers, and the curse of Night itself, so be it. Demons had been tormenting me for years. It made no difference if they were finally manifested. I forged on, and I will continue to do so until this world no longer has need of me.'

* * *

Taiyō glanced at the ronin as he processed his raw retelling.

'What happened to your wife?' Taiyō asked softly.

Hazukiro pursed his lips and held back tears.

'My first punishment. . .' his voice trembled. '. . .was watching her execution.'

With a defiant grunt, he composed himself, cleared his throat, and rose to his feet.

'Thank you,' Taiyō said. 'For sharing how—'

'Never again.' Hazukiro wiped his face and offered the girl a hand.

She nodded and he helped her up.

Taiyō echoed the words under her breath.

'Yes.'

The ronin and the girl, both former thralls of some maniacal master.

'*Never again.*'

CHAPTER XXXVIII

THE VIOLET PATH

TAIYŌ STIRRED THAT NIGHT.

She'd not brought up Simaro since that morning, but the image seared brightly behind her eyes. Unable to sleep, she lay on the cold cave floor, alone with her thoughts. A notion that sickened her.

When the chilled air drifted in from the cracks of the cave mouth, she thought of the snow-crusted peaks of Mount Shinok, and how she'd soon be back at the crucible of her making. And suddenly the Foremost was in her mind, so clearly that she felt as if he stood beside her in the dark, watching her fret over him. The inevitable flood of questions poured in.

He'd taken many girls and put them through all manner of trauma. She'd become this *Sunstrider*. Simaro, some towering, bearded beast. What had become of the others? Perhaps it was already too late for them.

She felt the oncoming headache and burst into silent tears.

'*I'm sorry I couldn't save you, dear sister.*'

More questions flooded in. They were loud, persistent and unforgiving. She rolled from side to side as they made themselves known.

How did Simaro get to Prowler's Rest? Would *she* become such a demon under specific circumstances? Was that process already underway?

She furiously silenced all of the maddening questions and replaced them with one answer.

'The Foremost needed to die.'

* * *

The following day proved to be a difficult one.

Without Akumo to share the brunt of the journey, Hazukiro's knees and ankles throbbed fiercely. Taiyō wrestled with her grief in silence, made doubly worse by the prodding pangs begging for her to divulge in crimson sin.

Each time the urge reared its snivelling head, she used the opportunity to practise the Hush. Washing out the present became simple enough, she'd found. But then again, the world was mostly silent as they moved by day. Especially as they travelled further north. It was at night, when her thoughts were louder than bells, that the real challenge came.

The further they found themselves from Prowler's Rest, the more animals they noticed about. Taiyō was able to stave off the worst of her cravings with some larger mammals.

Finding shelter became less of a risk as well, ever since their path through the wilds eventually joined with the Violet Path.

It was a large stretch of land that merged into Northern Ijihan, composed of rocky hills and white-barked smoke trees with deep purple leaves.

'At one point, it was the popular route on the island,' Hazukiro explained. 'A transport route to and from the dozens of silver ore mines that ran along the base of Mount Shinok. A pilgrim's path for others making their way to the temple at the summit. We'll see the torii gates in a few days.'

Most of the old trails to the mines were still marked, with cleared paths to and from each entrance.

Most of them were caved in or abandoned completely, by both man and oniku. Each night saw them stay in a different mine. Taiyō would sit and meditate, telling herself that no master controlled how much she needed to feed. Hazukiro would leave her to her thoughts and scout the surrounding area for danger and food. Luckily for them, the Violet Path teemed with the latter. Only the last mine towards the end of a week had two slumbering thralls. Taiyō practised her ability to mist, and tore through them within moments. They made camp there for the night, a few hours before sunset. The steep tread of the day's toll demanded it. Taiyō ate and drank as little as she needed from the forest.

'You've been pushing yourself these days past,' Hazukiro groaned, piling the last stone on their barricade for the night.

'I'm beginning to feel the strain,' Taiyō said, striking the flint above the wood she'd gathered. 'But I know when I'm nearing my limit. And you're not exactly in the best state to fight.'

'Sleeping on rock for days with bruises and cuts would drain anyone,' he replied. 'But I'm not entirely useless just yet. Just cold. And at this rate, winter will see us dead before the Blight.'

'There won't be a Blight before long.' Taiyō struggled with the flint, pursing pale lips in frustration. Hazukiro had noticed her increased anger. He'd acted the same in his youth, when he'd hidden his anger to focus on his goal.

'Taiyō.'

'*What*?' she flung the flint to the floor.

'With Simaro gone. . .' he stopped, gauging Taiyō's willingness to talk about her. 'It's likely that the other girls—'

'I know,' she said flatly, fumbling for the flint. 'But I can't be the only one like *this*. Even if I am, nothing changes the fact that *he* must pay.'

She sniffed, reached for the flint, and tried catching fire again.

'Are there no towns nearby?' she asked, doubtful and cautiously hopeful. 'We could steal a horse.'

'I'll not take more from these people,' Hazukiro firmly retorted.

The flint sent sparks into the kindle, and she carefully spread the flame about.

'Then at least somewhere warm to lay our heads for the next few nights. Eat a hot meal. Regain our strength. You need it, that much is certain.'

'Do I now?'

'I can hear your old bones creaking from here.'

'Am I to ignore the fact that you could also hear my heartbeat in a storm?'

'A deaf cow could hear your bones in a blizzard, old man.'

Hazukiro laughed. 'Why a cow?'

'I'm hungry.'

Hazukiro rubbed his nose, red and numb. 'Taodake isn't too far from here. If it's still standing we'll reach it before dusk.'

'A stroke of luck, then.' Taiyō sniffed and blew away a tuft of hair. 'Depending on—'

She stopped. Hazukiro took notice and drew his blade. She held a finger to her lips, closing her eyes and tilting her head.

'It's. . .humming?' she whispered.

'You're certain?'

She returned her finger to her lips, leaning into the wind.

'Yes. And it's only one voice.'

Puzzled, Hazukiro kept his weapon at hand, and Taiyō pointed the way. The path was wide, originally designed for horse drawn carts, though the warren of boulders prevented the road from being linear. Corners could mean danger, and Hazukiro found himself especially grateful for Taiyō's enhanced senses.

'Anything else?' the ronin whispered.

'He's still a little further on,' Taiyō reassured him. 'Nothing else stands out. He sounds. . .happy. I suppose that in itself is odd. What's a man doing out here alone? An hour away from sunset? And there's a strange scent too, one I can't place.'

The path straightened out, revealing a withered torii gate. An old man dressed in a faded blue robe hummed a tune as he dipped a bristled brush into a bucket. He lathered bright red paint over sections of the structure's fading colours. With kind eyes, he turned to face the duo, bowing deeply and continuing his song.

'Are you from Taodake, old man?' Hazukiro called out.

'A good evening to you too, travellers.' The man smiled. 'And I doubt I'm much older than you.'

Taiyō snorted and felt the back of Hazukiro's palm.

'Why are you out here?'

'Why are *you* so poor at introductions?' The old man gently placed the brush into a second bucket of water and wiped his hands on his red-flecked robes. He extended his hand freely as if the ronin's sword was sheathed and his forehead was unmarked.

'Naman Kio.' He bowed and offered a wrinkled smile.

'The man with no name?' Hazukiro raised a brow.

'You speak Bjoto?' Naman leaned in, intrigued. 'The language has been dead for some centuries, and is not even *of* our people.'

'Invaders reaching our shores prodded our academy to learn of our neighbours.' Hazukiro sheathed his blade. 'History. Tactics. Politics.' He sighed. 'Even dead languages.'

Taiyō was taken aback by that. Hazukiro was oddly quick to put his sword away.

'I suppose not all that's lost to most needs to *stay* lost.' Naman motioned to the torii gate, guiding them to it with alacrity. He flicked the bristles of the wet brush and dipped it in the paint, slathering it in red and twisting it with such finesse, you'd think he was weaving honey.

'But your phrasing is unidiomatic.' He coated a section of wood, gently gliding the brush along the wood like a seasoned captain steers his ship across a calm sea.

'The Bjotorii rarely expressed such form. They were quite literal people, and not all that descriptive. *Naman Kio* simply means *Nameless.*'

He paused and smiled, as if welcoming questions.

'And how is it that *you* come to know this language?' Hazukiro finally asked. 'And the name, or lack thereof, from it?'

'It is one of several monikers I've obtained over the years. My family learned and passed down plenty. Gifts of knowledge, among other things. What does it matter what I am called now?'

'Names live on,' Taiyō spoke up. Hazukiro shot her a curious look.

'Do they?' asked Naman Kio, piqued. 'Or do our actions?' He returned his brush to the bucket and coated it.

'*Who's* actions, though?' Taiyō asked. 'Who will be revered?'

'Who indeed?' Naman Kio's paint gleamed in the sun. 'Art, food, stories. Why name the invoker of these great works if their intent was to share the work itself?'

'There is honour in a name,' Hazukiro chimed in. 'The honourable will be remembered for their deeds.'

'Ah,' Naman Kio smiled knowingly. 'For their deeds.'

Hazukiro looked to the torii gate. In his youth, he'd travelled the Violet Path, and passed through its twelve gates, each larger than the last as the lilac road spiralled to the mountains. The structures were solid, and had always been maintained by the monks and priests of Kesyoka's temples across Ijihan. But ever since the Blight, caring for sacred things had become too great a risk.

'You would risk your life for the preservation of this structure?' Taiyō asked. 'This *deed*?'

'A life without a name, you mean? Lives *with* names have come and gone, and meant nothing.'

He planted his brush in the water again, stirring and shaking the bristles clean.

'Structures? They too have come and gone. But the torii gates are more than that. They are symbols. Ones that mark the advent of a journey towards something held sacred. If you stepped into the world and faced a tarnished symbol, one beaten by weather and peeling at its edges, you may yet turn back before you saw it through.'

He coated the brush again and took it to the wood. 'Or you could see something that some nameless person saw fit to preserve for the sake of those that will outlive them. And you will pause. You will remember the bright and beautiful things you've encountered. Most beauty is left forgotten or irrelevant to most that focus only on their demons. But while devils claw at your mind each night, the remembrance of something pure will carry you outside of your troubles for a moment.'

Hazukiro couldn't help but smile. The man exuded warmth and sincerity, something rare in these Blighted days. Taiyō smiled too, unsure of the feeling herself. They both looked to Naman

Kio, and to the symbol of a journey with divine conclusion, gleaming a terrific, bright red.

Hazukiro and Taiyō bowed deeply, and the Nameless Man smiled as they passed through the revived gate. The inevitable troubles beyond it had vanished, if for only a moment. Hazukiro's mind, swarming with the guilt of his past. Silenced. Taiyō, grieving and desperate for resolve. Hushed. They allowed themselves to remember the good.

Hazukiro thought of Hana, practising her shamisen, her biwa, in fields of white flowers. The memory of her soothing singing voice, smooth as honey.

Taiyō surfaced buried memories of Simaro, a treasured sisterhood like no other. The laugh of her parents as she danced for them on her mother's birthday. The taste of ripe peaches at the lake on a summer's day. The memories converged to the recent past, on that of an old man who'd risked everything to save her. A man who hated himself for his past. But a man who overlooked her curse before he even knew her name.

Remembrance could hurt, the pair found as they walked in silence, purple petals swirling about them.

But the pain of revisiting buried vestiges was worth enduring.

It meant that the good stayed surfaced too.

CHAPTER XXXIX

TAODAKE

PASSING THROUGH MORE PAINTED torii gates, Hazukiro and Taiyō eventually reached the foot of Mount Shinok. It loomed overhead, monstrous and white, like a titan wave at sea ready to crash.

Hazukiro turned to find Taiyō had stopped. Noticing that he looked on silently, she cleared her throat and averted her gaze.

'I know I've been up there, but. . .'

She left the thought alone.

'It must be a strange feeling,' Hazukiro offered. 'Come, Taodake is nearby.'

A road broke away from the Violet Path, leading down towards the foot of the mountain and the small town of Taodake.

A wooden bridge led to a large gate, mounted with watchtowers. Hazukiro bowed as two armed guards opened the gate, fixing cautious eyes on the pair.

'They are willing to let us in?' Taiyō whispered. 'Just like that?'

'Brigands rarely travel with children,' Hazukiro said. 'But we'll likely need to speak to whoever's in charge before poking around.'

Moss, creepers and general overgrowth were more common sights across the ruined remains of Ijihan homes. But these buildings sat in a silent cloister, with only blown autumn leaves blanketing the rooftops in bright yellow and purple. In the centre of the town, a large tower plumed black smoke.

Drawing nearer, Hazukiro noticed something familiar strung up in spirals around the buildings.

'What are those strange spheres?' Taiyō asked.

'*Baubles.*' He said surprised, passing under them.

Rows of them had been cast between buildings with rice straw ropes. It was a crude version of the lights that lined the Academy's walls, but still more impressive than any makeshift defences the ronin had encountered anywhere else on the island.

'Street lanterns?' Taiyō looked puzzled. 'They're so small.'

'They flare the violet protection.' He tapped the hilt of his sword, illustrative. 'It won't kill a thrall, but it will deter general interest.'

'How do they work? Surely every town would benefit from this?'

Hazukiro nodded, approaching the outskirts of Taodake's market.

'They would. The Academy has just now come to learn of the art, or so they say. Though it requires majik. Being illegal, you can imagine the difficulty in finding a *kijio*, or, arkinist.'

Taiyō looked to the ronin's sword.

'So there's one at the Academy,' she realised. 'He crafted that for you, didn't he?'

'Crafted it, yes. For me, no. Though I know not how or why the scholars are only now prepared to delve into taboo practices.

Perhaps they've finally come to realise the severity of the straits we're in.'

A breeze swept up the baubles, dangling light as feathers, reflecting the sunlight in their unused state.

'Taodake must have an arkinist too. If the Academy had bothered to scout this region, they'd have had more help in facing the Blight.'

'And that would've meant trekking across the island over many nights,' Taiyō scoffed. 'They must have felt these people were not worth the trouble.'

'Don't let your cynicism grow to my level,' he crossed his arms. 'But yes.'

Taiyō laughed.

'And for that reason,' the ronin continued. 'Do not speak a word of the Academy, the Blood Spectors, or the baubles. Speak as if you know nothing of them or their purpose.'

Taiyō halted and formed a frown.

'I knew nothing five minutes ago.'

'If you wish to remain ignorant, stop asking questions.'

They approached a group of women sitting in a circle on straw mats. They were humming old hymns and weaving rope.

'Nightspast,' Hazukiro bowed.

Taiyō awkwardly mirrored the gesture.

The women glanced and briefly looked them over, their hands still busy. The eldest of the weavers placed her materials aside while the others carried on.

'You don't look like bandits,' she narrowed her eyes. '*You* do.'

Hazukiro had lost his straw hat to the falls, and though his hooded cloak covered most of his forehead, he was still a stranger shrouding his face.

'But you travel with a child, and one not bound at the wrists.'

Taiyō quickly cupped her hands at her back, lest her silverburn scars be seen.

'Her rags are filthy.'

Hazukiro bowed again. 'We have been forced to douse ourselves in mud many a night.'

The woman said nothing for a while, studying them longer. Eventually, she decided on a more direct approach.

'Who are you?'

'Travellers, if you can believe it,' Hazukiro spoke softly. 'We seek only shelter for the night, and perhaps a meal. We've no qualms sleeping in the barn.'

He lowered his head, awaiting her response. He swatted Taiyō's arm, and she quickly lowered her head as well.

The old woman let out a wheezy sigh. 'Speak to the jito.'

'Jito?' Hazukiro looked up. 'Taodake is no prefecture.'

'It might as well be,' the woman spat. 'We've been abandoned by our own country.'

'So why not appoint a shogun while you're at it?' Taiyō shrugged, a conceited grin taking shape.

The ronin and the seated women shot glares at the girl.

'I apologise for my *daughter*.' Hazukiro tore the tension. 'She believes she is funny.'

'She can believe herself to be whatever she likes, so long as she keeps herself useful while you speak to the jito.'

The woman pointed to a straw mat. 'Fiwa will show you how to braid the shimenawa.'

Fiwa smiled and made a gesture with the twisted straw in her hands.

'Of course,' Hazukiro bowed again, then turned to Taiyō, whispering in her ear. 'Earn your keep. I'll return shortly.'

The weaver pointed towards the pluming tower further into town. She reached out and pulled on a string that had fashioned to a short pole. It sent a silver bell down a bamboo pipe and into the ground, clanging all the way.

'She'll expect you now.'

Puzzled but grateful, the ronin thanked her and stole away.

Taiyō took a sheepish seat among the women as they dropped straw into her lap.

* * *

Two guards stood at the foot of the tower, which Hazukiro now realised was actually an oblong, vertical furnace, though its intricate etchings and pointed curves resembled a small pagoda.

The guards crossed their naginatas at his arrival with a swift metal shink.

'What business have you, stranger?' one asked, stern as steel. Hazukiro recognised their armour, tarnished and dented as they were. Pauldrons of long-dead Mai-Ajin samurai, menpo visors of the southern Ajina Clans, and even the fur cloaks of fallen Njörkin invaders.

'I seek Sanctum for the evening, my daughter and I. She is assisting the nawa-shi, and I was told to speak to your jito.'

The guards kept their weapons crossed, eyeing him from his katana up to his branded forehead.

'Relinquish your sword.'

'I will not.'

The guard scowled. 'Then you are not permitted to speak to the jito.'

'My child sits in the open, unarmed. What guarantee have I that a town that sits below the cursed mountain itself can be trusted?'

The guards shifted back to their spots at the sound of approaching footsteps. The ground split in two, and a grass-covered door slid open behind them. The approaching person chuckled.

'You'd never approach a place you knew you couldn't leave alive.'

The figure emerged from shadowy steps, dressed in light leather armour. Her hair flowed white with age, and her mien was both curious and cautious.

'At least, that's how I've managed to stay alive this long.'

'Bow before Jito Yuriko!' The guard smacked the ronin with the blunt of his weapon. The woman patted the guard's shoulder as she approached the ronin.

'No need. We've much to do today.' She turned to Hazukiro. 'And you, who have hobbled into my town smelling of wayward toil. Speak your piece.'

'Jito Yuriko,' Hazukiro repeated respectfully. 'I seek—'

The jito walked off towards an inn.

'Over a drink,' she smirked. 'You look like the dead.'

The tavern emptied at the jito's entrance. Civilians bowed at their leader as she gave them an apologetic smile.

'A brief conversation with this errant man, good people. You'll be able to return to your drinks shortly.'

The floor housed cloisters of low tables and cushions. Lanterns of flowery hues hung from the ceiling, casting soft light against tapestries of Mai-Ajin warriors and legends. A counter comprised of sake barrels lined the wall across from the table that the jito had chosen for the pair.

A wrinkled man brought over two cups and poured, bowing deeply before he too left the building.

'You have private words for me?' Hazukiro raised his cup to his lips, drinking deeply.

'Or perhaps I'll not risk you massacring my civilians.'

She took a short sip.

'I'm sure your choice of seating would quickly amend that.' He pointed to the pipe at the corner closest to the jito. 'It is impressive. Ingenuitive. Is the entire warren of bells connected to your stronghold below the town?'

Yuriko took a long slip, fixing narrowed eyes on the ronin. She bit her cheek, choosing her words.

'You're no bandit,' her smile was wry. 'Unless you're scouting ahead for other idiots that follow an astute leader.'

'A fair assumption,' Hazukiro took another sip, savouring the taste on his lips. 'Anyone alive in these Blighted days without permanent dwelling is indeed dangerous.' He swivelled the sake in his cup. 'But *bandits* wouldn't know the first thing about maintaining arkinic defences. Taodake, and all its cunning, would be wasted on them.'

Yuriko raised her brows, then her cup. 'Yet still they try, thinking the grounds serve as some sort of blessed mark, anointed by Kesyoka herself.'

'It very well may be. Arkinists are no common thing.' He took another slow sip. 'Are not going to ask how I know of the baubles?'

Yuriko glanced at the ronin's forehead.

'I could hazard a few guesses. Is that what you want?'

'I *need* food and shelter for my daughter. I *want* to procure a few baubles for the road, and perhaps show your arkinist my blade. I'd like to unsheath it without you reaching for that string.'

'We both know a former samurai, even one as old as you, is quicker with a blade than any guard with a halberd is, no matter how well I like to believe I trained them.'

'You can tell I was one from a look?'

She scoffed. 'Your gait. Knowledge. Age. Scars. If you didn't serve, you've led a rather wasted life as a *traveller*, or whatever you'd have me believe you are.'

'Then perhaps you'd also be able to discern the fact that I'd not enter a town, kill its leader while my daughter weaved rope outside, simply for the pleasures it would bring. May I unsheathe my katana, Jito Yuriko?'

She swung her axe forward, pointing its silver head at his. The ronin hadn't even noticed it until it waved between his eyes. 'Slowly.'

Hazukiro complied, revealing the silver with care, setting it down on the table. The tavern's lanterns cast down a cherry glow that shimmered along the blade.

Yuriko leaned in, brushing her fingers along the runic etchings.

'You recognise the script,' Hazukiro said.

'In appearance, not understanding.' Yuriko leaned back, her eyes still fixed on the blade. She placed her axe on the table.

'It holds an enchantment,' the ronin explained, taking another sip, his eyes now resting on the katana. 'Though I'll not utter the words here. The weapon flares the light the thralls despise, and your guards may come running. It's quite bright.'

'*Thralls?*' she repeated. Hazukiro caught her glance out the window where the face of the snowy mountains stood.

'They've been taking people. Starting south. Moving north. Village by village. Victim by victim. And we know they're too mindless to coordinate anything themselves.'

Hazukiro hesitated, wanting to provide the full story.

The jito was experienced, and had proven to be successful at protecting her people. An ally would go a long way. But Taiyō's story was not one easily explained, especially while he sat in the centre of Taodake, in the maw of the lion. The jito could clamp down at any moment. Overwhelm them. Seize the girl. A bloodbath.

'We've heard strange noises from the mountain,' Yuriko said softly, as if the inn had ears to eavesdrop. 'At first I thought the cries were ones lingering from my nightmares, but others have heard it too. Reported it to me.'

Yuriko took one final swig, wiped her mouth, and placed her cup down.

'And here you are, walking right to it. With a child under your wing, no less. And a weapon of godlike proportion.'

Both of their eyes fell on the blade.

'And *you* wield its imbued power?'

She studied the ronin, a branded and weathered man.

'Just who are you?'

CHAPTER XL

RECKONING

SILVER BELLS RANG from the rafters.

'Jito Yuriko!' A voice cried out over the clamouring. 'Gorri has returned!'

Yuriko cursed and took to her feet.

'Lend me your sword arm and we'll arrange a meeting with my arkinist.'

She snatched her axe and stormed out of the tavern. Armoured guards fell in line behind as she marched with measured fury.

'Yuriko!' A man called out from beyond the town's gate. He sat atop a chestnut horse, wielding and waving a large spear.

'Form a line!' Yuriko spat at her men.

They were armoured head-to-toe in mismatched remnants of wars past. They positioned themselves along the town's gate. Civilians scrambled inside, sliding shoji doors shut. Taiyō darted past people, scouring the winding crowd for the ronin. Sprinting towards the gate, she spotted him among the soldiers, walking beside an axe-bearing woman.

'Hazukiro!' she called out. 'What's going on?'

'Get inside!' he called back.

'But—'

'Do as I say, child!'

Swallowing anger, she edged towards him. A concerned mother with a gaggle of children noticed Taiyō and snatched her hand.

'Quickly, girl! Come with us!

The horseman outside circled the foot of the bridge across the gate.

'Did I not warn you this would happen, Yuriko?' The man shouted, his voice carrying across the town. 'I told you I would return in force!'

He gestured behind him. A cohort of at least two dozen men, armed to the teeth, roared with fervour. They clanged swords and spears, inching closer to their leader, who trotted his horse in circles.

'This fool again,' Yuriko cursed.

The horseman raised his spear and encouraged shouts as if he were some esteemed commander out for glory. The very notion churned Hazukiro's stomach and sent a surge of rage across every fibre.

'Do you have archers?' Hazukiro asked the jito.

'We do. Stationed on the western wall.'

Hazukiro took in his surroundings, chewing them, blending them with the memory of his approach to the town.

'Is there an exit where the archers could sneak into the forest to the southwest, beside the bandits?'

'There is a passage to the woods, yes. But diverting them will—'

'I will stall. Send them off. Now.'

Yuriko whistled, and a burly guard bearing a longbow looked to his jito. Trudging over, he listened to the plan with scepticism, but nevertheless ordered the rest of his men over. There were only five archers, including their commander. It had to be enough.

'I will cry out three words,' Hazukiro explained. 'This is your cue to cover your eyes. Allow two seconds, then open fire on the bandits.'

'Cover our eyes?' the commander frowned. Yuriko looked at the imbued blade that rested at the ronin's side.

'Two seconds, commander,' the jito said in support.

Hazukiro proceeded with countenance.

'Yuriko, these words will also be your cue to open the gates. Have your swordsmen push forward after the arrows have flown. Strike once, pull back, and allow for a second arrow volley. If any still stand, charge again with the footmen. I will finish the rest.'

With a plan in place, the archers scurried off the walls and watchtowers as Hazukiro stepped towards the gate.

'Ha!' the horseman bellowed. 'Their archers flee! Have you finally come to your senses, Yuriko? I never offered a slaughter. I already told you, there'd be no point in killing the women. What good would that do my men?' he laughed. 'What good would a victory be without its spoils?'

'Run your mouth,' Yuriko shouted. She turned to Hazukiro. 'Let me go with you, ronin.'

'No,' he said. 'They know you and your people. Seeing me will seed some confusion, if only for a time. I'll try to draw it out.'

Yuriko nodded and began lining up her swordsmen behind the gate for the first charge. There were only six of them, some not much older than Taiyō. Hazukiro briefly empathised with the burden of the jito, but he quickly swallowed the sentiment, drew his sword, and entered the Hush.

'And ronin...' Yuriko clenched a white-knuckled fist. 'Bring me the horseman's head.'

* * *

The gates parted to reveal the lone ronin. The bandits murmured amongst themselves, some laughing, others looking to their leader for answers.

Hazukiro stepped onto the bridge and stopped halfway. This horseman wished to embody a bold leader, to seize some measure of self-proclaimed glory.

Hazukiro gave him the opportunity to try.

'Nightspast,' The ronin bowed. 'I am Hazukiro, a friend of Jito Yuriko. What may I call you?'

The horseman snickered and his whipped dogs echoed him.

'You may call me *master* if you'd like. Or you can open the gates, stand aside, and indulge in our scraps when we're finished.'

'I bear the appearance of a slave, it's true.' Hazukiro remained stoic in his stance. 'I'm old, tired, and hungry. And you sit tall on your steed like the shogun at the procession.'

Hazukiro drew his katana and swiped the cold air. 'And I will *still* kill you with ease.'

The bandits broke into laughter, jeering at their leader, poking fun and inciting him to finish the fool quickly.

'Quiet!' The leader dismounted and tapped his fingers along his spear's shaft. 'I want to spend my evening behind warm walls. And an even warmer bed. Now get out of my way.'

His men cheered in support. Their leader walked tall with broad shoulders and a sinister smirk. Resisting the urge to glance outright, Hazukiro noticed movement in his periphery. He hoped to all the gods that the bandits hadn't seen the archers settling in the trees.

'Well?' The leader pointed his spear. 'Are you going to step aside or can I stick your gut here and now?'

'Are you that confident?' Hazukiro said loudly, drawing attention to him and the bridge. 'Or is that arrogance? Usually, I can tell.'

The horseman shrugged. 'Stick your gut it is.'

'Allow me some final words?'

The leader halted his thrust and burst into laughter.

'How quickly the dog's tail slinks! Very well, but make them good!'

Hazukiro gingerly stroked the katana's hilt. A hasty stray arrow whistled over the leader's head.

'Damn it,' Hazukiro cursed. '*Too soon.*'

He raised his blade high and howled the mantra.

'*Soot and cinder!*'

The katana burst with the brightness of the sun. A volley of arrows rained over the squinting bandits, some hitting their marks. The ambushed brigands began to scatter like confused roaches.

'You stay put.' Hazukiro brought down the flaming blade, but one of the men ran to his leader's aid, longsword in hand. The ronin's blade struck him instead.

It tore through the horseman's skull, carving a straight line until its tip singed the bridge. Two searing halves of the horseman split like spliced fish. The fire simmered and the black of the blade began to return.

The horseman staggered back, fear washing his face white. 'A-attack!'

Hazukiro lunged and dropped down, slicing the backs of the horseman's legs, grounding him. He dropped his spear and writhed in pain.

'Forward!' charged Yuriko, her swordsmen pouring through the gate behind her.

The skirmish was brief. In the chaos of arrows and clashing swords, Yuriko's men managed to take down a third of the marauders. Yuriko and Hazukiro weaved through the rest. The ronin slicked his blade red, tearing through limbs and bellies. The jito brought down her axe into heads and sides, bringing the raid to its literal knees.

With a final scream, Yuriko pulled her axe from a skull and caught her breath. The archers emerged from the trees, cheering in victory. Some began boasting about which landed arrows were theirs.

Hazukiro swatted the blood from his blade and returned it to his sheath, smothering its remaining light.

'You've certainly earned that meeting.' Yuriko walked back across the bridge and gasped. The leader crawled on his belly, dragging limp legs, reaching for his spear.

'You left him alive on purpose?' A strange grin washed over her face.

'His fate is yours,' Hazukiro nodded, kicking the spear away.

'You may have earned a meal for the road and then some,' Yuriko smiled, fighting back a tear.

She placed a hand on Hazukiro's shoulder. 'I'm grateful.'

Spitting on the flailing marauder, she called over two of her men. 'Stop his bleeding and throw him in the pit.'

She glanced over the sea of bandit bodies.

'Feed him only his men's genitals.'

* * *

Hazukiro and Taiyō spent the night in the space above the inn. It was bare besides saké barrels surrounding two goza mats, blankets and food that had been prepared for them.

Jito Yuriko approached the attic the next morning, several hours after daybreak. Taiyō's bed was empty, but the ronin roused at her steps.

'I trust you are well rested?' she asked, seating herself on a barrel. 'I apologise that we couldn't offer you two something more comfortable.'

Hazukiro took his hand off his sword and sat up, pressing fingers into his lower back. Yuriko noticed just how many scars he wore. Both old and new.

'We do have a doctor, too,' she suggested.

'This is more than enough.' Hazukiro rubbed his eyes. 'It's been some time since I've had the pleasure of sleeping during the day. And on something other than stone.'

Yuriko looked at the platter beside the straw mat. The cup was empty and the plate had only crumbs and stems.

'I hope you've had enough food, too? We do have more.'

'I have, and I couldn't,' Hazukiro placed a grateful hand on his stomach. 'Thank you.'

'And your daughter? I haven't seen her, has she had her fill?'

'...Yes. I imagine she has. Thank you.'

CHAPTER XLI
EDGE OF THE BLADE

THE GRASS-COVERED DOORS near the furnace opened, and Yuriko led Hazukiro and Taiyō down the stone stairs. It was as the ronin had assumed. The tunnels below the town, once used for the mountain miners, remained a connected warren of passages and rooms. This was where the citizens of Taodake held up at night, allowing the baubles above to deter any thralls.

The smoke that the main furnace excreted served as the convergence point. All steam and smoke funnelled through iron ventilation systems to reach their shared plume point. The connected pipes kept the entire underground as warm as an onsen.

'And the grassed-over doors. . .' Taiyō wondered. 'They can be watered to muddy down the entrance?'

'Sharp one, aren't you?' Yuriko mused, lifting a torch from a stone wall sconce.

'She's older than she appears.' Hazukiro nodded. He was handed another torch and Yuriko led them through winding corridors.

'Come night this area will be crowded. The only thing keeping us on our toes on the surface, really, were those bandits.'

She stopped in front of a large stone door.

'Forgive me,' Yuriko said. 'I couldn't reveal the truth of the matter until I knew I could trust you.'

She turned to the doors and uttered the words that would open it.

'*Vora Bjaa Nokrii.*'

The grating slabs rumbled, scraped like whetstone wheels, and then parted like two roaring lions. A violet light ran up and along the doorframe when Yuriko walked through with her guests.

'The arkinist's workshop,' Yuriko presented.

Hazukiro frowned. 'And the arkinist?'

Yuriko sighed deeply. 'His skills were needed elsewhere. Made his way to the Teragaku after fortifying us.'

Hazukiro rolled his eyes. It did seem unlikely for Ijihan to have two arkinists. The smith would likely stay there, too, doing the Academy's will before helping the surrounding villages. He looked to the sword at his side. At least there was that.

'He did leave us his share of sunharnesses, though,' Yuriko offered, opening a crate in a corner of strange, mechanical contraptions.

The ronin pocketed a few, bowing deeply, then pulled at his withering kimono and cloak.

'I don't suppose someone would be able to provide us with something more suitable for the mountain? And something warm for the girl?'

'Of course,' Yuriko said. 'If you truly are adamant on going up that mountain, I'll muster something from the stockpile, and talk to our seamstress. You can sharpen your blade at the smithy near the inn, too. But the rest will be up to you. Your wits will need to be sharper than the edge of your blade.'

* * *

While Taodake's seamstress prepared attire, Jito Yuriko declared Hazukiro and Taiyō the town's guests.

On their second night there, Taiyō stole away into the woods, where she'd stowed two of the fallen bandits from the attack earlier in the evening. Sinking her teeth, she feasted in gallons, fully restoring her strength. A wave of warmth and relief swept over her. Her senses felt sharper than ever. The cold wind that washed over her exposed skin felt like nothing. Taking two empty vials she's scrounged, she filled them with blood and stowed them in her clothes.

Hazukiro finally felt some relief himself. Being able to rest with the comforting purple glow outside for several nights was beyond soothing. No thrall approached the town. No night came and went without the ronin eating his fill of warm bread and plump fruits.

One night, he even enjoyed the taste of salted pork and steamed rice, a favoured dish from his youth. He shook intrusive thoughts free, ones that declared him unworthy of enjoying the yields of hard-working townsfolk and farmers, not after what he had done to similar homes in the past.

He fought through the tearing memories, forcing down the replenishment his body needed for the remainder of the journey. He had come this far. He wouldn't allow his mind to falter his new purpose now.

Taiyō would find her fate up on the mountain.

And so would he.

* * *

'Fits her well,' the seamstress smiled.

'*Very* well,' Yuriko nodded, impressed.

Taiyō turned and admired her new attire. The kimono shone crimson red, and was made of a much thicker fibre than her withered threads. She wore loose-fitting trousers beneath it with black fur boots. The seamstress also managed to salvage the ronin's hooded cloak, shrinking it down to fit the girl.

'Thank you!' She bowed and looked at Hazukiro as he fastened the obi around his waist.

'You look less like a corpse,' she shrugged.

'Warmer than one, too,' he retorted. 'A fine fit.'

His attire was as slick and black as ravens. A straight-sleeve happi covered his torso, fitting into hakama trousers that nestled into studded leather boots with the same fitted furs.

'No sandals?' Taiyō wondered, pressing her heels to the floor.

'These are Njörkin,' Hazukiro realised.

The seamstress nodded, approaching him with a flowing, black fabric.

'Raven cloak furs from invaders. . .' Hazukiro grumbled.

'The Njörkin hail from frozen wilds, similar to the conditions of Mount Shinok.' Yuriko explained. 'Good grip. Good warmth. Toes will stay warm. Crevasses will stay ronin-free.'

'I am grateful.' Hazukiro bowed.

'It will do better than shredded rags,' Taiyō added. 'A *lot* better.'

'It will do fine,' Hazukiro nodded.

'And please, take these provisions.' Yuriko handed Taiyō leaf-covered parcels. 'There's plenty of that to be had under warm roofs, if you change your minds.'

'Thank you,' Taiyō said. 'But we will not.'

The seamstress excused herself with a bow and returned to work, while the jito led the travellers to the main gate.

'Thank you for everything, Jito Yuriko,' Hazukiro bowed.

'You two had better return,' she feigned a smile. 'I want to hear about what's so damn important on that mountain over a drink.'

Hazukiro smiled. 'I wouldn't miss it.'

Yuriko waved as the gate closed behind them.

Standing on the bloodstained bridge, Hazukiro turned to face Taiyō. He placed his hands over her shoulders.

'This is it,' he looked to the looming mountain ahead.

'He is within our reach.'

PART III
THE ENDLESS

CHAPTER XLII

HAZE

KESYOKA'S LARGEST TEMPLE sat nestled at the peak of Mount Shinok. Before Blightfall, followers of the goddess of Light partook in the three-day pilgrimage at least once a year. This usually took place in the springtime, when flaxen blue coldfoot flowers would bloom along the trees that sloped its stone steps.

Now the path was crusted only in snow, framed by frosted pines.

An hour into the climb, the air began to stretch itself thin. The stairs grew narrower and steeper, and by the midday mark, the burn of Hazukiro's calves forced them to rest up.

'How have your knees not detached from your legs at this point?' Taiyō panted.

'I am in pain,' Hazukiro huffed. 'But we've little daylight to move. Keep an eye out for a cave. And any signposts. We'll need to make camp at the first hollow point we find for the night.'

Another hour passed before the pair encountered their first obstacle. A large pile of rockfall blocked the steps, and it was too high to see beyond it.

'I could wisp over?'

'You should conserve that energy,' Hazukiro waved her off. 'There won't be anyone to. . .to consume up here.'

'I have a blood vial,' she insisted.

'Save it.'

He looked for a way around. For the most part, the obstacle looked climbable, but one misplaced step would send him slipping off the side of the mountain.

'We will have to backtrack,' Hazukiro concluded. 'The narrow paths we saw earlier. They were likely made for the miners to work around the pilgrims.'

'Is there no other way?' Taiyō approached the obstruction.

She peered through the boulders' fissures, trying to formulate a plan of her own. Hazukiro could see her thoughts racing. He felt a sudden surge of pride as he watched her. This was her journey, and she was grabbing fate by the throat, impasse after impasse.

'I trust you,' he said.

'You'll have to,' she gave a roguish grin. 'Because I'm going to have to wisp over this mess.'

Hazukiro sighed, telling himself to let the situation go. The narrow paths meant losing precious time before sunset. It *would* be better to maintain the direct course.

'This is her journey,' he told himself. 'Fine. But be careful.'

Taiyō took that to heart. She grinned with confidence, then burst into a scarlet cloud, smoking over the cluster and reforming on the other side.

The winds picked up, and a light snowfall tickled the air. Hazukiro peeked through a gap in the rocks. Taiyō was a distant haze beyond the debris. He knew he'd never hear her, but that she could hear him.

'If there's nothing to see, come back!' he bellowed into the wind.

Taiyō disappeared again, a distant red mist travelling through the air until she was out of sight.

Minutes passed and she still hadn't returned. Hazukiro gritted his teeth, pulling his feathered cloak up to his ears, searching the thin air.

'Damn it.'

Wrought with worry, he fastened his cloak tightly, then pulled himself up the first precarious boulder. It was smoother than it looked. His fingers slipped, walloping his gut with a chill. Grunting, he prodded for the next suitable foothold.

He moved up, little by little, grumbling at how slow he was forced to go.

'Taiyō!' he cried out, steadying himself, wind smacking his snow-crusted beard.

With limited options, he growled and gripped an ice-slicked rock with frozen fingers.

'Answer me, child!'

Stone gave way. His grip crumbled and sent rocks tumbling down the mountainside. He slid down and clasped the previous, more secure boulder, spewing curses to the cold.

'*Taiyō!*'

Snowfall swept against him. The winds whistled, sharp and loud. Through the muffled haze, he heard her cry out. Possibly the only thing more frightening than the sound was that it was cut short. Mid-scream.

'I'm coming, child!'

Hesitation left his mind. The careful climb turned into a mad scramble of uncertainty. He slipped often, almost spraining a wrist. He clamoured over fresh sleet and stone, then back down the other side with unbridled fervour.

'Taiyō!' he called out again, ripping his katana free. *'Soot and cinder!'*

Flaring through grey haze, the sword lit up against the rising storm.

He found Taiyō on the ground, wincing. A katana stuck out her spine, pinning her in place.

'Taiyō!'

Hazukiro lunged forward and felt the sting of a blade cut his neck. He howled and turned, brandishing light to reveal the attacker.

'Silkspinner...'

CHAPTER XLIII
OUR OWN TALES

THE ROPE DART RETRACTED into grey, and the assassin sprang from the murk. The blade soared through snow and clanged off a rock. Hazukiro realised that she was just as blind in the storm as he was.

He searched for Taiyō. Had she managed to remove the blade? Was it made of silver? The snow had grown too fierce to find her.

The Silkspinner offered no quarter. Her blade retracted and tore at Hazukiro's arm.

'Listen to me!' he called out, charging forward. He swung at the air, cutting only cloud.

'The Spectors would never venture this far north. They wouldn't go to these lengths for their own living people, let alone to exact vengeance for their dead!'

He swiped his blade again, this time deflecting the kunai that came hurtling at him.

'*Listen!* When we fought at the falls you called her a demon!' he shouted. 'I'd wager they told you nothing beyond that? Do not tell me this is what *you* want! You're risking your life to kill a child!' He roared to the wind. '*Is that truly what you want?*'

The Silkspinner leapt from an outcrop above, crying out.

'I don't want *any* of this!' She planted two daggers in the snow, inches away from the ronin.

Hazukiro seized the opening. The assassin was slouched, her blades stuck for a moment. It was easy enough to bring down his blade and cleave her head cleanly. Instead, he brought down his hilt, pounding her forehead. With a spin, he kicked her back against the icy rockface.

'Then let us *speak*.' Hazukiro commanded, quickly hugging his blade to her throat.

The Silkspinner grunted and conceded, dropping the kunai she had readied behind her back.

Bloodshot eyes glowed in the storm, charging her way. Taiyō leapt atop the assassin, digging claws into her shoulders. Her gob slobbered as she extended her maw, tearing the cloth from the woman's neck.

'Taiyō, no!' Hazukiro pulled her arm.

Taiyō's claws twitched. Her eyes fluttered. She forced herself to calm down until her eyes had rolled back into their pale hazel hue.

Hazukiro swiftly returned his blade to the Silkspinner's throat.

'You know what she is!' The assassin exclaimed.

'Do *you*?' Hazukiro growled.

The woman looked over to Taiyō and watched as she rose to trembling feet. Head spinning, she moved to stand beside the ronin, staring down the Silkspinner.

'When I first saw you at the falls. . .' the woman began, swallowing as the blade inched closer to her gullet. '. . .I was unsure. You were unconscious.' Her eyes moved to the ronin. '*You fought like a demon yourself.*'

'In defence of her.' Hazukiro said, studying the woman. She couldn't have been more than five years older than Taiyō.

'I see that now,' the woman continued. 'And the way she tore at me when filled with the thirst, but then stopped. And you? She's no danger to you. Are you her master?'

Taiyō punched the assassin square in the nose. The snow spackled red.

'I have no master,' she spat, wind howling at her back. 'And I'm not thirsty.'

Hazukiro made nothing of the outburst, staying only silent and keeping his blade steady.

'Then you are not as claimed,' the woman spat blood. 'You fight this curse yourself.'

Taiyō crossed her arms, pacing up and down. Hazukiro pushed the blade's edge deeper, forcing trickles from her skin.

'I wasn't aware Ijihan had *Silkspinners*.'

'*Ijihan* doesn't.'

Taiyō crouched, eyeing the kunai blade. 'Who sent you after me?'

'I do not know.'

The blade pushed deeper.

'I just need to get my husband back.'

Hazukiro eased off at the words. Taiyō's own gaze softened when tears swelled in the woman's eyes.

'Your husband?' Taiyō pressed.

'He's probably already dead. . .' she continued. 'The scroll said he'd be slaughtered if I didn't bring your heads to the peak of Mount Shinok before winter. I've already failed.'

She scrunched her face, fighting back tears. Her voice broke and swelled.

'I had to try. I know he's already dead, *but I had to try.*' She sighed, ignoring the silver pressed to her skin. 'What else was I going to do?'

Hazukiro pulled the sword away but kept it pointed in her direction. Taiyō had torn the Silkspinner's katana free. Her daggers lay in the snow. A few throwing kunai were visible on her bandolier, but one weapon was unaccounted for.

'Your rope dart,' Taiyō said, surprising and impressing the ronin. 'Toss it to him.'

She complied, defeated, wiping spittle and tears from her stained face.

'What else did this scroll say?' Hazukiro asked, still cautious.

'Just a promised pardon, forged, to get my husband in a boat to the mainland. Other than that, it came with a sack of gold to give to the ferryman who was to take him.'

'Join us, then.' Taiyō said, extending a hand.

'What?' Hazukiro stepped forward. The woman looked up, just as confused.

'The Foremost sent you,' Taiyō explained. 'He'd rather see me dead than living on her own accord.' She shook her head. 'You would never have been free of him, had you succeeded in your contract. Even now, you remain a slave to him. So I'll say it again. Help us end the Endless.'

The sounds of whistling wind filled the air as she mulled over the girl's words. Her demeanour. Her tenacity.

'What do I call you?' Taiyō asked.

'Nuruko.'

'Will you join us, Nuruko?'

She scoffed. 'Your fight will only end one way. The man commands the dead. It's foolish to try.'

Taiyō smiled. 'Maybe so. But I'd rather die a fool that did something than watch over my shoulder for the rest of my life, a slave to my own past.'

Hazukiro watched the two as they locked eyes, searching and recognising familiar feelings.

'I cannot bring the Foremost your heads. And for that, I've lost my husband. Losing him means I've lost all purpose.'

'No!' Taiyō lashed out. 'His life was dangled in front of you. The Foremost *used* him because he needed you. He needs thralls to do his bidding. He needed me too, and although I still don't know why, I do know what all of that means.'

Hazukiro crossed his arms. 'It means alone, he is not all powerful.'

'Exactly,' Taiyō spat, then turned back to Nuruko. 'He controls the dead, not us. He had to *pay* you to do his bidding. Do *not* let him wield the power he does have against anyone ever again. Do not let it evolve. *End* him.'

Nuruko chewed her lips, then shook her head blankly. 'There is no ending the Endless. . .' she sniffed. 'But I can finish my own journey here.'

'*How could you say tha—*'

'Taiyō. . .' Hazukiro held up a hand.

He understood that blank stare on Nuruko's face. Her life was her husband, and he was gone. Her life had been washed away with the blood that stained her hands over years of killing.

Hazukiro approached the Silkspinner. 'We choose the end of our own tales.' He handed her the rope dart.

'We will not stop you from finding yours.'

Hazukiro turned his back to her, sheathing his sword. Taiyō followed him and turned around, shaking her head at Nuruko. The Silkspinner hung her head, trudged through the heavy snow and disappeared into the grey of the storm.

CHAPTER XLIV

BLOOD MOON

'OUR SECOND NIGHT HERE.'

Hazukiro stood at the foot of the cave, staring out over the shrouded island of Ijihan below.

'And we've yet to see a single thrall.'

Thin clouds still hung in the frost-laden air, but the storm had subsided. Twinkling stars emerged to greet them amidst the peculiar silence, and in the centre of the eerie void above, the moon beamed bright and full.

'Not one,' Taiyō confirmed. 'They swarmed the entire mountain, peak to base when I escaped.'

The moonlight highlighted the wrinkles of the ronin's scowl. 'I don't like this.' He rubbed the chill from his calloused hands.

Hazukiro thought back to the sunken temple and the bereft woods beyond the lake. It had been quiet as graves, like the mountain was now. But to make mention of Prowler's Rest, and what Taiyō had lost there. *Learned* there. He felt it was not his place to dredge it up now.

'We cannot prepare any more than we have,' Hazukiro finally said. 'We know to be cautious, and worrying doesn't serve us.'

He unwrapped the thick-leafed parcel that Yuriko had packed for them, revealing rice balls, hardtack, and dried fish.

'You take the meat,' Hazukiro tossed it over. 'It's something.'

She thanked him with a nod, mindfully chewing and savouring the texture.

'Child,' Hazukiro began. 'We come to the end of our journey. If there is something you wish to discuss—'

'I just want him *dead*. Or is this where you scold me about vengeance being my downfall?'

Hazukiro wiped the hardtack crumbs from his beard, nodding slowly.

'Killing your oppressor will bring you peace,' he stated.

Taiyō raised a brow, ready to retort until he sighed and continued.

'For a time. A very brief time.'

The stars demanded his gaze, making him feel smaller than ever.

'If this self-proclaimed *Foremost* controls the oniku, then his death will not just ease your soul. It may yet bloom the seeds of peace for all of Ijihan. It could be a message to everyone that the curse need not hold us hostage in our own home.'

Taiyō smiled. The sentiment was something worth fighting for, beyond her desire to exact punishment.

'Hazukiro. . .' she said softly. 'Do you truly believe I still have a soul?'

She hung her head, unready for the answer the moment it left her lips.

'Taiyō.' Hazukiro placed his hand on hers. 'One without wouldn't bother with the question.'

She sunk into his arms, clutching at his clothes. For the first time, perhaps since her escape from the very mountain she lay on, she allowed herself to cry without judgement or worry.

* * *

The brisk wind woke them before the sun could. Moonlight still coated the steps. With the shine of snow, the journey to the divine temple could have been something spectacular. The Foremost capturing the historical peak as his dwelling was not only a twisted turn of fate that spat on the islanders of Ijihan, it was downright blasphemous.

But Hazukiro and Taiyō walked regardless, with fierce purpose alight in their hearts. Whether they failed or succeeded, their journey would end. They would come to know peace either way, a sentiment they repeated to themselves as they traipsed snowy stairs in the silence of Mount Shinok.

The second night was warmer than the first. Taiyō spotted a cave with enough of a curve to break the mountain breeze. The dried leaf wrappings made for some useful tinder. Hazukiro set about tending to the fire to smoke the cold from his bones while Taiyō leaned his katana gently against the cave wall.

The ronin removed his fur cloak and covered Taiyō as she huddled in the corner. She hadn't abated her thirst in a few days, and the cold began to seep into her pale skin.

Hazukiro found himself entering the Hush, even outside of battle. His mind was a tool like any other, and the higher they climbed, the more he felt it rust. And like his blade, his mind needed sharpening.

'Is this fear?' he whispered to himself when he looked to Taiyō, sound asleep. 'Yes.'

It was a new and strange sensation, fearing for someone else like that. Fighting it became a tiresome task.

After the cold air snapped at his sore bones and ushered him back inside, he crawled up beside the fire and searched for sleep.

* * *

'Something is wrong.' Taiyō shook Hazukiro awake. 'Quickly!'

'What is it?' He rose to his feet and snatched his blade, moving eyes around the cave.

'It should be day by now,' she said, pulling him by the hand. 'But the sky is dark and the sun is. . .*black*.'

Hazukiro glanced up. The celestial orb oozed onyx, like the ichor of demon blood drenched by night. A burning red ring outlined it.

'An eclipse?'

Hazukiro turned to the full moon, still beaming and bright, but flushed in scarlet lustre.

'Taiyō,' Hazukiro looked at the dark sky. 'I need to ask you about Simaro.'

'You think she has something to do with the Blood Moon?'

'Perhaps. Did she, the Foremost, or any of the others ever mention an *epoch*?'

Taiyō shook her head, baffled by the word.

Hazukiro sheathed his sword and helped her onto the stairs, now illuminated in a wash of red against the blackened sky.

'It was something one of the cultists mentioned. The ones who worshipped the oniku,' he shook his head. 'Come. We must focus on what lies ahead, not behind. Let's move.'

Taiyō nodded, then swiftly fell to her back as the mountain rumbled. Hazukiro slipped as he reached for her hand.

'An avalanche!' Hazukiro cried over the roar of the mountain. 'Get to the cave!'

The commotion stopped shortly after it began. No snow fell. No rocks shook loose to crush them. They took to their feet, squinting at the dark above.

A tremendous gust of wind warped the air, and a curdling cry like a choir of tortured tigers reverberated across the mountain air.

Far beyond the southernmost tip of Ijihan, over the horizon of shores beyond sailing, a green pillar of light pierced the heavens.

'Wha—what is that?' Taiyō froze, staring blankly at the light. Hazukiro had no answer to what he was witnessing either. All they could do was tremble, as if they were in the presence of something otherworldly.

Then the pillar ceased, dispensing upwards across the dome of the dark sky. And from the mountain they stood on, a dragon soared overhead, black as night.

Its wingspan was monstrous, at least eighty feet. Like a thrall, the wings were leathery, separated by stringy sinew, pumping with black blood vessels. Curved claws flapped at its ends. The body of the four-legged beast resembled some sinister hybrid of lizard and bat, a beast of black fur and grey scales, a long and thick neck, leading to a gargantuan gob, crowned with six stacked horns.

'W-what is that?' Taiyō clasped Hazukiro's arm.

'I do not know. Another thrall of this Foremost, it would seem.'

Taiyō swallowed, watching as the dragon soared down the mountainside, bending entire trees under the windy wake of its wings.

'That beast will—Hazukiro, it could raze this whole island to the ground.'

The ronin gestured to the snowy steps. 'The Foremost's tainted hands must have sculpted a new evil. Dark deeds need undoing. Come'

How do we do that?' Taiyō followed him, looking down at the dragon as it glided and screeched over forests.

Hazukiro scowled with focused intent. 'We cut them off.'

CHAPTER XLV
THE FOREMOST

THE FINAL STEPS WERE both the easiest and most difficult. The uphill trudge, and the fatigue that came with it, would end. What lay ahead would have sent anyone back down the mountain.

But Taiyō was not *anyone*.

She stormed ahead, fierce as the burning moon above.

'So this is what remains,' Hazukiro drew his sword. '*Soot and cinder.*'

The violet light seared again. Its hum was eerily prevalent. They stood at the summit, and through a thin layer of clouds, they spotted the decrepit, snow covered temple ruin.

Harsh, abrasive winds and rain had worn down its exterior over the years.

The temple pillars stretched high, housing its grand snow-peaked towers. The courtyard leading up to it was empty, nothing more than a flat field of snow and stone benches.

'Those vines have crept their way in,' Taiyō noticed. 'Why have the doors been left open long enough for that?'

Hazukiro edged towards the entrance.

'These vines are. . .' he squinted in disbelief. '. . .pulsing.'

The lattice of tendrils clutched the walls, throbbing with the drum of a heartbeat.

Hazukiro lit and led the way, stepping deftly into the temple. Taiyō followed closely, her red, hungry eyes shimmering in the dark.

'Drink that vial now,' Hazukiro whispered.

Agreeing, she indulged in the scarlet sin and held back shivers along her veins.

A groan from the walls caught the ronin by surprise. He swished his sword around, illuminating an iron-clad cage. Three pairs of bloodied, scrawny hands quivered and cried out to him. The words were nonsensical.

'What wickedness is this?'

Another voice moaned from across the room, seemingly induced by the first. In the far corner, a torch burned on a sconce.

'Taiyō, I need your eyes,' he whispered. 'Is the path to that light clear?'

She stood stunned, able to see everything in the room. *Every last, grotesque detail.*

'Yes. It's safe, but. . .'

Hazukiro stormed for the torch, retrieved it, and planted it in a nearby brazier. The fire fumed and ran along the walls, corner to corner, end to end until the room cast orange light onto the ungodly scene.

Villagers.

The islanders of Ijihan, some dead, some alive, some *both*, littered the floors and walls in various torturous contraptions.

Some had tubes and wires weaved into their skin. They sobbed softly. Across the room, in a walled pen, thralls thrashed at their silver chains. Limbs hung from the ceiling. *Human* limbs. It kept them hungry. Always reaching. Always depraved.

'N-nuruko?' a soft voice called.

Hazukiro turned to see the husband the Silkspinner had spoken of. He was as thin and brittle as a corpse, still somehow holding onto life.

'K-kill me,' he begged through cracked lips.

Hazukiro swallowed. It was clear that there was no saving him. But the weight of more death and decay at his hand. The very thought—

The man's head hung, the final breath leaving his lips. Taiyō gritted her teeth as she removed her clawed hand from his back.

'You shouldn't have to carry every burden,' she sniffed, composing herself. 'He deserved mercy and I gave it to him.'

Hazukiro nodded in thanks, taking in the sight of the other depraved bodies, all facing familiar fates. Starved and tortured souls, every one of them.

'This is where he kept you?' Hazukiro growled.

'No. . .' She couldn't bring herself to look away. 'We were kept in the archives, in our own rooms.'

'Why were you and the other girls kept separately?'

'You are slow to deduce things.' A voice rang from the shadows. Its baritone was deep, soft as silk, almost melodic in its resonance.

'They all reacted differently. And she's special.' The voice echoed around the room, reaching and rattling inside the ronin's head.

Hazukiro entered the Hush and fixed his stance. Taiyō extended her fangs and claws, fire burning in her eyes.

'Show yourself!' Hazukiro demanded to the dark.

'Not here.' The voice was stern.

Hazukiro felt its strictness inside his mind, easing through the Sanctum of the Hush like water to paper.

'I'd prefer not to make a mess of my progress.' The voice trailed off with the sound of soft footsteps.

'Don't let him get away!' Taiyō cried, lunging forward. 'It's him! It's the *bastard* that killed Simaro!'

'Taiyō! *Wait!*' Hazukiro chased after her.

They found themselves in a hall that looked as if it had been converted into a throne room. A chair of stone sat at the end. Beside it, a large open balcony faced the island below. At the edge, standing with hands folded behind his back, stood the Foremost. The same scarlet vines from outside pulsed along the floor and walls, converging behind the stone throne.

'I must thank you,' the Foremost began. 'You've returned one of my most promising results to me. No mindless thrall of mine could have achieved such a task. She'd have torn them in two. A smart Silkspinner though, I had my doubts, but it was worth a try. *You* on the other hand. . .'

The Foremost turned to face them. His skin was as pale as Taiyō's, eyes ink-black. His dark hair fell about his slender shoulders, running over his royal robes of red and black silks. He wore rings of gold on each finger, and when he smirked, his silver fangs gleamed red in the crimson moonlight.

'. . .You appealed to her human side.' He raised his brows. 'I honestly didn't believe that a mere man capable of surviving the Blight *this* long was *also* capable of such selflessness. Then again, you were once an honourable man. Is that what this is, Hazukiro?'

The ronin pursed his lips, studying the man like he did any opponent. What was he capable of? How did he know his—

'Everyone at the Academy knew your name, Hatamoto.'

Hazukiro's brain felt toyed with, addled and searing, as if the demon had moved it around like rice in a bowl.

'Yes, I'm rifling through your memories. And the minds of the dead that I've claimed as mine. It seems a lot of people spent many a night praying that the shogun's next village to face your wrath was not one where their wives, children and parents dwelled. Ha! And then you go and return my *favourite* girl.' A sharp and sinister grin formed across his face.

'I would say you have earned your redemption. It would have been better if you'd manage to kill the little failure yourself but,' he sighed. 'I suppose I could spend a little more time with her.'

'You will not *touch* me,' Taiyō spat.

'I don't need to,' the Foremost shrugged. 'You just need time to gestate. Like my dear Simaro, had she not been deemed *worthless*. I should have cast her out sooner. She could barely even use her *wings*, and her appetite was impossible to sate.'

He licked his fangs, looking out the open balcony.

'Now, Jiro, on the other hand. *She* was a *monstrous* success. Malleable, too.'

He gestured to the island and the dragon soaring overhead. 'As you can see.'

'What—' Taiyō shook, veins pulsing like black rivers across her forehead.

'Ronin, you may go.' The Foremost waved a limp hand. 'Unless you wish to bear witness?'

Taiyō snapped, bloodwisping and hurtling herself at the monster like a hellish wind let loose. In a flash, the Foremost's hand dissolved into the same red mist, swarming amidst the cloud that was Taiyō. His hand materialised, inside her reformed body, skewering the girl's gut. He effortlessly flung her against a wall, freeing his razored nails.

'Taiyō, wait!' Hazukiro called. 'I wish to speak to this man.'

She clamoured to her feet, clutching her bleeding gut as it slowly congealed and sewed itself shut.

'Do not let him inside your head!' she pleaded. 'He needs to *die*!'

'I only wish to speak. . .' Hazukiro breathed deeply, sheathing his sword.

The Foremost grinned, returning crossed hands behind his back.

'Quite a gambit. You are an interesting one,' he mused. 'I must admit I do appreciate a curious mind.'

'You mentioned the Academy,' Hazukiro began. 'The Teragaku? You worked there?'

'I did,' the Foremost said. 'As a scholar. For nearly two hundred years.'

Hazukiro frowned. 'The Blight is only seven years old.'

The Foremost shook his head. 'For Ijihan, yes. I sat with its knowledge for over two centuries, wishing to unveil it to the world. But the very notion of majik would have seen me executed. And the Academy provided me with the resources I needed to procure information on my own.'

The Foremost smiled nostalgically. 'Time and knowledge can open any door. And by gifting myself the Caeldriic curse, I unlocked many other talents. Sharp senses. Healing. *Immortality*. Oh, it simply offered godlike services that humankind severely lacked.'

'And the Academy knew nothing of this?' Hazukiro asked, slowly re-entering the Hush.

'Of course they did, my dear child,' the Foremost mused. 'Who do you think unleashed the Blight upon Ijihan?'

CHAPTER XLVI

EPOCH NOCTIS

'THE BLOOD SPECTORS WERE their way of covering up their own mistakes.'

The Foremost paced the balcony, admiring the fruits of his works in the form of the dark dragon below.

'It's true. Delving into blood majik finally stirred something inside of me, and though many hands partook in the process, the blame was pinned solely on me. I was to be executed, but by that point, there was no way they could have stopped me. I fled into exile, feasting on flesh as I traversed my new, open kingdom. All they could do was watch as villagers became my Vampires, homes became fortresses, and, cowering behind their walls, they deemed the curse a punishment from the divine goddess.'

'Vampire?' Hazukiro raised a brow.

'A more common name for the oniku I've heard whispered in my many visions, though it is often reserved for the more slender form you see before you.

'I began as a mindless beast, the kind you'd encounter at night. After that, a towering beast, akin to that of the older girl. I managed to exacerbate that decade-long debacle into a few months, but her growth stopped there, unfortunately. Useless. So I cast her out. Though I do believe some of the locals worship her as a demon lord now,' he laughed. 'She couldn't be further from it. Eventually, around the hundred year mark, I shed my skin for scales and became the soaring beast you see down there. Luckily that only lasted a month, because I was trapped in this accursed mountain, starved, unable to squeeze my way out. Another process I've since learned to expedite. And finally, I morphed into the exalted form of man, but with the power of a Caeldriic Lord.'

'But you still lack one thing,' Hazukiro said. 'Something the girl possesses.'

The Foremost nodded grimly.

'The girl, for reasons still unknown to myself, immediately assumed the final exalted form.'

He scoffed, turning to Taiyō. 'I had hoped that your blood would hold the answers into *sunstriding*. Gods know the lot in that room over there yielded no results on the matter. An army of thralls is useless if I cannot journey the distance between here and the continent in one night. But now...' The Foremost once again gestured to the dragon.

'To what end?' Hazukiro asked, now consumed in calm. 'What good is the world if you've nothing left to devour?'

'You misunderstand. This isn't *my* plan.' He gestured to the tendrils leading behind the stone throne.

'The line between the world of dormant Caeldriic and the mortal plane of ours is a thick one. It took centuries of blood majik to awaken even the *lowliest* demon lord. The first of many. And even he still awaits a suitable vassal.'

'Dormant demons?' Hazukiro interrupted. 'You speak of beliefs from the West.'

The Foremost shook his head as if disappointed by his spawn.

'Beliefs vary across common soil. They are there, known by different names across different planes. But Caeldriic, they are. Demon lords. Servants of the Dark Arbiter.

'That curse I conjured with blood majik, the one I inflicted upon myself, was the connection this particular demon needed to thwart his hellish chains, pierce the veil, and step into our world. Though free, he seeks a suitable host. Even I am considered unfit. And even a Caeldriic Lord serves a greater master, a thrall himself to something grander. And that something has requested the continent of Maija to be its first stronghold of this world. The reasons? Beyond our understanding until the Convergence of the Caeldriic. And that all begins with the *Epoch Noctis*. And for my loyalty to them, my willingness to merge my soul to their will, I will be spared, for I am no longer wholly human. Those tainted by demonblood will be spared, come the time. We are, all of us, saved. Though *none* of you can see that.'

The Foremost exhaled, smiling. 'Please excuse my ramblings, I've had nothing but monsters to commune with these many years, save the company of the girl.' He gave Taiyō a wink.

'And Jiro? Your unleashed beast?' Hazukiro urged him to continue. He shot a glance to Taiyō, ensuring her wound had sealed.

'The Blood Spectors are a nuisance. Give your enemy enough time behind walls, and they'll find a way to break down yours.

The Teragaku must burn, simple as that. Then I can be free to enthral enough people and crack the genetic code of sunstriding, given enough time. And time is what I have.

'The Blood Moon, an event marking the Epoch Noctis, signals that my master grows impatient in his restricted slumber. And so, after years of allowing the demons to simply feed, I've had to approach the situation more strategically. I allow them to feed, yes. After all, they are an insatiable lot that grow weak without blood. I've had to command them to feast on livestock from time to time, to make up for the people they had to turn to our cause, not to mention the live captures. Living specimens make for the best experiments. And I do have an affinity for the screams of women, I must say.'

He overlooked the island again. 'My dragon will burn the Academy to the ground, drink its fill, while the eclipse burns steadily for three nights. Plenty of time to finish this speck of land off. I do tire of this temple. The more prisoners I have, the quicker the results will come, in theory. And once the Caeldriic Lord is able to emerge from his dormant rest and seize the *continent*, the night will be Endless. Not even the Ithrae will be able to end the preordained. And those who served well will be spared. Rewarded, even. But first, darkness must rise.'

'This world *is* in dire need of renewal,' Hazukiro said, pensive.

'Hazukiro!' Taiyō cried. 'Don't *listen* to him!'

'I could begin anew,' Hazukiro continued.

'You could, child,' The Foremost said. 'If the girl stays, and we learn of her resistance to the accursed sun, the armies could soar for the continent, sooner than promised, with a force of living carrion more powerful than even the Caeldriic could have anticipated. Having been an integral part of the revival of the demon lords would bode well for you. Your reward would be *most* grand.'

'And. . .' Hazukiro wore a small smile. 'I could finally be free from my own torment.'

The Foremost grinned bright fangs. 'You could.'

Hazukiro looked to Taiyō. She shook her head with tearful eyes. 'But *she* won't be.'

The ronin's katana tore free. He howled the mantra and swung a violet stroke. The blade cleaved the Foremost in two. His legs toppled and sizzled, his torso scrambling as he screamed. Taiyō cried out in relief, running to Hazukiro.

A clasp like an iron vice gripped her ankle, twisting it. Beneath his severed torso, the Foremost began to materialise, illusionary clothing and all, pale skin warping over and around black veins.

'Why won't your will *bend* to me?' he spat, dashing at the ronin.

Hazukiro swiped to deflect, but the Vampire's speed was immense, and he was on him in an instant. He clutched his throat, a moment away from squeezing. Taiyō dug her claws into the Foremost's back.

'*Leave him alone!*' She slashed at his limbs, screaming spit. 'I'll kill y—'

A tendril snatched Taiyō's leg, dragging her along the stone floor. She wailed and scratched until she was pulled through the stone throne, crumbling rock before disappearing under it with a muffled scream.

'T-Taiyō!' Hazukiro choked out. 'W-what have you done with her?'

'As I said. . .' the Foremost snarled, malice and excitement behind black pooled eyes. 'The Epoch Noctis signals the awakening of the Caeldriic.'

CHAPTER XLVII
KYNZO

TAIYŌ SIMMERED IN SLIME like a gestating insect. Latched tendrils pumped blood into her mucus pod, swarming and drowning her as she floated, awake but dreaming.

'*Viiyaak uur Veaah. Greetings, Vassal. Kuundrea.*'

Taiyō's mind flickered in panic while her body floated calmly, her essence imprisoned in every sense.

'*Calm your mind. Huura, Vassal. You will serve.*'

'That voice. . .' Taiyō twitched.

Its hoarse words were foreign, laden with ancient undertones. But as they whispered like knives against her scalp, the speech morphed into her tongue, seeping into her brain, pilfering memories, moulding her mind to understand things beyond mortal understanding.

'My voice is yours,' the words continued, now weaving free from her lips like snakes through grass.

'*Witness, Scion of the Umbral. Witness how you will serve Kynzo.*'

Visions of worlds burning flooded behind her eyes. Lands far beyond the shores of Ijihan and Maija. At the centre of the destruction, a figure hung in the air, swathed in writhing flames. When their skin burned away, it revealed bones of ember. Masses of fearful people from all walks of life bowed before the being's swirling hurricanes of flame.

The fragmented portents slipped into darkness, replaced only with the persistent thrum of a rapid heartbeat that wasn't hers.

'First, we must leave this temple together,' Kynzo commanded.

* * *

'I've served *my* purpose,' the Foremost exclaimed, a thrill rising in his voice. 'And you've none left. Thank you. Truly commenda—'

The blade was fast. It pierced the Foremost's neck, straight through, then retracted back into Nuruko's hand. Hazukiro wheezed, free of the Vampire's grip.

'Do not relent!' Hazukiro cried. 'It recovers quickly!'

Hazukiro lunged once more, meeting the Foremost's claws with his blade, cleaving fingers clean. The other hand swiped.

Nuruko charged, flinging two kunai blades, piercing the jelly of the Vampire's eyes. It shrieked and blindly swatted with a black-blood hand of regenerating fingers.

'How do we kill it?' Nuruko cried out.

Hazukiro stepped to the side and brought his blade down, lobbing the Vampire's blinded head off. Nuruko recoiled and readied her rope dart. Hazukiro clenched his teeth, studying the headless torso.

'No...' The Foremost rose from the ground.

His fallen head burst into ashes as another materialised above his neck.

'*No human can kill an exalted demon!*' The Foremost shrieked and dashed forward. 'You are no *god!*'

The Foremost's claws stabbed like daggers, cutting deep into Hazukiro's belly.

He dropped to his knees, coughing up blood and spit.

'You see?' the Vampire scoffed. 'You bleed hubris.'

The Foremost turned to the Silkspinner. She'd sent her blade flying again. This time, he stepped into its tip, allowing it to pierce his shoulder. He pulled it out and crushed it into a fine powder. He shook his sizzling hand, wincing at the silverburn, not more than a mortal who'd touched a boiling pot would.

'That might've been my end, a century or two ago.'

The pointless rope dropped to the floor, and the Vampire turned to Nuruko with thirst burning in his eyes.

'Choosing mankind was a foolish choice, Silkspinner.'

* * *

Memories continued to haunt Taiyō. She was fighting a battle of the mind, and beyond the visions of burning worlds, she was flooded with the horrors of her past.

She saw Simaro's charred face. The Foremost's instruments of torture and experimentation, painfully vivid now. The notion of Jiro, little, quiet Jiro becoming an instrument of genocide.

'*Do not fight it,*' Kynzo echoed in her head. '*Your master calls for your submission.*'

'I will—' Taiyō screamed inside her mind, the voice drowning in voids of fire.

'I will. . .I—' She fought for the words, sour and hot on her tongue.

'*You will serve alongside your brethren when they are called upon.*' The demonic voice scratched like nails twisting inside eardrums, as if a legion of dark voices were chanting curses.

A fire rose in her chest, tightening her breathing as she swallowed the bizarre sludge that housed her. Panic set in. Immeasurable pain flooded her mind. Traumas sent to break her will. The sensation of the thick ooze strangled her senses mad with distress and disgust.

'*Submit!*'

She scoured her mind for a way out, scratching at surfaces. Her mind began to weaken as if it had been treading water at sea. She would drown before long, losing herself to something she'd been a slave to for far too long.

'No. . .' she clenched clawed fists, steel in her voice. '*I am not your weapon.*'

CHAPTER XLVIII

DEMONS AND DRAGONS

THE VAMPIRE APPEARED BEFORE Nuruko, snatching her by the wrist with fierce brevity.

'Do you see this hand?' He squeezed, crushing bones.

Nuruko cried out and thrashed to break free.

'This is the hand that defied me.' He snapped, scratched, and tore flesh and bone from the Silkspinner's arm in an arc of red.

'After I *generously* offered you the chance to wield your weapons *for* me. For the Caeldriic.'

Nuruko howled, clutching her severed limb, writhing on the floor. The Vampire dispersed into cloud and materialised in front of Hazukiro. The ronin was on his knees, wheezing sharply, hugging his gut.

'*You. . .,*' the Foremost leaned into his ear. 'Are already dead.'

He grabbed Hazukiro by the hair and effortlessly dragged him to the balcony.

'Watch your failure unfold,' he commanded.

The Vampire closed his eyes, veins dancing along his temples. A ringing rattled behind Hazukiro's eyes, then ceased sharply. The order had been given.

The Vampire forced Hazukiro's head up.

'*Watch.*'

The black dragon spewed fountains of molten red, shredding entire forests and ruins to melted mounds in moments. At his back, a thousand thralls swarmed from the mountain, spreading out and scouring the island for flesh. Frenzied wings blotched out the sun and moon.

Hazukiro's head spun, idling side to side. He grew pale and cold, dripping blood from the gashes in his torn gut.

A cruel reflection mirrored in his mind.

Burning homes.

Screaming villagers.

Genocide, not war.

'Y-you have no honour,' he spat, head reeling.

'Oh, I know,' the Vampire hissed. 'Honour and tradition? Those old notions breed no change. But *this*.'

The dragon rumbled and dove, scorching everything in its wake.

'This was always going to happen. And not just here on our soil.'

He looked down to the ronin, almost pitying him.

'Look at you. Bleeding out on my floor. Withered and weak from time. You could stalk this world as a fiend worth fearing, but you *wasted* it on petty wars against other petty warriors. The dark gods would laugh at us, if they could see how we've wasted this world. But they are not without pity. Mercy. They've not come to *slaughter* us. No. In fact, they are quite fond of us. We will be aligned with them, sharing each other's gifts for eternity.'

He sighed, satisfied, while the ronin faded further.

'Perhaps the lords of the Underworld will take pity on your soul,' the Foremost grinned grimly, the fire of the burning island reflecting in the shimmering black of his eyes.

'After all, you did bring me my prize. Her *will* proved difficult to crack, especially from all the way up here. She'd shut out my voice often. Luckily for me, and for all Caeldriickind, you marched her right up those snowy stairs into her rightful place. Perhaps she can still be of use to me.'

He licked pallid lips. 'At the end of my *leash*.'

CHAPTER XLIX

THE LAST FORTRESS

LINKU PLANTED HIS PAWS atop the Teragaku's tallest tower.

Noise and chaos ensued below. Bells rang, violet auras flared brightly, people panicked and doors were hammered shut. The full remaining force of the Blood Spectors lined the outside walls. The lilac glow of their defences bounced off their crimson armour.

Every Umawari was ordered to protect the daimyo, standing outside his locked temple, halberds in hand.

The Spectors readied bows and silverhead arrows as they fell into formation, staring at the distant carnage to the north.

Black smoke choked the sky, and against the backdrop of the beaming Blood Moon, the roars of the winged nightmare drew nearer.

Their captain was dead. Their new recruits had never stepped foot beyond the Academy walls. The soldiers cursed under their breath, silently begging for guidance from their cowering leader inside his temple of pillows and silk.

The last fortress of Ijihan would sear to ash under the reign of the rising Caeldriic.

And the first of the dormant demon lords, trapped without form inside Mount Shinok, was slowly creeping his soul into the perfect, sunstriding vassal.

Linku watched with one eye and slicked back ears as waves of overlapping magma drooped from the maw of the approaching dragon.

CHAPTER L

ASHES IN THE SKY

THE DORMANT ENTITY GREW desperate.

'*I command you to submit, Chosen Child!*'

Fighting off the right to be free tired her mind. Each time she pulled away, the nagging notion of servitude dragged her back. She recalled something that was spoken on the mountain.

They *needed* what she had.

The power to be graced by Kesyoka's Light without facing the punishment for stalking her plane. That grace had not been granted by the Foremost. Not by any dark words spewed while toying with blood majik.

Her strength lay in her humanity.

No demon had formed in the womb of a nurturing mother. None had danced and sang among good people. None had known the love of family. None had risked everything to protect a stranger.

She forced her mind to fill with all the good that remained.

'*What are you doing, Vassal?*'

The memories surged over the dark voice, smothering it with the strength of her will.

She was no one's servant.

Taiyō roared and emerged from the stone throne's rubble, drenched in blood and fuming crimson fury.

She shook a limp tendril free from her shoulder and spat black.

'The link has been severed. . .' she growled.

The Blood Moon waned. Darkness dissolved from the sun like the skin of a thrall, burning away that which Blighted it. Bright blue skimmed across the sky once more, brightening the island in beautiful daylight.

The Foremost trembled with rage.

'What did you *do*?' he fumed.

Taiyō panted, looking down in a cold panic. Hazukiro was on his knees at the Vampire's feet. Her hands shook and her claws unsheathed. Silver fangs grew like thin sabres.

'*Don't!*' the Foremost commanded.

He crouched behind the ronin and wrapped his arms around him, pressing claws against his chest.

'I will tear him to shreds if you *touch* me.'

Taiyō recognised the timbre shift. The elevated heartbeat. He was *scared*. Every fibre of her wanted to burst forward and revel in his cowardice.

Hazukiro closed his eyes, gently exhaling.

Taiyō mirrored his breath and entered the Hush.

'I—I will! *Get back*!' He hugged Hazukiro's weary body closer, his putrid, panicked breath falling onto the ronin's neck.

'I'll find another. . .' the Vampire growled. 'The realms are *riddled* with dormant demons. And *no* Ithrae. I'll find one. And then I'll make you mine.'

Hazukiro snarled, summoning the last of his strength to snatch up his sword.

'No, you won't.'

He drove the katana through his own chest. It burst through his back, impaling the Foremost.

'Hazukiro!' Taiyō screamed and ran to him.

Nuruko staggered to her knees. She flung her silvered rope over the Vampire's throat, tightening her grip with her remaining hand, throttling and holding him in place.

Taiyō burst into red mist, pushing the pinned Vampire onto the open, sun-soaked balcony.

Kesyoka's boon burst forth.

Writhing in place, the Foremost squealed as his pale skin peeled off of his body. His muscles set alight, burning and twisting into embers.

His wail wandered into the wind with his ashes.

'And everything you created with it. . .' Taiyō trailed off, watching the thralls in the sky burst into balls of flames.

The meteor shower of fallen demons pummelled into trees and rivers all across the island. Jiro's monstrous form crashed into the ground, dispersing into ashes at the foot of the Teragaku.

The Foremost, and all of his enslaved thralls, were no more. Taiyō looked at her own hands, wondering if she too would fade away into nothing.

But no deliverance came.

She dropped to the floor, gingerly placing the ronin's head on her lap.

'You've done the most honourable thing, Hazukiro,' she whimpered, tears falling down her bloodied cheeks. 'You've saved our home.'

His voice was soft.

Weak.

'It does not make up for the past. . .'

'Stop that!' Taiyō exclaimed. 'You've ended the Blight. They will all know that *you* did this. I'll make sure of that. *Nothing* can change that! You saved the citizens of Taodake. You spared Nuruko. *You saved me!'* she sobbed, clasping his hands.

'No one can change who you are.'

Hazukiro stifled a laugh. 'Thank you for not using *what.*'

Faces flashes before the ronin's fading eyes.

A wounded woman at Fushumaka, grateful for his medicine and his discretion. A small boy playing with a toy tiger, young enough to enjoy the ignorance of youth. A skilled arkinist who kept hope and sought to combat the Blight. A doctor who adopted a shy boy. A jito, herself burdened, looking out for her people. A nameless man with a love for beautiful things. A desperate assassin. A curious one-eyed cat in a prison cell. A faithful mare named Akumo. And a scared, pale girl, who was far more than she thought she was. With a will so strong that she foiled the Underworld.

These were the faces of those who would live a Blightless life. Those children would grow old without bloodshed born of needless schisms. Without the greed of masters whipping their young minds.

Hazukiro finally felt that his actions had meant something. He had given himself.

'It's enough,' Taiyō pushed away tears, squeezing his shoulders.

'It's more than enough.'

Hazukiro brimmed with tears as he locked eyes with Taiyō.

His ears pricked to the sudden sound of songbirds. The smell of white flowers that calmed his senses. Eased his pain. Then, the soft strings of a biwa.

A honeyed voice called him home.

Printed in Great Britain
by Amazon